Julia Reynolds h̲ Whittingham's sharp ton̲ ̲ ̲ ̲ ̲ ̲ ̲ ̲ ̲ ̲ ̲ was not prepared for
what she was hearing now.

"You must get yourself a lover, or two, or three," the
lady said. "You will be happier, believe me."

Julia had had enough. "I find it most unusual for you
to be instructing me, ma'am. After all, you are a
spinster yourself."

Miss Whittingham's faded eyes twinkled. "I do assure
you, my dear, my single state does not mean I have
not enjoyed a man's company many times. In every
way." She paused, then went on. "The Earl of
Bradford might do very well for you. True, he has
never married, but it is not because he does not care
for feminine company. Or there is Robert Hammond.
He is definitely attracted to you. Naughty man! But
they can be the most exciting, you know. Then there
is the Prince, though his stomach grows daily, and that
is so unpleasant in a lover, is it not?"

Listening aghast, Julia told herself that the warmth
flooding through her must be rage—and not that far
more dangerous emotion. . . .

*(For a list of other Signet Regency Romances by
Barbara Hazard, please turn the page.)*

The
Royal Snuffbox

Barbara Hazard

A SIGNET BOOK

NEW AMERICAN LIBRARY

SIGNET TRADEMARK REG. U.S. PAT. OFF. AND FOREIGN COUNTRIES
REGISTERED TRADEMARK—MARCA REGISTRADA
HECHO EN CHICAGO, U.S.A.

SIGNET, SIGNET CLASSIC, MENTOR, ONYX, PLUME, MERIDIAN and
NAL BOOKS are published by New American Library,
1633 Broadway, New York, New York 10019

First Printing, March, 1987

1   2   3   4   5   6   7   8   9

PRINTED IN THE UNITED STATES OF AMERICA

Author's Note

There was a great variety of beautiful and valuable snuffboxes made during the Georgian and Regency periods. There were different boxes for men and women; boxes to be used in the morning or the afternoon, at balls or masquerades.

One of the more unusual boxes showed a fashionably dressed lady reclining on a sofa on the cover. When the box was opened, the same lady, in the same pose, appeared nude inside the lid. It was a subtle way for a gentleman to discover if the lady he fancied was interested, not in snuff, but perhaps in something else.

1

"My dear Fanny! Thank heaven you have come!"

The lady being bowed into Lady Julia Reynolds' drawing room by her very correct butler barely had time to step within before her hostess came forward in a rush, her hands outstretched. It was most unlike her.

"I knew you would not fail me, dear Fanny," Lady Julia whispered. "I am in the most *dire* straits!"

Mrs. Fanny Lowden smiled at her friend as she took her hands and squeezed them a little. "Of course I came, you goose," she said. "Who would not have, after receiving such an impassioned and—dare I say it?—almost incoherent note? Only an illiterate could have stayed away. Now, just let me remove my gloves and bonnet, my dear, before you tell me what is troubling you."

Her hostess, who was attired in a stunning lavender silk afternoon gown with a sarcenet overskirt, sighed and nodded. "I do beg your pardon, Fanny," she said, trying to resume her normal, unhurried manner of speaking. "As you can see, I am truly up in the boughs. But I promise, not another word until we can be private." She moved gracefully to the bell-pull as she added, "I shall order you some sherry."

"Sherry?" Mrs. Lowden inquired as she laid her

bonnet on a Chippendale side table and patted her smooth coiffure. "Surely a cup of tea would be more appropriate for our coze?"

Lady Julia shook her head. "When you hear what I have to tell you, Fanny, you will be glad of the wine. Ah, Hentershee, sherry, if you would be so good."

As the butler bowed and left the room, Lady Julia returned to a sofa beside the fire and patted the seat beside her. "Sit here, Fanny," she said. "I fear what I am about to reveal were better whispered than spoken in a normal tone."

Mrs. Lowden made no comment as she took the seat indicated. Instead she chatted lightly of the weather, and the play she had attended the previous evening until the butler had returned and served them both.

"That will be all, Hentershee," Lady Julia said. "Leave the decanter, and if anyone should call—anyone!—I am most definitely not at home."

"Certainly, madam," the butler agreed.

His mistress did not take her hazel eyes from his back as he made his stately way from the room and closed the doors behind him. Beside her, Mrs. Lowden began to feel distinctly uneasy. Julia Reynolds was not a woman given to dramatization or alarums. She was generally composed and even-tempered, but now it was obvious she was in some sort of distress, for she almost quivered with tension.

As the door closed at last, she turned to her friend, and without preamble began, "I doubt you will believe me, Fanny, even after I tell you the whole. I can hardly believe it myself! I am in the brambles, and all through no fault of my own." She paused, and appeared to be thinking hard, for a frown wrinkled her smooth forehead. "At least I do not think it is my fault," she added.

Mrs. Lowden took a delicate sip of her sherry. "You must be plainer, Julia. Whatever has occurred to put you in such a state?" she asked.

Lady Julia leaned closer. "I had a visitor this morning," she said, her gentle voice filled with doom.

Mrs. Lowden shrugged her thin shoulders. "But you have many visitors, my dear. Indeed, I vow most of London travels in and out of your drawing room on a regular basis. And today was your at-home day, was it not?"

Lady Julia nodded. "Yes, but this visitor came long before the other callers. Why, I had barely finished interviewing my housekeeper when Hentershee brought in his card." She waved a hand toward a huge and magnificent arrangement of long-stemmed red roses and added, "And that bouquet as well."

"Who was it, Julia?" Mrs. Lowden inquired archly, her thin lips narrowed even further as she smiled. "A suitor?"

"*No!* Oh, dear, yes, I think . . . No, I am sure of it!" her friend replied, sounding a little desperate as well as confusing. Then she leaned closer and whispered in Mrs. Lowden's ear.

Mrs. Lowden, who was known throughout society as the Imperturbable One, for once looked startled. She had earned the sobriquet many years before when dining at Lady Booth's one evening. One of a large company, she had been enjoying a string trio when the butler entered the room to announce that the kitchen was aflame and the fire was spreading rapidly. Amid the hysterical cries and sobs of the other guests as they rushed headlong for the stairs, she had been heard to remark languidly to Colonel Gates that it was fortunate they had already dined, and she was one of the last to leave the smoky premises, and one of the few guests whose dignity was intact as she did so.

Now, however, her dark eyes narrowed in her thin, homely face, and both carefully plucked black eyebrows rose in astonishment.

"How . . . how very unusual," she said when she could speak.

"Unusual, you say?" Lady Julia repeated. "It was terrible, terrible! I could not refuse to see him, how

could I? And, Fanny, he came alone! I remember
thinking how fortunate it was that Edwina had gone
on that expedition to Richmond with Lady Rogers and
her daughters today, so she was not here to witness my
awful predicament. Oh, my dear, what on earth am I
to do?"

"First, sip your sherry and calm yourself," her
friend advised her, before taking a healthy gulp herself. As she put the glass on the table beside her, she
added, "But why did he come? Did he say, Julia?"

Her hostess stared at her. "Not in so many words,
no. He gave me a number of polished compliments in
that deep, musical voice—you know his way, Fanny—
and he chatted of the impromptu concert we had both
participated in at Lady Cowper's last week. But he
smiled and looked at me in such an intimate way that I
did not know where to look myself!"

She put her sherry down to wipe her lips with her
handkerchief. As she inspected her friend, Mrs.
Lowden saw how twisted it was, and she did not
wonder at it. Lady Julia Reynolds was a tall woman in
her early thirties, with a graceful, lush figure. She had
been a pretty girl when she made her come-out four-
teen years previously, and now she was a serenely calm
and beautiful woman. She had an abundance of curly
chestnut hair and speaking hazel eyes, and her late
husband had adored her. Over the years, many people
had remarked how sad it was that Lady Julia had
never attained motherhood, for with her generous
curves and good nature, to say nothing of her concern
for others, she seemed made for the role. Society
nodded wisely when they saw how much time she
lavished on her nieces and nephews, one of whom,
Miss Edwina Ogilvie, was staying with her for the
current Season.

Mrs. Lowden reached out and patted her hand.
"But my dear Julia, perhaps you are making too much
of the incident. It is true he often has sudden passions,
and sometimes for the most unsuitable females as well,

as we both know. But surely you have only to avoid him for a few weeks, and it will all pass over. He must be aware that you are not in the least promiscuous, for never in the past five years since your husband's demise has your name been linked with a man's. Perhaps, in your apprehension, you mistook his intent?"

"It was not only that, Fanny!" her friend exclaimed. "He made the matter much plainer. He . . . he offered me snuff!"

"Offered you snuff?" Mrs. Lowden echoed, looking more than a little confused. "But you don't take snuff, do you, Julia? And what has such a gesture to imply?"

"Of course I do not! I have always considered it a disgusting dirty habit. But it was not so much the offer of his box as . . . Oh, dear!"

She leaned forward again and whispered for several moments in that attentive ear. The Imperturbable One could be seen to start, one hand going to her heart as her dark eyes widened in shocked surprise.

"No!" she exclaimed.

"Yes!" Lady Julia cried. "And the lady looked very much like me. Oh, whatever am I to do, dear Fanny?"

"What did you do then?" Mrs. Lowden inquired, absently reaching for her sherry and draining the glass.

"I am sure I blushed, before I begged him to close the box. And then I told him I did not care to indulge. Indulge, Fanny! I must have been scarlet! I thought I would sink right into the floor before he finally obeyed me, making a light comment that perhaps he would be able to change my mind. And he went on and on, becoming even more complimentary, more wild in his declarations. He claimed he had been smitten the instant he heard me sing at Lady Cowper's, and that he had been fighting his attraction for me ever since. Alas for me that it was to no avail! And then, when he finally took his leave, I barely had time to dash off a note to you before I had to endure an afternoon of callers. I pray I was coherent, for I was so distraught and unnerved, I cannot even remember who came!"

Mrs. Lowden rose absently and went to refill her glass. She was so preoccupied, she did not even ask permission. "It is unfortunate that you sing so well, and look as you do, my dear," she mused as she returned to her seat.

"Whatever can you mean?" her hostess inquired.

"Why, he is not only a patron of the arts, and an accomplished musician himself, he has always had a fateful attraction for women of your type, although they have generally been older than he is himself," Mrs. Lowden explained. "But you are tall, and, forgive me, my dear, built on queenly lines, as all his mistresses have been. You must remember that even as a young man, besides being attracted to Mary Robinson, the actress who played Perdita to his Florizel, he also had other women. There was Georgiana, Duchess Devonshire, Lady Melbourne, and Madame Hardenburg, all before he reached the age of nineteen!"

Her friend looked down at the lavender gown that showed her soft shoulders and white bosom, and she frowned. "I cannot lose two stone, but perhaps if I never sing again?" she asked in some distress. Before her friend could reply, she went on, "The whole situation is more than ludicrous, it is degrading! Why, I will be thirty-three in September, and I have been widowed five years. To have a man, any man, proclaiming his love and begging me to be kind to him would not be believed even on the stage. And you know very well, Fanny, I throw out no lures. I do not flirt or employ innuendos with any gentleman, for I am past the age for such foolishness!"

"Widgeon!" her friend said fondly. "Of course you are not past the age, nor is love at any age foolishness. However, lures are not necessary, not when *he* is hot on the trail! Probably your very modesty has inflamed him, for most men are like little boys, crying for what they cannot have." She sighed. "His rank is most unfortunate. You could repulse any other man with ease, but in this case we must find another way."

The two sat in frowning silence for several moments. "Perhaps if I were to leave town for a few weeks?" Lady Julia suggested at last.

"How can you do that?" Mrs. Lowden asked. "Especially since you have Edwina to stay for the Season?"

"You are right," Lady Julia admitted, a little smile curling her lips for the first time. "She is not here at my invitation, however. I hope I love all my nieces and nephews as I ought, but I suspect my sisters Anne and Mary send them to me with such great regularity because they do not consider it seemly for me to live in town alone. It is ridiculous, of course, but both of them, being older, have been overprotective of me since I was a child. I have long resigned myself to being chaperoned by a series of young relations."

"Julia, we must not stray from the subject," Mrs. Lowden admonished her, very like a severe governess with an inattentive pupil. "Since it is not possible for you to go out of town, may I suggest you eschew any festive evenings that you know he has been invited to as well? And you must engage in no more musicales, nor receive him when he calls unless others are present. If he writes, and I am sure he will, for I have heard it is one of his favorite ploys when wooing, return his letter with only a cool, formal note. Tell him you cannot be easy with such an indiscretion in your hands."

"Will he not be very angry, Fanny?" Lady Julia asked, looking doubtful.

"Perhaps. He is much more likely to become even further enamored, and renew his pleading. You must be firm with him. Firm, but ever conscious of his status. After all, he cannot force you into an affair. No, not even *he* can do that!"

She swallowed another healthy sip of sherry before she added, "Oh, I almost forgot! Julia, you must not accept any presents from the man, not so much as a fan or a pretty bracelet, and most certainly not his miniature."

"Of course I will not!" Lady Julia exclaimed. "I am not such a bubblehead! But, Fanny, why, oh why, did his eyes have to light on me? When I think of the women he has had, has even now, I cannot believe this new passion he claims. What of Mrs. Fitzherbert, pray, to say nothing of his lawful wife?"

"Her!" Mrs. Lowden said, her voice scornful. "Any man married to her would be glad to find satisfaction in someone else's arms. Especially someone like you, my dear. Besides being so handsome, you wash regularly."

"I have heard she is most . . . er, untidy," Lady Julia agreed.

"Untidy?" Her friend snorted. "Not to put too fine a point on it, she is dirty! But enough of them both. I must leave you now, for I promised to call on old Mrs. Jennings this afternoon, and she will be wondering where I am."

As she rose and went to don her bonnet again, she added, "Do keep me informed, my dear Julia. And if there is anything I can do, you know you have only to ask."

Her hostess smiled as she came to hug her. They were an incongruous pair, one so tall and stately and fair-skinned; the other short and dark and lean, but in spite of their physical dissimilarities, they had been the best of friends for almost four years.

"Indeed, you are too good, my dear Fanny," Lady Julia told her. "I do not know what I would do without you, my faithful friend. Somehow, just telling you the whole has eased my mind. I am so glad Edwina was not here. We could never have spoken freely in her presence. It would not have been seemly."

Mrs. Lowden smoothed her neat kid gloves. "I suspect she will find out in a trice. She is very precocious for barely sixteen, is she not? And from what I have seen of that young miss, she might well make a valuable ally. I advise you to tell her the whole, so she might help you. After all, your suitor can hardly attempt any lovemaking with a wide-eyed young girl in the room."

As she kissed her friend good-bye, Lady Julia Reynolds began to consider. It was true that Edwina was precocious, and in spite of her flighty ways, somehow mature for her years, but she could never burden her with this horrible situation. Why, every feeling must be offended!

After Mrs. Lowden left her, Lady Julia wandered back to the sofa, trying to ignore the sweet scent of the roses that perfumed her smart drawing room. She wished she might have ordered them thrown into the dustbin, but she had not dared. Somehow, *he* might have found out.

And Lady Julia would be the first to admit that as a loyal subject, she had the utmost reluctance to offend His Royal Highness, George Augustus Frederick, the twenty-first Prince of Wales and the next King of England.

2

She was still sitting before the fire deep in thought when she heard her niece's somewhat gruff contralto in the hall. Lady Julia made an effort to put her problem from her mind, and look as serenely normal as possible.

"Dear auntie, such a time as I have had!" Miss Ogilvie exclaimed as she came in, to remove her riding hat and toss it onto a chair. It slid immediately to the floor, and Lady Julia hid a sigh. It had been her experience that most of the young were untidy at heart, but Edwina Ogilvie appeared to have made a fine art of the failing.

As she bent to kiss her aunt, Lady Julia inhaled the cool spring air she had brought with her, and she admired the girl's round cheeks that were glowing from her exercise, and her dancing blue eyes.

"Just imagine, if you please, ma'am," Edwina said. "The Marquess of Cartley joined our party." She giggled before she added, "I thought that Miss Rogers would fall from her horse, she was so excited, and Evelyn blushed scarlet. How silly they are!"

Lady Julia smiled at the criticism, spoken in that scornful, gruff little voice. "Should you care for some tea, Edwina?" she asked. "I can easily summon Hentershee."

Her niece took the seat across from her and stretched out her legs to the fire. It was a very unladylike position, but Lady Julia did not reprimand her, since they were alone.

"Pray do not bother, ma'am," Edwina said. "We had a sumptuous spread at Richmond." Her brows rose a little as she spotted her aunt's half-empty glass of sherry. "Good heavens, dear auntie! Imbibing at this time of the afternoon?"

Lady Julia started, almost guiltily. "Fanny Lowden came to call. She . . . she had some distressing news to impart, and I thought the sherry would be welcome."

"Oh, Mrs. Lowden," Edwina said with supreme indifference as she stripped off her gloves and dropped them beside her.

Lady Julia studied her niece carefully. Edwina Ogilvie was girl of medium height, lithe and slim. She would never be called beautiful, or even passing pretty, but in spite of her long nose and heavy eyebrows, there was an air about her that must always be remarked. She was as supremely indifferent to her looks as she was to her aunt's best friend. Suddenly, as she watched, a little frown creased Edwina's brow, and she looked around as if puzzled. Lady Julia swallowed when she saw her gaze go to the vase of roses. In one quick motion she jumped to her feet to go and admire them.

"And may I inquire where this luscious bouquet came from, dear aunt?" Edwina asked, closing her eyes as she bent to inhale the scent. "It was not here when I left this morning," she continued. "Someone obviously admires you very much, for it is such an enormous tribute, is it not?"

"You would not believe me if I told you," Lady Julia said somewhat glumly, quite forgetting her determination to keep Edwina in the dark about her most unsuitable suitor.

Her niece came back to sit beside her and take her hands. "Who was it, ma'am?" she asked.

As her aunt folded her lips and tried to look severe, Edwina chuckled and said, "Very well, I shall guess. Now, let me see."

Fascinated, Lady Julia watched her wrinkle her nose and screw up her eyes in thought.

"I have it!" she crowed. "Beau Brummell! No? Perhaps Sir Walter Scott? Mr. Wordsworth? Hmm. Mr. Almack of the famous rooms? Prinny?"

Throughout this ever increasing list of ridiculous candidates, Lady Julia had shaken her head, but as the last name was uttered, she paled, one hand going to her mouth as if to restrain the gasp that had escaped her.

"No, you do not mean it, dear ma'am!" Miss Ogilvie exclaimed, her blue eyes shining. "The Prince of Wales himself? My word!"

Lady Julia shrugged. "Yes, the Prince called this morning. He was kind enough to congratulate me on my singing last week." She watched her niece's face, praying the girl would accept her story and ask no more about it. To her relief, Edwina nodded carelessly.

"I saw the Prince in the park last week," she said. "He paused, very near me, to speak to a friend. I thought he had beautiful gray eyes, so animated and intelligent, although, to be sure, he is a little portly." Edwina shrugged. "Of course, at his age that is only to be expected, I guess."

Unwilling to discuss the royal gentleman any further, Lady Julia rose. "Very true, my dear, but I think you have forgotten we are engaged in a theater party this evening. So kind of Lady Barr to include you! I really think you should have a bath after all your exercise, don't you agree?"

Miss Ogilvie rolled her eyes heavenward. "I had a bath two days ago, aunt," she said. "Mama does not believe excessive bathing at all necessary, or . . . or healthful."

Lady Julia wondered how many times she had had

this same argument with each of the young relatives sent to stay with her, and she stifled a sigh. "Nevertheless, Edwina, I believe a bath is in order. Unless, that is, you do not care to attend the theater this evening?"

For a moment aunt and niece stared at each other, but it was Miss Ogilvie who lowered her eyes and that stubborn chin first, and nodded her consent. As she went to the door, completely forgetting her hat and gloves, she said over her shoulder, "Alas, that you must make do with the company of mere mortals, after receiving our Exalted Highness, ma'am. It is too bad!"

She was chuckling again at her own wit as she turned and winked. Before Lady Julia could call her to order, she was gone in a swish of skirts.

At least the child does not hold a grudge, nor sulk, her aunt thought as she picked up the discarded articles of clothing. As she followed her upstairs to begin her own fastidious preparations for the evening, she prayed that the Prince would not be attending the theater too, for she much preferred consorting with mere mortals.

Lady Julia did enjoy herself that evening, for the play was splendid, and the party she was with, witty and amusing. And only a cursory glance at the royal box as they took their seats showed her she might relax, for her unwelcome admirer was nowhere to be seen.

Her happiness was short-lived, however. The following morning when her maid brought in her tray, there was a thick letter on it addressed to her.

Lady Julia eyed it as she poured her coffee, much in the way she would have eyed a fat black spider sitting beside her plate. She made no attempt to open it until she had fortified herself with two cups of steaming coffee, a roll, and a piece of ham. She always had breakfast in bed, for she had discovered she did not enjoy companionship or conversation first thing in the morning. But if she had some time alone to gather her

wits and plan her day, she found she could face the
world with impunity.

At last she could delay no longer. She could hear her
maid moving about in the adjoining dressing room,
where she was laying out her clothes, and Lady Julia
knew she must get up shortly. She took a deep breath
as she broke the ornate seal that secured the letter.
Several finely covered sheets fell into her hand. In
some trepidation, she picked them up and began to
read. Anyone watching her would have surprised a
number of emotions crossing her face. Reluctance
first, then disbelief, irritation, surprise, and even a
trace of satisfaction.

At last she lowered the sheets to the velvet coverlet
and leaned back on her pillows deep in thought.

The Prince had written of his love in a most elegant
way. And even though she had no intention of suc-
cumbing to him, what lady would not be pleased to be
told she was "the loveliest, most adored of women,
whose love would crown me with bliss forevermore"?

Suddenly remembering something that had puzzled
her, Lady Julia frowned a little as she took up the
sheets to search them. Yes, here it was! Whatever
could he mean by it? she wondered as she read the
lines again.

"Dear lady, as you accepted my flowers yesterday, a
humble tribute to your beauty and grace, I beg that
you will also accept that object that we admired together. I shall pray that you will show it to me again
when next I call. Believe me when I assure you that I
shall kneel at your feel if it is open, and cover your
white hands with a hundred fervent kisses that you
will grant me my heart's desire."

Lady Julia's hazel eyes widened. He must mean that
terrible snuffbox, but she did not have it in her possession. Perhaps he had sent it with the letter? She
searched the breakfast tray, but no package came to
light, and her maid, when questioned, knew nothing
about one.

Frowning now, Lady Julia rose and dressed. She would have to ask her butler, and the housemaids. Perhaps the Prince had placed it on a table, purposely forgetting to take it with him. Remembering the scene inside the lid, she flushed, hoping that if the servants had found it, they had not opened it.

Her most assiduous questioning was in vain. No one had seen a snuffbox, either in the drawing room or in the hall. Puzzled, Lady Julia retired to the library to write a cool, formal note to the Prince that would accompany his own letter that she fully intended to return. In it, she planned to deny not only her love but also any knowledge of his expensive gewgaw.

Several streets away, in a small antechamber of Carlton House, Trevor Whitney, the Earl of Bradford, sat thumbing through one of the morning journals and wondering as he did so how long he would be kept there cooling his heels. He had little expectation of seeing the Prince, for he had been summoned by one of the equerries on a matter of some importance, or so Colonel Lake had claimed. The earl sighed and ran a hand over his dark brown hair. His idea of a morning's amusement did not involve wasting time in an over-ornate, overheated anteroom, not that he had not done so many times in the past. The Prince—indeed, everyone in the royal household—valued his assistance on matters of delicacy, and he himself found it amusing to untangle the knotty situations the Prince seemed destined to embroil himself in over and over again. At least you can train dogs, the earl thought with a cynical smile. If only someone could train the Prince to learn from past mistakes! And he would be willing to wager any amount that the reason he was sitting here at Carlton House, instead of busy with his own pursuits, was that the Prince's roving, amorous eyes had discovered yet another lady he could not live without, however momentarily.

The earl stood and stretched his long, rangy body,

shaking his head as he did so. Just then the door opened, and Colonel Gerard Lake entered the room. He was an older man than his visitor by many years, and the time he had spent serving as the Prince's equerry had caused permanent lines to score his forehead, and given his thin mouth a distinct downward cast.

"Ah, my boy, how good of you to come," he said with old-fashioned courtesy as he bowed.

"When did I ever not obey a royal summons, sir?" the earl asked, his unusual blue-gray eyes crinkling shut in amusement. His smile transformed his lean face. In repose he appeared a more serious man than most, and one not given to informality, but his flashing smile made him appear years younger, and a great deal better-looking.

The colonel gestured to a chair. "As always, I am grateful for your help, m'lord," he said.

"Prinny in the suds again?" Lord Whitney asked as he sat down. He and the colonel had had a long association and they stood on no ceremony.

"*He* doesn't think so," the equerry said sharply.

"Ah. Blond, brunette, or redhead?" the earl asked lazily.

Colonel Lake leaned his elbows on the table between them and made a tent of his fingers. "I believe the lady in question has chestnut hair this time, m'lord," he said. "The Prince is greatly attracted to her, and is in hot pursuit."

"It was ever thus," m'lord remarked, sounding bored.

"He does not appear to be at all concerned that any scandal at this time, especially involving the fair sex, is apt to land him in a scrape. You are aware, m'lord, of Princess Caroline's latest indiscretion? Not content with taking lovers herself now that she and the Prince live apart, she has got herself with child!"

"But I do believe she must have had some assistance in the matter, sir," the earl said, his voice grave.

The colonel looked at him sharply, and when he saw the twinkle in those deep-set eyes, he was surprised into a tiny smile.

"Just so, m'lord, but of course there can be no question that it was the Prince who was so . . . ah, obliging. But if he behaves in like manner, and causes a new scandal, he will lose support. Support that comes to him because there are those disgusted with the immorality and loose behavior of the princess, and who now are prepared to choose his side. If only the Prince could be brought to realize how important that support will be when he assumes the throne! And if a whisper of this should come to the ears of the king . . ." He shuddered and ran a hand over his thinning gray hair, patting it carefully to hide his growing bald spot. "One would think that at the age of thirty-nine, the Prince of Wales would be content with the affections of one lady at a time. True, Lady Jersey's star has fallen, but Mrs. Fitzherbert is once more in ascendance. Why does he feel the need for yet another mistress?" He snorted in disgust.

"If the affair is conducted quietly, I fail to see that this is a serious problem, sir," the earl pointed out in the silence that followed these remarks. "And it might well cool as rapidly as it heated."

The older man waved an impatient hand. "I am most concerned with the lady in the case. From something he let drop, I fear she has a weapon she could use against the Prince."

The earl raised his brows. "More passionate letters?" he asked.

Again came the wave of the hand. "I am sure there will be those—the Prince is a tireless correspondent. No, it seems that he called on the lady yesterday morning. He went alone, clutching a bouquet, like any smitten swain. Ha! But while he was with her, he had occasion to offer her snuff, and when he returned to Carlton House, he discovered he had left the box behind. Of course, he is convinced it was a fortunate accident, and by reminding her of him, will speed the happy conclusion." There was a pregnant pause before the colonel concluded, "It was not one of his more—shall we say?—innocuous cases."

"Ah, one of the naughty ones, was it?" the earl asked, his eyes twinkling again. Really, the Prince was impossible, he thought as the equerry nodded, his face grim.

"What is more, the Prince just commissioned it this past week. Although a hurried job, I am told the lady represented looks very much like his newest passion. And, as you are aware, a box like that is such an obvious invitation to dalliance, it could hardly be considered subtle. And if the lady is determined to be expensive, it must surely come to the king's attention. You will remember how furious he was at the Prince's staggering debts only a few short months ago. His Highness must not incur any new ones at this time, over and above his usual extravagances. The problem is that the lady may well realize that she has a valuable object at hand, one by which her fortune could be made."

"You think she might try to blackmail the Prince?" the earl asked, sounding grim.

Colonel Lake shrugged. "I have no idea. I know little of her besides her name."

"And what are your orders, sir?" Lord Whitney asked.

"Get it back!" the colonel said rapidly. "And that as quickly as you can! I have spoken to His Highness, but he fails to see how serious this is. He claims he is content to leave the box in her hands, hoping the sight of it will speed her capitulation."

"Who is she? Do I know her?" the earl asked.

"You may. She is the Lady Julia Reynolds. She lives in Charles Street, near Berkeley Square. I believe she is in her early thirties, and a widow of some five years' standing." The colonel paused and frowned a little. "That is unusual, now that I come to think of it. His Highness generally admires women who are older than he himself. And this lady, besides being younger, is highly thought of in society. I discovered that never in the years of her widowhood has her name been linked with any man's. She seems content to travel life's paths alone, now that her husband is dead."

"As you say, most unusual," the earl murmured, suddenly mindful of his own ambition to do the same thing. Trevor Whitney was thirty-nine, the same age as his Prince. He had never married, nor felt the least compunction to do so in spite of his mother's ever-increasing comments about fleeting time and her desire to retire to the dower house at long last. He supposed he should get himself an heir, but the prospect of tying himself to one woman for the rest of his life was distasteful to him. He admitted freely that he preferred to be solitary, and since he had several promising nephews, all bearing the Whitney name, saw no reason why he had to marry to ensure the continuation of the line.

Colonel Lake interrupted his reverie. "Take whatever measures you feel necessary, my boy," he said. "Up to, and including, paying her to relinquish the box. And if we can keep our activities from His Highness, so much the better."

"You may rely on me to be discreet, sir," the earl said, rising as the older man got to his feet in dismissal.

As Colonel Lake strolled with him to the door, the earl mused, "How strange it is that the Prince continues his intrigues with the same intensity he had as a youth of nineteen. Then it was no wonder that he embraced the fleshpots with such fervor, not when you consider his almost monastic, sheltered boyhood. But surely now his endless love affairs are excessive."

Colonel Lake paused, his hand on the doorknob. He seemed to be lost in memory. "He must ever seek love, m'lord. He will do so all his life," he said at last. "I have been the Prince's equerry for many years. I believe he does so to make up for the love that has been denied him."

The earl stared down at the serious gray-haired man

as he went on quietly, "That love he knows he can never have, no matter how hard he tries to attain it, from the one person he himself loves best in the world."

There was a short silence, and then the earl asked, "Do you mean his father's love, sir?"

The colonel nodded. "Just so. I do not know why His Majesty dislikes his eldest son and the heir to the throne, for he adores his other children. Perhaps it is jealousy for the one who will succeed him." He shrugged a little. "I only know that that dislike has always been a part of his life since His Highness was a child. The Prince loves his father very much, but unfortunately, there is nothing he can do to make the king return his own, very real regard."

3

In spite of Colonel Lake's request for expediency, the earl did not rush into action at once. In such a delicate matter he knew it would be better to move slowly, with great caution, and he wanted some hard facts to hand before he accused the lady of intrigue.

Accordingly, he spent the rest of the day secluded in the library of his town house in Portman Square, making his plans. With more interest than usual, he riffled through the vast number of gilt-edged cards of invitation that lay on his desk, and he wrote a number of notes and sent his footmen running to deliver them.

It was late afternoon when he heard his mother's assured, commanding voice in the hall, and he went to the library door to ask her to join him. Lady Millicent Whitney looked surprised, but she agreed with a smile. Tall and as slim as when she had been a girl, she was white-haired now, but she held herself proudly erect. She had only recently arrived in town, for she claimed a woman of her advanced years could not endure the rigors of an entire Season without endangering her health. This sentiment always caused the earl's eyes to crinkle with amusement. His mother came from long-lived stock, and she had a wiry endurance. He would be willing to wager that except for her failing hearing, she was almost as healthy as he was himself.

"Trevor, my love," she said now, as she reached up to kiss him. "I did not know you were home. Shall I order tea?"

"Have a glass of wine with me instead, Mama," the earl invited, strolling to the drinks table. As he raised the decanter and his eyebrows simultaneously, she laughed.

"Very well, if you prefer it, my dear," she agreed, sitting down in a comfortable wing chair near the fire. "How delightful this is," she went on as she took the glass from his hands. "We should see more of each other."

"But we live in the same house, Mama," Lord Whitney reminded her.

"Quite so. But between my engagements, and your engagements, we never seem to have a moment alone together. Do you dine in, by the way?"

"Not this evening," the earl replied, leaning against the mantel, glass in hand. "And you?" he asked.

His mother shook her head. "No, I, too, am engaged. There is a soiree at the Rogerses', and dear Lady Rogers has kindly invited me to bear her mother company." The countess paused, and then she said, "Although it might be because Miss Nancy Rogers has made her come-out this Season, and her mother is aware of my bachelor son. I cannot say."

"I would remind you, Mama, that at the age of thirty-nine, I am much too old for a miss of eighteen," the earl said, coming to sit across from the countess, and crossing his long, well-breeched legs. "Why, I could be her father!"

His mother looked at him fondly. "I hate to disillusion you, my son, but you would not be too old at forty-nine or even fifty-nine. Lady Rogers has her eye on the main chance, and as long as a rich titled bridegroom can totter down the aisle unsupported, would welcome him to the family with open arms."

"Poor Miss Rogers," the earl murmured.

"What did you say, Trevor?" the countess demanded. "Please do not mumble. I have told you so many times before."

"I said that Miss Rogers was to be pitied, Mama," the earl replied, raising his voice a little. His mother refused to accept the fact that her hearing was failing, claiming instead that people in this modern age garbled their words, mumbling and drawling in the most distressing manner. It would never have been permitted in her own more polite youth.

"But now I think we will put the Rogerses and their ambitions, as well as any more social chitchat, aside," the countess said next, putting her glass of canary down. She folded her hands in her lap and fixed her son with a steady gaze. "What was the real reason you asked me to join you, Trevor?"

The earl shook his head. "I never could bamboozle you, could I, Mama?" he asked. "Very well. To get straight to the heart of the matter, I wish you to tell me everything you know about a Lady Julia Reynolds."

The countess leaned forward, her faded blue eyes glowing with her delight. "Dear boy, never say so!" she breathed. "And just when I thought it was useless to hope anymore! Why, I cannot tell you . . ."

The earl held up one strong, powerful-looking hand. "You most certainly cannot, Mama," he said. "My interest in the Lady Julia does not involve *amour*. Not mine, at any rate," he added softly.

His mother's face fell, but she said no more. There was no sense getting the man's back up, she told herself. But since this was the first lady he had shown any interest in in some time, she would not be discouraged. And Lady Julia was such a lovely woman, so tall and graceful. What a pair they would make! She would not despair.

Putting her dreams aside, she called to mind everything she knew of the lady, and related it to her son.

"You say she was married to Nigel Reynolds, Marquess Hastings?" the earl asked when her recital was concluded. He frowned. "I do not believe I ever knew him."

"It would be unusual if you did, Trevor," the countess said. "He was many years your senior. It was one of those May-December marriages we were just discussing. But I have it on good authority that he adored her, and they were such a happy couple, they were together constantly. After his fatal illness and death, everyone expected her to remarry, but she has not done so. She lives alone, except for the visits of her relatives, especially her young nieces and nephews. How good she is to them! A most superior woman, besides being so very lovely and talented."

"Talented?" the earl prompted.

"Yes, she has a clear, true soprano. I have never heard a finer voice even on the concert stage," his mother assured him.

"An excellent woman all around, I see," her son said, trying to forget the Prince's love of music and his expertise on the violoncello. "Have you heard nothing to her detriment, Mama? No faults of any kind? No discreet liaisons?"

The countess shook her head, and then she said with dignity, "I can see by your expression, Trevor, that you think me gilding the lily, in hopes of interesting you, but that is not true. Julia Reynolds is truly lovely and good. A lady in the best sense of the word."

"A veritable paragon," the earl murmured, and his mother leaned forward.

"She most certainly is not!" she exclaimed. "Whatever can you mean? An irritable parasite, indeed!"

The earl chuckled as he came to draw his mother to her feet and hug her. "Never mind, ma'am," he said close to her ear, and then he explained.

They parted in perfect accord, the earl to change to evening clothes, and his mother to dream for a while beside the fire in her boudoir, of a rosy future that promised several more handsome, intelligent grandchildren bearing the Whitney name.

That evening and all the following day, the Earl of Bradford was seen here, there, and everywhere. His appearance occasioned no little comment, for he was not in general fond of society and its amusements. But although he attended not one, but four parties that evening, and rode, strolled, and chatted all the next day, the lady he sought was nowhere to be found.

He knew his mother was attending a reception of Lady Jersey's tonight, and knowing how this particular hostess insisted on a perfect crush at her parties, decided he would escort his mother there. Perhaps the elusive Lady Julia would also be in attendance.

As the two entered the crowded rooms, the earl raised his quizzing glass and looked around. There was not a hint of anything but insouciance on his lean face, but he felt his heart quicken a little when his mother said, "Why, there is Lady Julia now."

"Where?" he asked, looking around again.

"Are you blind, my son?" the countess demanded. "The tall chestnut-haired beauty in emerald green, of course, standing with Lord Alvanley and Fanny Lowden."

The earl raised his glass again for a careful inspection, and his heart sank. The woman was undoubtedly handsome. As he watched, she smiled a little at something Lord Alvanley was saying, and he watched her turn into a beauty. Intently he inspected that alluring form. Ah, yes, he thought. The soft white skin, the smooth shoulders and arms, and the magnificent deep bosom would all attract the Prince, as would the slim waist above a pair of rounded, swelling hips. She had long legs and a neat ankle as well, he noted.

"If you are quite through, Trevor?" the countess said beside him, sounding a little annoyed. "One would hate to rush you, but such a detailed inspection is rude, and besides, we are blocking the door."

The earl lowered his glass and offered his arm. "Shall we, Mama?" he asked meekly, as if stricken by her lecture. The countess was not fooled.

"Let us stroll about the room," he went on. "And then, perhaps, you would be so good as to present me to the lady."

The countess stopped dead, upsetting an elderly gentleman behind her, who almost skidded into her. "Do you mean you have not even been introduced?" she asked, her voice awful.

"Not as yet," the earl said cheerfully, drawing her onward. "But that can soon be rectified, can it not?"

The countess sniffed, her visions of chestnut-haired grandchildren fading slightly.

It was some time later before the Whitneys found themselves near Lady Julia Reynolds. As she curtsied to the countess, her expression was thoughtful. She did not know the elderly lady very well, and she was surprised to be sought out by her.

"May I present my son, Trevor, Earl Bradford, Lady Julia?" the countess asked.

"M'lord," Lady Julia said, curtsying again. The earl bowed, and as he studied her, up close this time, a delicate color washed over her cheeks. She looked back at him almost defiantly as she studied him in turn. She realized that she had never seen a pair of eyes quite like his. They were an arresting blue-gray in color, and they were surrounded by such a pure white, it was obvious the gentleman had little use for late nights or debauchery. They were also piercing in their intensity, even deep-set as they were in his lean face. She did not consider him a handsome man in spite of his fine eyes. He was too severe, his haughty expression almost cynical.

"An honor, m'lady," he said, his deep voice holding nothing more than slight interest.

As Lady Julia turned to the countess to ask her how she did, she wondered why she felt such a tremor of unease. The two ladies chatted briefly, and then Julia felt a hand touch her arm, and she looked up to see the earl holding out a handsome snuffbox. It was made of green porphyry mounted in gold, and decorated with a marble mosaic depicting a classical landscape.

As she watched, her heart beating a little faster now, he deftly opened the box, using only his left hand, as gracefully as ever Beau Brummell did. "Lady Julia?" he asked with a little bow.

"Thank you, no, m'lord," she said. "I do not take snuff."

The earl, who was listening carefully, could have sworn her voice was slightly constricted, and he smiled to himself.

Taking a pinch himself, he closed the box, ignoring his mother's frown. "I do assure you, you are missing a treat, m'lady," he said easily. "My mixture is from Fribourg and Treyer. It is called the King's Carotte, and I have it in good authority that it is our Prince's favorite. He, as I am sure you know, is a connoisseur of snuff. Why, his cellar is worth thousands of pounds, and his collection of boxes superb."

Lady Julia seemed to draw clower to the countess as he spoke, but she did not look away from him. "Indeed?" she murmured, before her gaze went past him. He was sure her hazel eyes brightened. "I must ask you to excuse me, Countess, m'lord," she said. "Lady Jersey if beckoning."

"How very unfortunate! And at her own party, too," the countess remarked.

Lady Julia looked confounded, and the earl took a hand. It was several moments before his mother discovered her hostess was "beckoning," not "sickening."

"Run along, my dear," the countess said after all had been made clear, but this Lady Julia was not allowed to do until the earl had lifted her hand to kiss. There was no hidden pressure of the hand that held hers, nor did his lips linger on her fingers, but still Julia was delighted to leave his side. She had come this evening only because she was positive the Prince would not attend a party given by his former mistress, but there was something about the Earl of Bradford that seemed to warn her of a danger just as real as any His Highness offered. She did not care for the feeling.

"And what was that bit of nonsense all about,

Trevor?" the countess whispered harshly as Lady Julia moved gracefully away. "I have never known you to take snuff in my life!"

"Ah, one acquires all kinds of habits, Mama, some good, some bad," the earl said as he escorted her to a set of chairs nearby. Two of her friends were already ensconced there, and he knew, once he had her safe in their company, he would be free to mingle in the crowd.

The earl did not approach Lady Julia Reynolds again. He saw her popularity with members of both sexes, but although he watched her carefully, albeit as inconspicuously as possible, he did not see any indication that she was a flirt. She was pleasant, she chatted and smiled, but he wondered if he were imagining a slight formality in her manner, a touch-me-not attitude in her posture and demeanor that seemed to say she would not welcome any gentleman's attentions. Lady Julia was a puzzle, and he found himself warming to his task. He would discover what made the lady tick, he promised himself, just as he would discover what she meant to do with the Prince's snuffbox.

The following morning, he sent his valet to Charles Street with careful instructions. Hennings had been with him for years, and had proven an invaluable assistant on many occasions before this. When he reappeared to help the earl dress for dinner, he had several interesting developments to report.

"I rather thought the lady's butler would be impossible to approach, m'lord. He has been with the family too long," he told his master as he carefully pared his nails. "It was just a lucky chance that I followed one of the younger footmen to his pub this afternoon. I bought him a pint or two and enlisted his aid, claiming that the gentleman I served was in love with the lady and would pay well for information about her engagements."

"Quick work, Hennings," the earl complimented him.

The valet smiled a little as he took up the earl's other hand. "You will like to know that Lady Julia rides in the park tomorrow morning with her niece, a Miss Edwina Ogilvie, that she is engaged for tea with her friend Mrs. Lowden, and that she has a dinner engagement with Lady Browning. The next day she plans a shopping trip, and she will attend a concert of sacred music, again with her niece, that evening."

"Excellent, Hennings!" the earl said, clapping his man on the shoulder now his hands were free. Hennings looked pleased as he went to get m'lord's dark blue jacket and ease him into it.

"Ply him with all the pints necessary to keep him talking," the earl said as he settled the jacket on his broad shoulders, and Hennings fussed around him with a clothes brush, dealing with imaginary specks. "And do not hesitate to offer him money, if he appears to be having qualms of conscience."

"Certainly, m'lord," the valet agreed, as he bowed his master to the door of his room.

The earl strolled down the stairs, well pleased with the progress that had been made. His butler presented him with a note.

"This has just come, m'lord," he said.

The earl recognized Colonel Lake's handwriting on the inscription, and he was quick to take the note to his library to study.

A few minutes later, he was frowning, all good humor gone from his face.

"M'lord," the note began abruptly, "It has become known to me that the lady we were discussing the other day denies any knowledge of the object we seek. That in itself is disturbing, but she has also returned all correspondence sent her by the principal in the case, and she refuses to see him. I fear she is playing a deeper game, although I cannot imagine what it could be. I do, however, believe haste to be imperative."

The earl sat tapping the note on his desk for several moments before he nodded to himself. He would write to her and ask for an appointment sometime after her ride in the park, and before her engagement for tea tomorrow. And he would phrase his note carefully, in such a way that she would be unable to refuse to see him.

This was a more difficult task than he had imagined, for they were, after all, barely acquainted. At last he nodded again, and sacrificed his mother's name to the cause.

A footman was sent running to Charles Street, and in an hour he had her formal reply, agreeing to the meeting. He was able to enjoy his dinner with a good appetite, therefore, and he allowed himself the luxury of staying home that evening, reading a good book.

Early the next afternoon, he arrived in Charles Street a little before the appointed time. He had chosen to walk from Portman Square, and his long legs had covered the distance quickly. As the lady's butler Hennings bowed him inside, he saw at once why Hennings had not approached the man. He fairly reeked "old family retainer."

"I beg your pardon, sir," this austere individual was saying now. "Lady Julia told me you were expected, but she herself is not here. Would you care to wait in the library? I am sure m'lady will soon return. She is always prompt to her appointments."

The earl nodded his assent to this plan, and the butler escorted him to the library. After refusing any refreshment to help while away the time, Lord Whitney stepped inside. He was a little surprised to find himself being regarded by a young girl whose rather homely face was further disfigured by a ferocious scowl. She was curled up reading in a chair near the fire, and she rose most reluctantly. He noticed she kept her place with one finger.

"And who might you be?" she asked in a gruff little voice.

Lord Whitney checked in astonishment. He was sure he had never met such an abrupt young miss. Strolling toward the fire, he said, "I am Trevor

Whitney, the Earl of Bradford. And who might *you* be?"

As she curtsied, she said, "I am Edwina Ogilvie, Lady Julia Reynolds' niece. Have you come to see my aunt?"

The earl nodded. He was a little amused when he saw her suppress a tiny sigh and put her book down with the great air of one about to do her duty, no matter how difficult or tiresome that duty might be.

"Won't you be seated, m'lord?" she asked. "I am sure Aunt Julia will return soon. She had an errand she had to run, and she has been gone for some time now."

The earl sat down across from her. "Are you enjoying your stay in London, Miss Ogilvie?" he asked politely.

"Yes, I am," his reluctant hostess replied. "It is interesting to observe society. Of course, I am not out yet, being just turned sixteen." She paused, and then asked, her voice even gruffer, "Although what difference it will make when I am, I cannot see."

The visitor must have looked a question, for she went on, "It is obvious that I will never take, no matter how much town bronze I acquire. My mother sent me to Aunt Julia this Season, hoping, I am sure, for a miracle. But even if I were interested in such paltry things as *haut couture* and courtship, it will never happen. Not even with my aunt as a model."

"I do not think you should disdain society so quickly, Miss Ogilvie," the earl felt compelled to say, even though he was certain she was right. She was such a funny little thing with her gruff voice and plain face. Perhaps if something were done about those heavy eyebrows? he mused.

Miss Ogilvie shrugged, her face contemptuous. "I don't care," she said airily. "I have no interest in cutting a dash. In fact, I think it all silly beyond belief."

She stared at the earl. "Are you married, sir?" she asked.

The earl stared back. How gauche she was, he thought as he told her he was not.

"And you are very old, are you not? Quite past the age to consider it now," she said.

Lord Whitney had trouble controlling his expression.

"Neither is my aunt married," she went on. "Why can't I emulate her?"

"But Lady Julia is a widow, Miss Ogilvie," the earl reminded her. "And I know that single ladies do not have anywhere near the freedom enjoyed by wives and widows. Perhaps you should reconsider?"

His young hostess put her head to one side, deep in thought. "You mean marry some old man like Julia did, and hope he dies quickly?" she asked. "Well, that is a possibility."

"I meant nothing of the sort!" the earl snapped.

"I'm sure I beg your pardon," the irrepressible Miss Ogilvie said. She did not sound at all regretful at her lapse of good taste.

Trevor Whitney decided a change of subject would be most welcome, even as he wondered what the devil was keeping Lady Julia. "I saw you reading when I came in," he said smoothly. "Is it a good book?"

Miss Ogilvie looked down at it, and her eyes lit up. "Oh, yes, it is the most exciting tale!" she said, and then she chuckled. "Not at all serious or moral, you know. That is one thing I really enjoy in London. The circulating libraries are so fine! And unlike my mother, Aunt Julia does not supervise my reading. It has been most . . . most educational."

She grinned at the earl, and he smiled back. There was no denying Miss Ogilvie had a way about her, he thought. In spite of her outspoken manner and lack of polish, she was a taking little thing.

The door of the library was thrown open then, and Lady Julia swept in. Not a hair was out of place, nor was her smart gown disarranged, but somehow she seemed a little flustered. The earl rose and bowed.

As she gave him her hand, she said, "I do beg your pardon, sir, for keeping you waiting. There was a carriage accident and I was held up in the resulting traffic."

Before he could speak, she turned to her niece. "Thank you for entertaining the earl for me, dear Edwina," she said. "But now I think we will excuse you. Do take your book into the drawing room. I shall be with you presently."

Obediently the girl curtsied. Her eyes were bright with curiosity, and the earl saw Lady Julia shake her head in silent warning. He was a little surprised when Miss Ogilvie left them without blurting out some impossible remark or asking some daring question. From what he had learned of her the past few minutes, he was positive there was one hovering on her lips.

4

As the door closed behind the unprepossessing, yet preposterous Miss Ogilvie, Lady Julia turned to her guest with a formal, welcoming smile. "Won't you please be seated, m'lord, and tell me how I might assist you?" she asked in her clear soprano, indicating a chair as she did so.

Lady Julia had not wanted to receive the Earl of Bradford. She was unnerved and unsettled, and she felt enough confusion at the continued attentions of her royal admirer without adding another difficult, dangerous man to her life. Some little intuition, however, had warned her it might be most unwise for her to refuse to see him, her problems with the Prince notwithstanding.

Every day the Prince sent her another letter, pages and pages of compliments and fervent declarations of love, all interspersed with pleading that she become his mistress. The one she had received this morning with her breakfast tray had even hinted of his possible illness and death if she would not be kind to him. He claimed he could not eat or sleep, nor hardly breathe because of her refusal to surrender. And he had sent gifts. Yesterday there had been the most beautiful gauze fan that was set in a jeweled mounting so magnificent that Julia had gasped. Today there had been flowers accompanying an emerald pendant as big as a bird's egg. She had returned everything, both the gifts and the letters, and she had implored the Prince to believe her when she told him she would never love him with anything more than the love any loyal subject gave her sovereign. But even as she sealed her note and sent the footman running to Carlton House, she had known despair. It seemed to her that the colder she acted to the Prince, the hotter and more abandoned he became. She did not know what to do, nor where to turn.

And here, taking the seat she indicated, was this enigmatic earl with his cynical expression and piercing eyes that seemed to see a great deal more than most men. As she picked up Edwina's handkerchief and an apple core the girl had left behind before sitting across from him, she took a deep breath.

"I do hope Edwina behaved herself, but somehow I am sure she did not, m'lord," she said lightly. "I shall ask you to forgive her before I even inquire."

The earl smiled a little, but the watchful look in his eyes did not change. "I have forgiven her already, ma'am," he said. "She was quite outspoken, but I do not think I shall reveal the content of our conversation. Does she remain with you for long, Lady Julia?"

He crossed his legs, leaning back perfectly at his ease. Still wondering what he had come for, Julia said, "I expect she will be with me for the duration of the Season, m'lord. Unless, of course, she does something so outrageous I shall have to send her home. With Edwina that is a distinct possibility. But come, enough of my niece. Your note confused me; I do not understand exactly why you requested this interview."

"It is simply explained, although I hesitated to commit it to writing," the earl said, never taking his eyes from hers. "I have come as an emissary, if you like, to recover an object you have in your possession. An object, Lady Julia, that has the potential to create all kinds of difficulties. Mostly for you."

Julia's chin had come up as he spoke, but he noted she still looked confused, and she had not started or shown any sign of consciousness as he spoke.

"You will have to be plainer, sir," she said. "If you speak in riddles, I fear we may never reach an understanding."

"Very well," the earl said, his deep voice harsher. "I want you to give me the snuffbox the Prince left here, so I might return it to him, and that's a plain statement for you, ma'am. However you planned to use it, for profit or for scandal, can come to naught, since we know that the box is in your possession."

"But I do not have the snuffbox!" Julia exclaimed, leaning forward now as she endeavored to make him believe her. "I have not seen it since the Prince showed it to me that first day he called."

In despair, she saw the earl shake his head, and knowing he did not believe her, she added swiftly, "Have you any idea how unpleasant all this has been for me, who never wanted to be pursued by royalty? I do not love the Prince, and I shall never become his mistress. And that's a plain statement for *you*, m'lord. But no matter how many times I tell him so, he will not believe me. Besides, I have returned all his gifts and letters. Surely I would have returned the snuffbox, too, if I had it."

Throughout this impassioned speech, Trevor Whitney had looked only mildly interested. Now he leaned forward in turn to say, "But since, as I understand it, the box was commissioned for you, you might well consider it your own. It is worthless to anyone else. And, of course, it has great . . . er, value to you. But it will not do, Lady Julia. The box must be surrendered."

Lady Julia rose to her feet, unable to sit calmly anymore. The earl followed her example in leisurely fashion, and he watched her as she took a few uncertain steps, her hands clenched tightly at her sides.

She turned and faced him again at last, to say with

dignity, "I do assure you on my honor, m'lord, I do not have that snuffbox in my possession. I can say nothing more."

The earl stepped closer, but she held her ground. He was so near her now she could smell the soap he used, and the scent of his skin that was not masked by the heavy lotion or perfumes so many gentlemen affected. "But where is the box, then, Lady Julia, if you do not have it?" he asked softly.

She threw out her hands. "I have no idea."

"The Prince is positive he left it here," the earl continued, his eyes locked with her.

As she stared up into their wintry depths, Julia saw how they had darkened with suppressed anger, and she shivered a little.

"I do not like to contradict the Prince, but he cannot have done so," she said through stiff lips. "I have questioned my servants, and searched myself, and there is no snuffbox to be found." She paused for a moment, and then, as if tired of being on the defensive, she asked, "But what is your interest in all this, m'lord?"

"As I told you, I am an emissary. Not of the Prince, to be sure, but of his royal household advisers, and of the king's." He stopped, as if to give her time to consider the implications of what he had just said. "I shall be open with you, Lady Julia," he said, when she did not speak. "This is a dangerous time for the Prince. No new scandal must attach to his name—not now. And that box is damning evidence that he intends to set up yet another mistress—you. What could be more plain that *maya vestida* and *maya denuda?* Especially since the lady depicted has titian hair and your identical features? Surely you can see why it must be returned before it falls into unscrupulous hands."

His lips twisted in a cynical smile, as if he really believed it was already in those hands. Julia flinched.

"I would give it to you in a moment, if I had it. I do not," she said quietly, her clear hazel eyes never leaving his face as she willed him to believe her.

The earl shrugged. "I see. Perhaps a period of reflection might be wise, ma'am? I shall return tomorrow. At that time I shall hope you will be more amenable, especially when I tell you then the sum we are willing to pay you to recover the box."

As she gasped at his audacity, his hands enclosed her upper arms. His grasp was not painful, but still she felt threatened.

"This is a dangerous game you play, m'lady. You cannot win," he said, as quietly as she had spoken. But in his voice were iron determination and a proud assurance that he would not fail. Julia felt despair. "We really must have that box," he went on. "I warn you now, we shall stop at nothing to regain it. Believe me when I tell you it would be to your advantage to cooperate. Otherwise . . . well, who can say what unpleasantness might occur?"

Suddenly he dropped his hands and stepped back. Julia took a shaky breath as he bowed.

"Until tomorrow, m'lady," he said. "Expect me at noon."

Julia heard the door close softly behind him, but she remained standing exactly where he had left her. She fancied she could still hear his threats, still feel his hands on her skin, and she looked down, as if expecting to see ugly bruises. But of course there were none, for he had not hurt her. She wondered what on earth she was to do? It was impossible for her to return something she did not have. But since not only the earl but also the king himself—the king!—thought she had that terrible snuffbox, she was in serious trouble. What might they not do to punish her for defying them? Royalty could do anything, even in 1801. Her difficulties repulsing the Prince's advances seemed very unimportant now.

There was a knock on the door, and Edwina ran in. "I could not wait another moment, dear auntie!" she crowed. "What was that all about? Have you acquired another admirer?"

Lady Julia's heart sank. Not for the first time, she wished her sisters would let her lead her own life, and cease burdening her with difficult, inquisitive young relatives. She had to make herself smile. "Only a small commission the earl wishes me to undertake for his mother, Edwina," she said as casually as she could.

She saw further questions in her niece's eyes, and she added quickly, "But do look at the time! I must change lest I be late. You do remember that I am expected at Mrs. Lowden's for tea, do you not?"

She patted Edwina's cheek and left the room, suddenly feeling some little relief that at least she could discuss this problem with her dear friend. Perhaps Fanny would know what she should do, she thought as she hurried up the stairs to change.

She was disappointed when she entered Fanny's rooms a little later to discover old Mrs. Jennings and her sister already settled in around the tea tray. She had so hoped Fanny would be alone! None of her feelings showed as she removed her things and made pleasant conversation with the two elderly ladies, however. As she took her seat, and her hostess poured her a cup of tea, she looked around. Fanny's rooms were very pleasant with the late-afternoon sun streaming in to illuminate the scene. Julia knew that the woman who rented the rooms was careful about which tenants she took, and that Fanny considered herself well situated here in Wimpole Street. When her husband had died many years before, leaving her childless, Fanny had not cared to continue living alone in a large house. Julia knew she herself would not have liked taking rooms, but then, she knew that in many ways, and even as close as they were, she and her friend were very different.

It seemed an endless time before the two old sisters took their leave. Fanny winked at her over their heads as she collected reticules and shawls, Mrs. Jennings' cane, and Miss Eudalia's parcels before she ushered the ladies out.

"There!" she said as she closed the door behind them and made shooing motions with her hands. "Now we are quite private, my dear Julia, and you shall tell me without another second's delay what has been bedeviling you this past hour."

Julia smiled. "You read me so well, Fanny," she said. "Yes, I do have a problem—as usual, it seems these days."

"The Prince continues relentless?" Fanny asked, offering her the plate of tea cakes.

Julia shook her head. "No more, thank you. Yes, he is still in hot pursuit, and I, of course, in rapid retreat. Nothing has changed there."

"What did he sent you this morning, my dear?" Fanny asked.

"An emerald pendant as big as that piece of sugar," Julia said, pointing to the tea tray. Her hostess gasped.

"And another impassioned letter," Julia added, her voice glum. "But it is not about the Prince that I am concerned today. No, indeed. The Earl of Bradford called on me this afternoon. He came as an emissary of the Prince's advisers, and of the king, to demand the return of the snuffbox."

"Never say so!" Mrs. Lowden breathed, losing more of her imperturbability as she arched her thin brows.

"Whatever am I to do, Fanny?" Julia wailed softly. "The earl returns tomorrow for the snuffbox, and how can I produce something I do not have? And he refuses to believe me when I deny any knowledge of it."

Her friend looked thoughtful as she sipped her tea. "Bradford, hmm?" she asked as she set her cup down. "I know of him, although he does not often seek society's amusements. But however unlike they may be, he is in the Prince's retinue. He is an educated man, and I believe became acquainted with the Prince when he first came to London. Their tastes in literature and music are similar. And it seems to me that I have also heard that the Prince has trusted him in the past with delicate missions."

She seemed to be thinking, and then she shook off her abstraction and said, "What else did the earl say, Julia?"

"Any number of things," her friend admitted. "He was most unpleasant, although at all times the perfect gentleman, even when he as good as threatened me! And he had the audacity to tell me that tomorrow he will let me know how much money he is prepared to give me to recover the box."

Mrs. Lowden's eyes narrowed. "That is audacity indeed," she said.

"Fanny, I cannot help being frightened," Julia went on. "Might they not put me in the Tower if I do not give them the snuffbox? After all, the king is concerned in the matter . . ."

Her friend considered this for a moment. "But I cannot believe that he is," she said slowly. "The Prince has a separate household, and his own loyal servants and advisers. I understand that it is common practice for them to shield him from his father's wrath. No, I do not think the king knows anything about this, for there is no gossip as yet. I questioned both Mrs. Jennings and her sister about that before you came. You know how they love to relay the latest *on-dit!* I have to believe, therefore, that the earl mentioned the king only to frighten you. It seems to me that you must just continue to deny any knowledge of the box, and all this furor will die away."

Julia looked doubtful. "Well, I suppose it might happen that way," she said, and then her hazel eyes brightened. "And, Fanny, if I continue to refuse the Prince, surely he will grow tired of wooing me and find some other, more melting, agreeable lady! And when he does not want me anymore, his friends will see I am no longer a threat to him!"

Mrs. Lowden leaned back in her chair to avoid a stray sunbeam that was shining in her eyes. "I had not thought of that," she said. "Yes, you are right, my dear. When Prinny ceases his attentions, you will be safe."

"*Dear* Fanny, do pour me more tea," Julia said, her voice happier now. "I feel so much better!"

As she took the cup her hostess held out, she added, "But if I am taken to the Tower in chains and under heavy guard, know that I shall expect you to get me out!"

Mrs. Lowden's lips curled in a smile. "You are funning, are you not, my dear? I am sure you will never be put away in that ugly place, for you are guiltless. But I must hear everything that happens to you, if I am to advise you. Do say you will take me up in your carriage for a drive tomorrow afternoon. We can be private there, if we speak softly, and I would hear any new developments. I am so worried about you, Julia!"

"I should be glad to, but won't Edwina think it very strange that she is not included too?" Lady Julia asked. "I have not told her anything, by the way, about this terrible matter."

Mrs. Lowden shrugged. "You must not let her impose on you so, my dear Julia. After all, you are taking her to a concert tomorrow evening, are you not? The girl cannot expect to hang on your sleeve every minute, for it is not very amusing for you, or for your friends."

Julia considered her remark before she said, "You do not like Edwina, do you, Fanny?"

Mrs. Lowden sniffed. "To be honest, I do not. She is pert, and not at all respectful to her elders. I consider her a badly brought-up, encroaching miss. Her parents will have a hard time launching her, for even putting aside her plainness, her manner is such that it must always give offense."

"I pray you are wrong," Julia said. "However, she remains with me only until July, and I am thankful I am not responsible for her future."

"Take care that your sister Mary does not insist that you bring her out when she turns eighteen," Mrs. Lowden warned. "I would not put it past her to lay that burden on your shoulders too. I can hear her arguments now! After all, dear sister, you move in the best circles of town, and I am so busy with the other children!"

Julia laughed as she put down her empty cup to pull on her gloves. "I shall stand firm, never fear! Three months of Edwina are all any mortal woman should have to stand, although in many ways I am very fond of her. She is such a funny little thing, how could I not be?"

Mrs. Lowden walked with her to the door, her arm around the supple waist of her taller friend. "Goose!" she scolded. "You are too softhearted, Julia, as I have told you time out of mind."

An hour was set for their drive on the morrow, and Julia tripped down the stairs, her heart much easier. She was so glad she had Fanny to confide in. She always felt so much better after a dose of her cool common sense.

Because of her talk with Fanny Lowden, Lady Julia was able to enjoy her dinner party at the Brownings' that evening with much of her old enthusiasm. It was a small, select group, and one that did not include either an amorous Prince or a threatening earl, which certainly added to her pleasure.

She would not have fallen asleep so easily later if she had had a glimpse of the Earl of Bradford's face when he returned home from an evening at White's, however.

Just as she was laying her head down on her pillow, he was entering his house in Portman Square, to find his butler holding out a note.

On learning that it had come from Carlton House only an hour before, and that the footman who had brought it had said it was most urgent, the earl's enigmatic expression turned to a ferocious scowl, and he only nodded curtly before he retired to his library.

His face as he finished reading the note was taut with emotion, and his deep-set eyes dark with anger. Colonel Lake had written to tell him that an anonymous letter had been delivered at Carlton House that evening, a letter that claimed its writer had the snuff-box safe. It also stated that a large sum would soon be demanded for the return of the box, and if such money was not forthcoming immediately, the scandal would be leaked to the journals and to the political satirists who had in the past taken such great delight in depicting every one of the Prince's peccadilloes in their crude cartoons. The colonel begged Lord Whitney to call on him the following morning, so they might discuss this new development, and the earl might see with his own eyes this damning, dangerous letter.

5

The next morning the earl chose to go to Carlton House by shank's mare, as he almost always did when he was in town. He was a man who insisted on regular exercise, for he felt it kept him fit and alert.

As he walked briskly along Park Lane, he found himself recalling his interview with Lady Julia Reynolds the day before. He was surprised that she had troubled his dreams, and that somehow he found himself wanting to believe that she was as innocent as she claimed. This was so unprofessional of him that he was disgusted with himself, but putting aside the uncharacteristic sympathy he felt for her, it was plain that she was either a consummate actress or she was, indeed, without guilt. Could she have written the letter he was about to see? It did not seem very likely, for why would she take the risk, when she knew he was coming at noon to tell her the amount they would give her for the box? Surely it would have been much more prudent for her to wait and hear it from his own lips. Then if she did not consider it enough, she could have written, demanding more.

He heard someone call to him, and he touched his hat to Lord Alvanley, who was about to enter the park with a party of friends, all mounted on restless thoroughbreds.

Park Lane was noisy this morning, for there were
many people and riders abroad. Carriages and carts
rumbled over the cobbles, giving the crossing sweepers
more work to do, and adding to the din. A little way
ahead, people had gathered to watch two tradesmen
involved in a loud argument, while footmen pushed
their way through the crowd, intent on urgent
errands. Nearby, a nanny waiting to cross the street
was busy instructing her young charges to cover their
ears, lest they hear words unsuitable for children of
their station. He saw a sweep coming toward him,
carrying his long brushes in one hand, while the other
gripped his climbing boy's collar tightly. Two ladies
gave them a wide berth, holding their skirts aside to
prevent any contact with the grime that clung to
them.

This was London, the London he had known for
years, bustling and thriving, and sometimes raucous
and bawdy as well. On this fine spring day its inhab-
itants went about their business with their usual gusto.
Trevor Whitney wondered what they would think if
they knew of the predicament their Prince was in, and
his expression grew more cynical. Some would laugh,
he knew, and make lewd jokes, but many would nod
and tell their friends how unstable the Prince was, and
how much better off they all were with good old King
George.

As a coachman cracked his whip and shouted loudly
to his team, the earl pictured in his mind's eye the
quiet serenity of Lady Julia's well kept house in
Charles Street. He had noticed and approved its
quality. There was nothing second-rate about either
its furnishings or its appointments. Obviously the late
marquess had left Lady Julia a rich widow. And was
that also not an argument in the lady's favor? he asked
himself. She could not need money, unless her house
was only a facade, and she was desperate because of
unpaid bills or gambling debts. He reminded himself
to ask the colonel to check on the state of her finances

as he made his way past the arguing men, not even hearing their bullying shouts.

As he strode along, he admitted he had been struck as well by the lady's behavior. She was a lovely woman, calm and self-assured. Indeed, her home seemed a reflection of her own excellent attributes. He had found himself wanting to relax in her presence— at least he had until he began his questioning. Yet even now, he could still hear her clear voice denying any knowledge of the snuffbox's whereabouts, and he had seen how she kept her hazel eyes firmly on his as she proclaimed her innocence. And once again he had noticed her formal manner, a manner that seemed to say, "You are allowed to approach me this far, but I will permit you to come no further." She was a mystery indeed.

The earl was so lost in his thoughts that he was surprised when he saw he had arrived at Carlton House. After he had been admitted, he found he did not have to wait very long today for the colonel to join him in the small antechamber.

When the usual courtesies had been exchanged, the two men took their seats. The colonel, without further ado, handed him the letter that had been delivered last evening.

He sat quietly watching the earl's face as he read it. It was as cryptic as ever, and the colonel thought what a shame it was that the earl had never considered entering diplomatic service.

At last Lord Whitney put the letter down on the table between them. "Who knows of this, sir?" he asked, tapping it with one finger.

"Myself, and one of the Prince's secretaries," the colonel said. "I have not shown it to the Prince. Frankly, I hope he never learns of it, and of the treachery of the lady he thinks he loves."

"How was it delivered?" the earl asked next, his eyes intent.

"It was brought to one of the back doors by a ragamuffin of a boy. The maid who took it from him did not understand its importance, you understand. Not that she could have detained him for questioning in any case, however, for she says he was off like a shot as soon as he put it in her hands."

The colonel frowned and rubbed his forehead, as if he were weary. Knowing his devotion to the Prince, the earl was sure he had not slept well this past night. He picked up the letter again, to study the handwriting. "Does this look like a woman's hand to you, sir?" he asked.

"I cannot tell," the colonel admitted. "It is obviously disguised, for see how it has been printed, rather than written in script. I believe it was composed by an educated person, however, for the sentences are lucid and there are no misspellings. You might ask Lady Julia for a sample of her handwriting, not that that would be conclusive of guilt or innocence in any case."

The earl raised his dark brows, and the colonel explained. "She could very well have had a confederate write the letter for her. I think you should take it along with you and show it to her. Observe her reactions carefully—ah, I don't have to tell you that, my boy, now do I? I beg your pardon, my wits have gone begging!" He shook his head before he went on, "You may tell her we will pay her a thousand pounds for the snuffbox. Hopefully, she will accept our offer, although it is worth much more to her."

Trevor Whitney shifted a little on the ornate gilt chair. "Do you know, I find I am beginning to doubt that the Lady Julia has the box at all," he said slowly.

Colonel Lake's faded blue eyes opened wide as Trevor Whitney told him everything he had discovered in his interview with the lady the day before. "This theft is so out of character for her," he concluded. "If you were to meet her, I am sure you must agree with me. She is not at all the type for blackmail. She is too fine."

"Can it be that you are falling under the woman's spell too?" the colonel asked in astonishment. Before the earl could deny it, he went on in a rush. "Think, my boy, think! The Prince took the case to her house. He showed it to her. When he returned here, he did not have it. Of course she has the snuffbox! Never underestimate the power of greed, m'lord. No matter how wealthy they are, there are some people who can never have enough. Greed is one of the most unattractive failings of the human race. I beg you, do not feel sorry for this Lady Julia. She is as contemptible as any snake, no matter how gentle and lovely she may appear."

He shook his head. "Women, my dear earl, can be deadly creatures, worse than the blackest blackguard who ever lived. There is no treachery too evil, no deed too foul, for them to plan and carry out. I am an older man than you by at least a score of years, and you must believe I have seen more of women's weakness than you have. Sometimes I have thought their very fragility and softness make their acts twice as despicable as any man's."

The earl tucked the letter in his notecase and rose. "I shall remember what you said, sir," he said, although privately he thought the colonel too harsh in his judgment of the sex.

As the older man rose as well, he leaned heavily on the table for a moment, as if to steady himself. His color was not good, and the earl was concerned.

"Try to get some rest, sir, I beg you," he said as he came to take the colonel's arm. "I do not think you can be well."

The colonel smiled slightly. "After all these years, I believe I am getting beyond these intrigues, m'lord. Each one seems to take more out of me than the one before."

"Will the Prince never be still?" the earl asked in some despair.

"Someday perhaps, when he is allowed to use the

brains and intelligence with which he was blessed at birth," the colonel said. "Ah, what a good fairy attended his christening, m'lord! So many wonderful talents as she showered on him, before she outdid herself giving him a tall, strong constitution and handsome good looks, as well as a charming manner that is found in few men. You know him yourself. He is unique. But I believe that since he cannot put his brains and education to good use, he wastes his powers on the will-o'wisps that are his collections, his mistresses, and his drunken sprees. England shall not see a man who could have attained such heights of greatness soon again. It is too bad, and if that is treason, so be it."

He reached out to open the door, and the earl stayed his hand. "One moment, sir. Tell me, if you please, is the Prince still hot for the lady, or do you see signs that his ardor is cooling?"

"Unfortunately I do not," the colonel said. "He remains in a positive frenzy since she continues to refuse him. Oh, she is a canny one, is she not? She must know how her shrinking reluctance feeds the Prince's desire."

He turned quite red as he shook his fist in the direction of Charles Street. "She-devil!" he hissed. "Get the snuffbox, m'lord, and get it soon!"

The earl bowed, and after begging the elderly gentleman to try to get some sleep, he took his leave. He noted that it was almost twelve, and he beckoned to a hackney cab. It might make Lady Julia nervous if he were late, but he did not care to delay.

She received him in the drawing room. He wondered if she felt its grand formality would help her cause. Of Miss Ogilvie there was no sign, for which he was grateful.

As he came close to the lady to bow, the earl studied her carefully. She was wearing a rather severe gown of dark green. It had long, tight sleeves, and lapels cut like a man's waistcoat that were open to show a high-necked bodice of pleated white lawn. Her only jewelry was a handsome brooch, and she wore her chestnut curls dressed high.

She was pale, so like Colonel Lake, she did not appear to be sleeping very well. "M'lord," she said as she curtsied, but she did not ask him to sit down.

"You have had time to consider, ma'am?" he asked abruptly.

"I have thought a great deal of our conversation, that is true," she said, holding her head high. "I am afraid this further visit is fruitless, for I can add nothing to what I told you yesterday, sir."

The earl took out his notecase and removed the letter he had brought with him. "And I suppose you will tell me you have no knowledge of this?" he asked, wishing he might shake her out of her calm, reasoned tones. "No doubt you have never seen it before?"

His words were sarcastic, and she stiffened as he spread the letter out on a table, holding one edge of it as if she might snatch it away and throw it on the fire.

She was forced to come nearer in order to read it, and she was very aware of that tall, lean masculine body so close to hers. His arm brushed hers as she bent over the letter to peruse it.

"But this is terrible, terrible!" she said, one hand going to her face in her distress. The earl listened carefully, but there was nothing in her voice but revulsion and dismay.

"Who could have done such a dastardly thing?" she asked, almost as if she spoke to herself. And then she straightened up, and with more animation than he had ever seen her display, she said quickly, "And you will have the goodness not to tell me that it was I myself, if you please, sir! I did not write this filth! Furthermore, it is nothing like my handwriting."

Before he could speak, she went quickly to the bell-pull. He put out his hand, sure she was going to ask the butler to show him out. As she turned toward him again, however, she said, "I shall ask Hentershee to bring a sample of my hand, and then you shall see!"

She stared at him triumphantly, and he leaned back against the table and folded his arms across his chest. "It would not matter if it were not your hand, m'lady," he said. "You could have asked an accomplice to write it for you. And it is printed, too. Do you normally print your correspondence?"

Before she could answer, the butler came in, and she sent him to fetch her account book and a letter she had been penning to her sister in the library.

The old retainer bowed, his face carefully expressionless. As soon as he was out of earshot, Lady Julia said, "You are the most cynical man I have ever met in my entire life! Are you so determined to convict an innocent person that you will destroy all my arguments without believing a word I say? I would hate to be so negative, so cold as you, m'lord! Is there no one in the world you trust?"

He made himself pause for a moment before he replied, for he was angry now. "My trust or mistrust of humanity is not at issue here, Lady Julia. No. We are only concerned with the return of the Prince's snuffbox. As soon as I have it in my possession, I shall trouble you no more. Until that time I am afraid you must expect to see a great deal of me."

The butler knocked then, and brought in the items she had requested. She put them on the table next to the blackmailer's letter.

Lord Whitney riffled through them. She had a fine hand, her letters well formed and very feminine. He took the opportunity to read a few lines and saw that she had been writing of Edwina Ogilvie to her sister Mary. From her affectionate tone it appeared they were very close. He put that sheet aside, and turned the pages of her account book. He could not study it too obviously, but it showed the lady was careful and precise. Her numerals bore no comparison to the print of the letter.

"I agree you did not write this letter, ma'am," he said as he straightened up.

For a moment wild hope shone on her face, and she smiled. The smile transformed her face into stunning beauty, that same beauty he had noted the night of the Jersey reception. His own face remained as cold and enigmatic as ever, and the light in her eyes faded. He wondered why, for one brief second, he had wished he could bring it back.

"I see you still hold fast to your belief in an accomplice," she said. "But wouldn't that be very foolish of me, to trust another with my secret, m'lord?" she asked.

The earl shrugged. "Perhaps it was a risk you felt you had to take, ma'am. And there will be enough money for two. I must tell you that we are prepared to offer you a thousand pounds for the box. Generous, don't you think?"

Lady Julia swept up to stand before him, her hazel eyes flashing. "You insult me, sir! Let me tell you again, that even if you offered me a *million* pounds, I could not accept it. I . . . do . . . not . . . have . . . that . . . snuffbox!"

She leaned forward in her intensity, and he took her shoulders in his hands. "I cannot tell you how you disappoint me, ma'am," he said in a voice as harsh as any she had ever heard. "Do you think to make us raise the price by prolonging this innocent act?"

Lady Julia took a deep breath, and in spite of his anger, Trevor Whitney was very much aware of her beautiful breasts as they swelled the white lawn tucker she wore. "We have nothing further to say to each other, sir," she said.

"You are wrong. We have a great deal more to say to each other," he replied quickly. "Let me tell you what a wise old man pointed out to me this very morning. A. The Prince came here. Will you agree that is an unquestionable fact?"

He shook her a little, and she nodded, biting her full

lower lip. "B. He showed you a snuffbox, here in this very room, did he not?" he went on, his voice driving, relentless. "Both closed and open, ma'am. Do you deny that?"

She shook her head, those hazel eyes, which stared at him as if she were mesmerized, beginning to fill with tears. Trevor Whitney steeled his heart against them. He had seen women cry many times before, he reminded himself. He knew they could make themselves into veritable watering pots at a moment's notice, if it served their purpose.

"C. When the Prince returned to the palace of Carlton House, he did not have the box anymore, and that is also true, as I know," he said, shaking her harder now. One of her chestnut curls came unfastened and lay against her throat. He grasped her shoulders harder, to keep from touching it.

"You see, it is as easy as ABC, m'lady. Where else could the box be but in your possession?" As he finished speaking, he let her go. Julia staggered a little, and she reached out to grasp a chair back to steady herself.

"I am aware how damning it looks for me, m'lord," she said, her voice husky now with the tears she promised herself she would not shed. "I cannot help that. I only know I do not have it, that I did not write that terrible letter, or order it done. There is nothing more I can tell you."

The earl glared down at her, his lips tightening as one hand came up. She paled, thinking he meant to strike her, and he lowered it at once.

"I shall give you a further period for reflection, ma'am," he said, sounding as if the words were torn from him against his will. He picked up the letter he had brought and restored it to his case. "If, when next I call, you continue to prate of your innocence, we shall be forced to take further steps," he said. "I do most earnestly assure you, you will not care for them. The Tower is such an unpleasant place, is it not? And that is only one action we might take."

Julia gasped, her hand going to her throat in her distress. The earl bowed. "Even the Prince will not save you, not after we show him this letter. I advise you to have done with greed, and accept the thousand pounds."

He waited, but when she only stared at him, he turned and left her without another word.

Lady Julia did not remain in the drawing room for long. At first, all she wanted to do was sink down in a chair and weep those tears she had been so valiantly repressing. She felt as vulnerable as any newborn babe. There was nothing she could do, nothing she could say, to prove her innocence, and the earl had told her plainly what her fate would be.

But she knew she must not give in to despair so quickly. She was not a weak, helpless woman. There had to be some way she could solve this problem, and she set herself to thinking of what it might be.

The Prince claimed he had left the snuffbox here in the drawing room. She accepted the fact that he had probably done so, for if he had dropped it in the hall or on the steps, her dear old Hentershee would have restored it to him at once. So, other than herself and the Prince, who had been in the drawing room that day?

She began to pace the room, deep in thought. Of course, the servants. Not the maids, she reminded herself. They had already cleaned the room early that morning. But Hentershee might have come in, or the footmen.

Suddenly she stopped, an arrested expression coming over her face. How could she have forgotten? That had been her at-home day, and several people had come that afternoon. Why, she had even mentioned it to Fanny herself!

Picking up her skirts, Julia almost ran across the hall. She could not imagine what her butler thought of all this strange activity, but she was relieved he was nowhere in sight as she entered the library. She sat down at her desk and took a piece of paper and a pencil from one of the drawers.

Now, who came first that day? she asked herself. For a moment she was lost in thought, and then she nodded in triumph as she began her list with Lady Beaton and her son Percy. She remembered hoping they would not stay long, for although the lady was one of the London's most revered hostesses, she had a piercing, disagreeable voice, and her tongue-tied son was difficult to entertain.

She nodded again as she remembered that Lord Alvanley and his elderly relative Miss Whittingham had come a short time later, and she added their names to the list.

She closed her eyes for a moment then, trying to recreate the scene in her mind. Lady Beaton had settled down on the sofa beside the fire, Lord Beaton in solicitous attention behind her. Miss Whittingham had taken the wing chair across from them, while she herself and Lord Alvanley had exchanged a few words some little distance away. She frowned, but she could not recall the conversation. Just a few pleasantries, she was sure. And then she had left him when Hentershee announced the two Miss Hammonds, and their nephew, Robert Hammond.

Julia's eyes glowed as she entered their names. The middle-aged sisters were distant relations of her late husband's, and although they had never been intimates of hers, she certainly knew them better than she knew their nephew. Robert Hammond was a rake, whispered about by many for his compulsive gambling and endless love affairs. As Julia sat tapping the pencil on the desktop, she recalled that she had not cared for him, and wished his aunts had not brought him with them. She had found his knowing, leisurely inspection of her face and figure, and his slightly suggestive conversation, offensive. He was, however, a man with a quick wit and a sharp eye. Had he seen the snuffbox? Had he picked it up?

Julia studied her list, and added one more name. She had asked a Mrs. Andrews to come, for she had felt sorry for the lady when she had met her the week before. She was newcome to town, and her acquaintance in society was slight. Now she recalled that the lady and Robert Hammond had spent a great deal of the visit in conversation *à deux*.

Julia put down her pencil and sighed. In her head she could hear the earl's remark that it was as easy as ABC. Her mind told her the thief had to be one of her guests, but her heart found it hard to believe.

She remained in the library until it was time for her drive with Fanny. Edwina had gone shopping and sightseeing with her maid that morning, and she could only be glad that her niece was still absent as she tied the ribbons of the dark green bonnet that matched her gown under her chin.

Fanny was suitably horrified by her tale. Julia told her everything the earl had said, and answered all her questions, and she was comforted when Fanny took her hand and held it tightly throughout the telling. But later, after she had left her in Wimpole Street, all her doubts and fears returned. Fanny had had no new ideas about how Julia was to free herself from this coil, even when she mentioned her list of suspects, and her suggestion that Julia only continue to maintain her innocence did not seem particularly helpful.

When she reached home again, Julia fully intended to retire to her room. But as she was chatting with Hentershee about some notes that had arrived, she heard Edwina's gruff little voice.

"There you are at last, dear auntie," she said from where she stood at the door of the library. "I have been waiting for you this age! May I see you for a moment? I assure you it is very important."

6

Lady Julia hid an impatient sigh as she went to join her niece. She hoped whatever the girl wanted to talk about would not be serious, for she did not think she could deal with any new problem. Still, she noticed that Edwina sported a little frown between those heavy eyebrows, and she put her own troubles aside to hug the girl before she took her seat. "Whatever is the matter, Edwina? How can I help you?" she asked as she removed her bonnet and put it down on the sofa beside her.

"There is nothing you can do for me, dear Julia," Edwina said. "It is what I can do for you!"

Before Julia could ask a question, she went on, her voice indignant, "How long did you think you could keep me from finding out what is going on and why you have had all those letters and presents from the Prince? The entire household is buzzing with it!"

Seeing her aunt's white, concerned face, she added quickly, "Of course Mr. Hentershee and the house-keeper have not said a word, but everyone else, from the scullery maid to the footmen, is whispering. That is how I found out. My maid, Bess, let something slip this morning as we were shopping. You may be sure I had the whole story from her in a twinkling!"

Julia was sure she had, not only the story, but a

good deal of needless speculation and gossip as well. "You do see I could not like to mention it to you, Edwina," she said as calmly as she could. "It is a private matter, and a story that is not seemly for a young girl your age to hear."

"Pooh!" Edwina exclaimed, tossing her head. "What fustian! I am sixteen now, aunt, and so of course I know what women do, and men, and . . . and everything of that nature," she finished with a grand gesture. "Besides, I might be able to help you—indeed, I am sure I can."

"Thank you, my dear," Julia made herself say. "But there is nothing you can do. In fact, it appears there is very little I can do either."

She shook her head, and Edwina ran to take the seat beside her. She swept Julia's new bonnet to the floor as she did so, but her aunt could not bear to remonstrate with her, not when she saw the love and concern in her blue eyes, and felt how tightly her hands were held.

"Please tell me, dear auntie," Edwina said more quietly. "Not a word of what you disclose shall escape my lips; you need not fear I will gossip."

Julia realized she had no choice. She knew Edwina. The girl would not rest, nor stop importuning her until she was satisfied. Accordingly, Julia gave her a very condensed version of the past few days' happenings. It was no use. Edwina read between the lines with ease.

"You mean the earl has been badgering you, aunt?" she asked, her scowl ferocious now. "And he has accused you of keeping the snuffbox and asking money for its return? What a disagreeable man!"

Julia was not permitted to agree, for Edwina swept on, "And I cannot believe the Prince would . . . Why, he is married and has a child! And you . . . you are so old!"

Julia's brows rose, and her niece flushed. "I mean, I know you are very lovely and charming and all that, but surely at your age, such things as love and romance are a thing of the past?"

If Julia's heart had not been so heavy, she would have laughed out loud at this ingenuous statement. And perhaps, she mused, I might even have asked the girl to fetch me my shawl in a quavering, elderly voice. Now, however, she had no such inclination for levity.

"That is what has happened, my dear," she said instead, pressing Edwina's hands. "I am so glad I have told you, for you do see that you might have to return to Kent in the near future."

"But why would I . . . ? Oh!" Edwina gasped. To Julia's surprise she took a deep breath and rose to stride up and down the room. "No, it will never come to that, I know it," she said at last.

"I see no way of preventing it," her aunt remarked. "I have made a list of all the people who came to the house that day, but I am hardly competent to investigate them. All I can do is continue to state firmly that I am innocent."

"But that is paltry, dear auntie!" Edwina exclaimed. "There is so much more we can do! For one thing, now that we know someone *does* have the box, that it is not just lost, I mean, we can set about finding out that person's name."

"Lost?" Julia asked. "That never occurred to me. But how could His Highness lose such a valuable object between here and Carlton House?"

"Easily," her niece said. "I lose things all the time. Much bigger things than a snuffbox, too. Now, aunt, show me your list, if you please. It must have been one of your guests. After all, we know *I* don't have it, and *you* don't have it, and I am very sure the servants had nothing to do with it. Why, not a one of them even suspects a snuffbox is involved!"

Julia put both hands to her head. She could feel a headache coming on, but she made herself say, "You will find it in the top left-hand drawer of the desk."

"I remember being glad I was going to Richmond with the Rogerses that day," Edwina remarked as she went and sat down at the desk and searched for the paper. "I did not want to have to pass plates of cake all afternoon and make polite conversation, but now I am sorry. If I had been here, I might have caught the thief red-handed!"

The list in her hand at last, the two began to discuss the guests, one by one. Edwina asked many eager questions. Julia had to hide a smile in spite of her worries, for her niece managed to find something suspicious about everyone.

Lady Beaton's disagreeable voice was surely only a way of blustering to hide her guilt. As for Lord Beaton, anyone as quiet and submissive as he was, was particularly sinister. Who knew what dark thoughts went through his mind, what terrible deeds he was planning? She reminded her aunt that still waters ran deep, nodding as she said it.

Lord Alvanley was wealthy and a leader of the *ton*, that was true. He probably had any number of beautiful snuffboxes, suitable for every occasion. Perhaps he had not been able to resist adding to his collection? And Miss Whittingham had to be eccentric in her old age. Perhaps even absentminded to the point where she had taken the box, thinking it was her own.

As for the Hammond sisters, who knew what lay in their past? Just because they were distant relations did not eliminate them from suspicion.

"And isn't Robert Hammond a great rake, ma'am?" Edwina asked brightly as she reached the gentleman's name. Julia must have looked startled, for she went on, "Evelyn Rogers pointed him out to me in the park. She said he's no better than he should be, for besides his gambling, he has fought several duels, and broken hundreds and hundreds of hearts!"

"He has not always behaved as he should, perhaps, but I rather think 'hundreds and hundreds' is an exaggeration, Edwina," Julia said dryly.

"But he does sound promising, does he not?" Edwina persisted. "And what is Mrs. Andrews like?"

she asked next, for the moment abandoning the eligible Mr. Hammond. "I do not think I have ever met her."

"She is about twenty-five, I would say, and a very attractive blond. Her husband was wounded in a naval battle; he remains at their home in the country," Julia told her.

Edwina propped up her chin with one hand, her eyes deep in thought. "And you only met her a short while ago, aunt?" she asked. When Julia nodded, she went on, "Then you know nothing about her. She might be capable of worse things than theft and black-mail!"

Before her aunt could remonstrate with her for this sweeping statement, she picked up the list again and waved it. "Well, it has to be one of them, auntie," she said cheerfully. "We must be glad there are only eight suspects!"

Edwina jumped up then and began to stride about again, as if she thought better on her feet. "Let's try to picture the scene, aunt," she said. "The Prince visits you, and he puts his snuffbox down on a table. When he leaves, he forgets it. You do not notice it there, but someone who came to tea must have seen it. It would take only a moment to slip it into a pocket or a reticule."

"You know, Edwina, I find all this hard to believe, even now that I have made the list," Lady Julia said in a musing voice. "I would swear no one in my drawing room that afternoon was the light-fingered type."

"You would not think so, would you?" her niece asked. "But maybe they couldn't resist. I'm sure it was a valuable box. What did it look like, by the way? Was it encrusted with jewels, and heavy with gold?"

She looked at her aunt eagerly, her eyes shining in anticipation, but Julia had no intention of telling her any more about that suggestive box than she had to. "It had a gold filigree, but there were no jewels except for some small ones on the clasp," she said, and then she closed her lips tightly.

Edwina did not seem to notice her reticence, she was so obviously disappointed. "Even so, I am sure it *looked* valuable," she said stoutly. "And everyone knows you do not take snuff. Perhaps this person thought he or she had a golden opportunity for just the kind of blackmail that has occurred, for surely it must have been some gentleman who left it here. How delighted they must have been to discover the Prince was the owner!"

"Now you go too far in your suppositions, Edwina," Julia said. "The Prince's name was not on it. There was no way to tell to whom it belonged."

Edwina refused to be daunted by this logical statement. "But one of our servants might have mentioned his visit and that handsome bouquet," she said. "You know how they gossip! It would be too much to expect for them not to spread the word of the Prince's visit. I imagine they were all puffed up with reflected glory, such an exalted person coming here." She paused, and then she asked eagerly, "Did any of the ladies leave the room or require a maid, Aunt Julia?"

Julia recalled that both Lady Beaton and Miss Whittingham had excused themselves at different times, and she had asked Hentershee to summon a maid to assist them. As she told Edwina this, she saw the girl nodding. She knew everything Edwina had said about the servants could well be true.

"Perhaps the servants did gossip," she said. "I will never be able to get them to admit it, though. But do look at the time! I must go and change if we are going out this evening."

As her niece ran to put her arm through hers and walk her to the door, she added, trying to treat the whole matter in a casual way, "I am sure the real culprit will be discovered in time. I am not a bit worried, nor must you be."

Edwina was quick to say she was not, but if Julia had not been so preoccupied, she might have been suspicious at the girl's meek acquiescence. It was most unlike her.

After Lady Julia went upstairs, Edwina returned to the desk to study the list again. Of course she was worried! Who wouldn't be? And she had no intention of letting that nasty earl reap all the glory. No, indeed. She would find the thief herself and make sure he or she was brought to justice. She put any serious consideration of how she was to do this from her mind, and spent an agreeable hour dreaming of one scenario after another where she confronted the blackmailer, and he confessed, weeping copious tears and begging her to let him go. From this it was a small step to being received at Carlton House by the Prince and awarded a casket of gold as thanks for all help.

Although both Lady Julia Reynolds and Miss Edwina Ogilvie attended the concert of sacred music that evening as planned, it would be fair to say that neither lady heard more than a note or two.

When Julia came downstairs the following morning, she discovered that Miss Ogilvie had left the house with her maid sometime before. A tremor of unease swept over her, for she knew Edwina would not let the matter of the missing snuffbox rest. She only prayed she was not even then marching up to a number of smart London doors demanding to see those who had attended her aunt's tea party.

Lady Julia was not far wrong. Edwina had decided to do just that, but first she rather thought she must make a study of snuff and snuffboxes. It would be too difficult to introduce the subject if she knew nothing about it.

Innocent of her niece's plans, Lady Julia went to Bond Street for a final fitting on the gown she intended to wear to Lady Beaton's ball that evening. She had spent a great deal of time vacillating over whether to attend it, for if the Prince should come, it would cut up all her peace. And even if only the Earl of Bradford was there, she did not see how she was to enjoy herself, not with his wintry, accusing eyes following her every move.

At last she decided she was being a coward. Besides, she had never seen the earl at balls, and, recalling Lady Beaton and her ineffective son, she hardly thought them the types to invite royalty to their party, or have that royalty accept. And, she told herself as the carriage conveyed her home, the large box containing her new gown on the seat across from her, I refuse to be intimidated. Am I to miss all the fun of the Season because of two impossible men? It was not in the least fair, and she would not stand for it. She tried to forget that it had also occurred to her that if she disappeared too obviously from the social scene, the earl might take it as a sign of guilt.

The day passed in normal fashion, and was marked only by the absence of any visit from Trevor Whitney, for which Lady Julia was more than grateful.

That evening, after she had bathed and had her hair dressed à la Sappho, her maid lowered the new gown carefully over her curls. It was made of dark brown silk, shot through with gold threads, and confined under the breasts in the Empire style made so popular by Empress Josephine of France. At the hem there were two deep flounces of the creamy lace which also trimmed the low neckline and sleeves.

Julia knew the gown became her, and although the color was unusual, it complemented her chestnut hair. She wore a gold-and-topaz set with it, and had topaz combs for her hair.

Edwina was loud in her compliments when Julia came downstairs to dinner. "How very fine you look, dear auntie!" she enthused.

Julia felt a little pang. "I am sorry that you do not go with me, Edwina," she said. "It does seem too bad that you must wait two more years before you are out and can attend balls."

Edwina waved her fork. "Pooh! I shall enjoy myself so much more reading à good book, ma'am," she said.

She seemed excited somehow, and Julia remembered her apprehension of the morning. "What did

you do today, Edwina?" she asked. "You were quite
the early bird, were you not?"

Her niece nodded to where Hentershee and one of
the footmen were busy at the sideboard, and then she
winked at her aunt. Lady Julia's heart sank. "I had a
most educational morning, dear aunt," she said, her
eyes twinkling. "I am sure you must applaud my
industry."

Lady Julia looked thoughtful, but when Edwina
changed the subject, she did not persist in questioning
the girl. She did, however, dismiss the servants after
dessert had been served. As soon as the dining-room
doors closed behind them, she asked in a stern voice,
"Now, just what have you been up to, Edwina? You
will tell me at once!"

Edwina took a last spoonful of pudding before she
replied. "I have been learning all about snuff, Aunt
Julia," she said. "It is the most interesting subject! Did
you know there are two basic kinds? One is called
rappee, which is moist snuff, and the other, which is
dry, Irish or Scotch snuff."

"I had no idea. What I want to know, however, is
where you had this information?" her aunt persisted.

"I went to Fribourg and Treyer, of course," Edwina
answered, scraping her spoon carefully around her
dish so that not even the tiniest bit of pudding would
escape her.

"What?" Lady Julia demanded, horrified. "Why,
how could you, Edwina?"

As her niece looked a question, she continued, "You
must have been the only female in the place!"

"I was," Edwina admitted cheerfully. "At first the
clerks were not very nice, but when I told them I was
looking for a gift for my godfather, they soon settled
down. And Mr. Treyer himself came and told me so
many things! Did you know that the firm makes
periodic visits of inspection to the royal snuff cellar,
even though it is supervised by the Prince's chief page?
And there are so many kinds of snuff, aunt, you would

stare! Queen Charlotte's mixture, that's for morning, and Etrenne, Old Paris, Martinique, Bureau— hundreds and hundreds of them! Some gentlemen even have their own sorts, as they are called. And the boxes! They are gorgeous! Gold and enamel and silver gilt, even tortoiseshell. Why—"

"What did you purchase for your godfather, Edwina?" Lady Julia asked, trying hard to keep her voice even.

"I didn't. I said I would have to think it over," her niece replied. Sensing Julia's disapproval, she added quickly, "I did thank them kindly for all their time."

"And may I ask why you made this study, niece?" Julia asked next.

"So I might use it when I begin to question the people who came to your at-home day, of course," the girl explained. "I am sure the culprit will give himself away. Maybe by a startled word or a self-conscious look. You do see I had to know something about snuff, though, before I could begin."

Lady Julia leaned forward and caught her niece's wrist. "Edwina, listen to me!" she commanded. "I positively forbid you to do any such thing! It cannot be tolerated, a young girl not even out, questioning the likes of Lord Alvanley or Lady Beaton! Come now, I'll have your promise on it, and at once!"

Edwina scowled. "But someone must make a push to discover—"

"At once, or I shall send you home to Kent tomorrow," Lady Julia said. Her voice was so implacable, Edwina knew she was beaten.

"Very well, I promise not to speak to anyone who was at your tea party, aunt," she said in a voice that seemed to say she had lost her good opinion of her aunt's courage.

There was a knock on the door then, and Hentershee came in to announce the carriage was waiting, and their conversation, of necessity, came to an end.

All during the drive to the Beatons' town house,

Lady Julia could not stop thinking of Edwina, and what she had done. Thank heaven she had thought to extract the girl's promise, she told herself. And then she could not help wondering what Edwina would conjure up to do next.

Lady Beaton had outdone herself this evening, Julia noted as she went slowly up the stairs among the other guests. She had invited a perfect crush of people, and it appeared that most of them had accepted. After greeting her hostess and listening to Lord Beaton's stammered compliments on her appearance, the more awkward because they were made under his mother's beady eye, Julia moved into the ballroom.

She was quickly hailed by a group of friends, and it was not long before she was able to put her problem from her mind, for a little while at least. A few minutes later, Julia was surprised to find Robert Hammond at her elbow, an intimate smile on his face.

"My dear Lady Julia, how lovely you look tonight," he whispered, bending close. As he spoke, his narrowed eyes slid over her shoulders to linger on the low, revealing neckline of her gown before he took her arm and indicated a sofa nearby. "Will you be seated, ma'am?" he asked.

Julia was annoyed that he did not even wait for an answer before he led her away from her friends. As they sat down, he continued, "I count myself very fortunate to have captured even a moment of your time, dear lady. Especially now that I know how admired you are—how *ardently* pursued. I am more than pleased that that is the case, however. I had thought you a hopeless Puritan, you see. I cannot tell you how delighted I am to discover that you are not averse to a *warm* relationship, ma'am."

"I don't know what you are talking about, sir," Julia said, wondering where he had ever received the impression she would welcome a lover.

She had no time to discover it, however, for Percy Beaton appeared then, bowing and stammering as he asked her for the first dance. Julia was quick to smile and agree, and she put Robert Hammond and his strange remarks from her mind as they took their place in the set, and she set herself to draw her shy host into conversation. She felt so sorry for Percy Beaton; she always had.

After the dance, as he was leading her from the floor, there was some little commotion near the doorway, and the majordomo rapped his tall cane on the floor for silence. Julia felt her heart sinking, even before he announced in ringing, sonorous tones, "Milords, miladies, His Royal Highness, the Prince of Wales!"

Lord Beaton excused himself quickly, to hurry away to welcome his unexpected royal guest. Julia stood alone, wondering what she was to do. All around her, ladies were jockeying for position before sinking into their deepest curtsies. The gentlemen, too, were preparing their most reverent bows. Julia looked around in dismay, searching desperately for a way to escape. To her surprise, she encountered the steely eyes of Lord Whitney. He was observing her from where he stood by an alcove a little distance away. As their eyes met, he held out his hand, and, not even taking time to think, Julia picked up her skirts and fled to his side.

The earl himself was astonished at his behavior. He had seen the panic in her eyes, how frightened she was, and he had come to her rescue as quickly as any knight in tales of old. Guilty of blackmail or no, he could not stand by and watch the Prince compromise and embarrass her, he told himself.

When she reached him, he moved aside a little, holding up a drapery that hid most of the alcove from sight. Julia brushed by him, and in a moment the heavy brocade came down behind her.

She leaned against the wall, her hands to her heart. She could see the Prince entering the room with his gentlemen, and she observed his charming smile as he moved easily among the guests. She hoped he would not remain long; it was very warm and airless in the alcove.

And then, almost as if he had been able to see her hidden there, he came directly toward her, his smile deepening and his arms outstretched. Julia, thinking her heart must stop, it was pounding so in her breast, shrank back against the wall.

"But, my dear Bradford!" the Prince exclaimed. "How delightful, yet unexpected, to see you here."

"Your Highness," the earl said in his deep voice as he bowed. He sounded so amused by the situation and her predicament that Julia had the greatest urge to kick him.

"I was not aware that you were to grace the festivities, Your Highness," he went on. "Surely I have heard rumors that you have not been well?"

"A fever, my friend," the Prince confided. "A consuming fever I had hoped to ease this evening. Alas, the lady I seek is not here. Strange, that," he went on. "I had it on good authority that she would attend. My disappointment, Bradford, is severe."

"But you may take heart that at least you have made Lady Beaton's party a triumph, sire," the earl remarked.

"Is there a card room, my friend?" the Prince asked next. "I do not wish to remain here. It would sadden me beyond belief to have to watch others dancing with their ladies when the lady I desire is denied me."

"I believe there is a card room set up in the salon at the end of the hall, Your Highness," the earl told him.

The Prince asked Trevor Whitney to join him and his gentlemen, but he was gently refused, and in a moment Julia sensed that her nemesis had moved away. She dared to peek out again, and she was vastly relieved to see the Prince strolling toward the ballroom door.

"A moment more, m'lady," the earl murmured.

As it turned out, it was several more moments

before she was released, for two other gentlemen came up and engaged the earl in conversation. Julia's cheeks were red when they finally moved away, for they had had several earthy comments to make about the ladies present, and their availability for dalliance.

She was sure her face was still red when the earl held the drapery aside for her and offered his arm. She thought his deep-set eyes were amused. "One can only be glad you have been married, ma'am," he remarked as he led her to a side door. "Marcus can be very blunt, and Lord Sendell positively scurrilous, don't you agree?"

Julia made no answer as they passed into a smaller salon. As she looked around, she did not know whether to be glad or sorry that there was no one in the room.

She stood indecisively for a moment, and then she put up her chin. "I must thank you, sir," she said, looking him straight in the eye. "What you just did for me was very kind."

The earl strolled over to a table containing drinks, and poured them both a glass of wine. "No doubt you think it out of character?" he asked as he handed her a glass. "But I am a gentleman born and bred, and the habit is hard to break. Besides, you looked quite desperate. And no matter what you have done, or plan to do, with Prinny's snuffbox, I have never thought it fair that royalty was able to take advantage of an unwilling subject. You have convinced me, you see, that at least you have no intention of taking the Prince as a lover."

"Thank you," Julia made herself say.

"Won't you be seated, ma'am?" the earl asked politely, indicating a pair of chairs.

Julia wished she might refuse, but she had no idea what she was to do next. A little frown played between her brows as she obeyed. She knew it would be most unwise to go back to the ballroom, for the Prince might return. But how could she escape the house?

Surely it would be dangerous with him only a few rooms away. And if one of his gentlemen should see her, she would be lost.

"What do you intend to do now?" the earl asked, almost as if he could read her mind.

Julia sipped her wine to give herself time to think. "I would like to go home," she said softly. The earl bent closer to hear her, as she added, "I do not know how I am to do that, however. If the Prince should see me, learn that I am here . . ."

Trevor Whitney finished his wine and put his glass down before he rose. "But nothing could be simpler, ma'am," he said. "I shall have your wrap fetched and your carriage called, make your excuses to our hostess —a sudden indisposition, don't you think?—and escort you myself when all is in train. You will not object to leaving by a side door, I trust."

"It will not be necessary for you to escort me . . ." Julia began as the earl strolled to the door. He turned and stared at her. His lean face was expressionless, but she thought she saw a little light deep in those wintry eyes. For a moment there was silence in the room. Faintly Julia could hear the strains of a waltz coming from the ballroom, and, unable to remain seated while he stared down at her from his great height, she rose.

"But it will be my pleasure, ma'am," he said at last.

Julia took a deep breath as he closed the salon door behind him. His voice had been cold and without inflection, in spite of his courteous words. She knew that whatever emotion he felt at seeing her home, it was not pleasure.

7

Lady Julia woke early the following morning. She read the latest passionate letter from the Prince in some abstraction, for she was pondering the behavior of the enigmatic earl the previous evening. He had deftly extracted her from the Beatons' town house without anyone but servants seeing them, and he had handed her up to the waiting carriage himself. After taking the seat beside her, he had made no attempt at conversation, which surprised her a little. Instead, he had stared out the window of the carriage, lost in thought as they rumbled over the cobbles. Julia had sat quietly as well, although she had been very much aware of the tall gentleman at her side. Only when they had arrived at her home, and he stepped down to help her alight, had he said a word.

"I trust the time you are being given to consider our proposal has been profitable, ma'am," he said, holding her hand in his. "I shall call on you in a few days' time, unless, of course, you send word before then that you are agreeable to the terms."

For a moment Julia had been tempted to cry her innocence again, but the presence of her coachman and groom forced her to remain silent. Instead, she had curtsied, and begged the earl to make what use of her carriage he desired to take him on to his next destination.

Now, as she lay in bed lingering over her breakfast, she decided she must try to discover who had taken the Prince's box herself. What she had forbidden her niece to do was well within reason for her. She went over the names of her guests again, trying to forget Edwina's wild speculations about them as she did so.

Lord Alvanley she could dismiss as a possibility at once, she knew. A wealthy gentleman of the first stare, it was inconceivable that he would take a snuffbox that was not his own, for whatever reason. Gentlemen had their own codes as regards snuff. It was considered a politeness to offer a pinch from your box, and the height of discourtesy to request one from someone else. The recipes for the various sorts were carefully guarded secrets as well.

But even crossing Lord Alvanley from her list, there was still his elderly relative. Miss Whittingham was a dotty little thing, and Julia was well aware that sometimes as people aged they did things they would have condemned when younger.

And then there was Robert Hammond, or Red Rob as he was called for his brilliant hair. He had done any number of *outre* things in his lifetime; might he not have added theft and blackmail to his repertory? Julia shifted uneasily, suddenly reminded of his incomprehensible remarks to her last evening. What had he meant by them? In a way it was too bad Lord Beaton had interrupted them and that the Prince's arrival had made her flee the ball. If she had stayed, she might have been able to discover why Mr. Hammond thought her fair game. Did his sudden revision of her character have anything to do with the snuffbox?

She sighed, as the rest of her guests ran through her mind. The problem was, she still could not imagine any one of them doing it, not even the infamous Red Rob.

Telling herself that since it had to be one of them, such negative thinking was defeatist, she rang for her maid. She would begin her investigation this very day, and she would call on Alma Andrews first. Of everyone who had come that fateful afternoon, she was the least known, and therefore the most suspect.

Julia came downstairs half an hour later for her customary interview with her housekeeper before she went out. As her butler bowed, she asked for Edwina. She was feeling a little guilty about neglecting the girl, and she had had the thought that perhaps she might enjoy a drive in the park that afternoon.

"Miss Ogilvie has gone out," Hentershee said.

Julia nodded carelessly, and would have turned away, except he coughed a little and said, "If I might be so bold, madam . . . ?"

At her nod, he went on, his face carefully expressionless, "I fetched a hackney cab for her myself, madam, and I overheard Miss Ogilvie asking to be taken to the Earl of Bradford's house in Portman Square."

Seeing his mistress's look of distress, he added quickly, "She had her maid with her, milady."

Julia ignored this sop to propriety, for she was thinking hard. "Be so good as to tell my maid to bring me my bonnet and reticule at once," she said crisply. "Then fetch me a hackney cab as well. I cannot risk delay, waiting for the carriage to be brought round."

Less than ten minutes later, Lady Julia Reynolds was heading for Portman Square. While she had waited for the cab, she had questioned Hentershee, but besides telling her that Edwina had left the house quite an hour ago, he had no further information.

When her hackney reached the square, Julia was somewhat relieved to discover the earl standing outside his house. Dressed for riding, he was talking to a groom, and patting the horse he had obviously just dismounted. Perhaps he has not seen Edwina yet, she thought as she paid her cabby.

Still he had not noticed her, and as the groom tipped his hat and began to lead the horse away and the earl prepared to mount his front steps, she called to him.

Trevor Whitney turned, astonishment crossing his lean features before he resumed his usual unreadable expression. He stood still, making no move to approach her, but she saw how intently he watched her as she drew near.

"M'lady," he said, bowing a little. "Can it be that you have come to see the wisdom of giving up the snuffbox at last?"

Julia was angry at his words, so angry that she missed the curious note of regret in his voice. "Of course not!" she snapped. "I cannot give you something I do not have, as I have told you, time out of mind. No, I have come because my niece Edwina was heard to give this address to her cab driver over an hour ago. Have you seen her this morning, m'lord?"

The earl could not hide his astonishment. "Miss Ogilvie came to my house?" he asked before he held out his arm and added, "Come, let us go in and see if she is still here."

As they went up the steps, he said, "I went out riding some time ago. I must have left the house before she arrived."

Julia could tell he was waiting for her to explain the girl's unprecedented visit, but she was loath to do so. If he had not seen Edwina, she could have had no opportunity to mention the list of people at her party to him, nor tell him what she thought of him for falsely accusing her aunt. All was not lost.

As the two entered the front hall, the earl looked around and saw a wide-eyed maid seated in one of the straight chairs against the wall, and he said to his butler, "I see that I have had a visitor this morning, Ford."

The butler bowed. "Indeed, m'lord. The, er, the young woman came over an hour ago. I told her you were out and that I had no idea when you would return, but she insisted on waiting. That is the young woman's maid, sir," he said, waving his hand. Julia saw Bess flush bright red and lower her eyes.

"And where is my visitor now, Ford?" the earl asked, handing him his gloves, hat and crop.

"She is in the morning room with the countess,

m'lord, taking some refreshment," the butler said.

"Shall we join them, m'lady?" the earl asked, coming to take her arm again.

Julia had been thinking quickly. "If I might have a few moments of your time in private, m'lord?" she asked.

Trevor Whitney bowed. "Certainly, ma'am. We shall be quite undisturbed in the library. I am sure my mother can entertain even the unusual Miss Ogilvie for as long as you require."

Neither spoke as they walked across the hall, and he opened the door and stepped back so she could precede him into a large book-lined room. Julia looked around in some surprise. Besides the usual appurtenances of a gentleman's book room, the earl's library also contained a large piano and several music stands and chairs. There was even a cello leaning against one wall, and the piano top was covered with scores. It was not an especially neat room, but rather one that looked as if it were in constant use. Several books were stacked on the large desk, along with a quantity of paper, and another heavy tome lay facedown on a chair beside the fireplace.

"I must beg you to excuse the untidiness, ma'am," the earl said as he led her to a chair. "Not knowing you were coming, I gave no orders to have it made ready for a lady."

Julia shook her head, as if to deprecate the necessity of any such nicety, and he went on, "Now, how may I serve you, ma'am?"

She looked up to see him leaning on his desk, his booted legs crossed, and she wished he would sit down so she did not have so far to look up into that strong, lean face with its cynical little smile.

"First, I must apologize, m'lord," she began. "It was inexcusable for Edwina to come here alone this morning, and I do beg your pardon."

"But she did bring her maid, which is more than you did, m'lady," the earl pointed out.

"I am not sixteen, and I am a widow," Julia was quick to remind him.

As he nodded, she went on, "Edwina has discovered this business about the snuffbox, although I tried to keep it from her. The servants have been gossiping, you see, not only about the Prince's gifts and letters, but your visits as well. I could not deny it when she taxed me with it, as you may be sure she did." She paused and looked down at her tightly clasped hands for a moment before she went on, "She has decided to help me. And when Edwina decides to help, everyone in the vicinity had better beware." She shook her head. "She is still young, of course."

"But why did she come here, m'lady?" the earl asked.

"I am very much afraid she came to take you to task for harassing me, sir," Julia told him. "Then too, since I made her promise not to question any of the guests who were in my drawing room that day the snuffbox was taken, she might well have come to lay their names before you herself." She sighed. "I cannot help but wish Edwina was not quite so . . . so . . ."

"Busy? Meddlesome? Attentive? Fierce?" he suggested.

"All of those, and several more," Julia said, her clear voice tart. He smiled a little.

"What guests do you refer to, m'lady?" he asked next. Julia thought he sounded almost uninterested in them, as if he considered them merely a diversion she intended to use to confuse the issue. Her color deepened, and her chin came up in defiance, and in spite of himself, Trevor Whitney thought her very lovely.

"I remembered after your last call that the day the Prince showed me the snuffbox was my at-home day. Several people came. If the Prince did leave the box, any one of them might have picked it up."

"Knowing by some miraculous emanation it gave off that it belonged to the Prince?" the earl asked. His voice was as carefully expressionless as his features.

Julia stared at him, completely forgetting she had made the same objection to Edwina. "It must have happened that way," she said quickly. "Oh, of course the thief did not know it was the Prince's box, but he or she had to know it was a gentleman's belonging. I do not take snuff, I never have, and we are an entirely feminine establishment. They might have planned to blackmail whoever it was who left the box. And you know the way servants gossip, how they brag about any illustrious visitor. It would be a small matter for the thief to discover that its owner was none other than the Prince of Wales."

The earl appeared to be lost in thought. Julia could think of nothing more to say, and she sat quietly, waiting.

"Who did come that day, ma'am?" he asked at last.

Julia gave him the names of her eight guests in a steady voice, and he went around his desk to write them down. "Anyone else?" he asked, frowning down at the list.

"No one but Mrs. Lowden, who came much later, after everyone else had left," Julia admitted. "She is my best friend; I wrote and asked her to come, for I needed her advice."

Trevor Whitney nodded. "And can you remember if anyone in your drawing room seemed excited or behaved in an unusual way, m'lady?" he asked, almost, she thought, as if he were sure she had a suspect ready to hand.

"No, no one," she told him. "Of course, I cannot be positive, for I barely remember the afternoon. I was still upset about the Prince's visit, you see."

He nodded again, but although she searched deep into those wintry blue-gray eyes, she could see no sign that he either believed or disbelieved her.

He rose then. "This must be investigated, of course. I suppose one can only be grateful that there were not more guests that afternoon."

Julia stared at him. His voice had been noncommittal; she could read nothing in it but the coolest of interest and concern. Her heart sank, for she could tell he did not believe they would find the culprit among her guests.

The earl stared back at her, and then one dark eyebrow rose, as if to remark her steady gaze. "Shall we rescue my mother now, ma'am?" he asked in the deepening silence.

Julia shrugged, putting away the uneasy thoughts she was having. As she rose, she made herself say, "You must not allow Edwina to bother you, m'lord. I would not put it past her to insist on helping you herself in finding the thief."

"Miss Ogilvie will be firmly repulsed," he told her as they walked to the door. "However, it occurs to me that your help would be very welcome. You see, although I know some of the people on your list, I have never met Mrs. Andrews, nor do I know the older ladies. And I know Robert Hammond only by reputation." As Julia glanced sideways at him, looking surprised, he explained, "I am not much involved with society, ma'am, in a general way."

Julia could not help wondering why, but he gave her no opportunity to question him, for he went on, "It would be easier for me if we could meet some of your guests together."

He saw Julia nod, almost reluctantly.

"I intended to call on Mrs. Andrews today," she said. "She is the least known to me, and I thought to begin with her."

The earl paused, his hand on the doorknob. "You were going to investigate these people yourself?" he asked in disbelief.

Julia's gaze did not falter. "Yes, I was," she said. "It seemed the only thing I could do, for you have made it so very plain that you consider me the blackmailer. And since you believe you have already found the culprit, why would you be bothered to look for another? That is the truth, is it not, m'lord?"

Her voice challenged him to deny it, but to her surprise he shook his head, his mouth quirking in a rueful little smile. "I cannot tell you how delighted I would be to discover you were innocent, ma'am," he said, and then, as if he felt he had revealed too much, he turned away from her abruptly and opened the door.

They did not speak as they went together toward the morning room. Julia wondered what he could possibly have meant by that last statement. He had accused her and threatened her; surely he still believed her guilty!

The earl, as well, was wondering why he had expressed himself that way. It was most unlike him. But then, he had surprised himself last evening when he had rescued her from the Prince. In fact, he had been so stunned at how quickly he had come to her rescue, how strongly he had wanted to protect her, that he had sat in the carriage in a brown study all the way back to her house in Charles Street. It was hardly the way he generally behaved. Could it be that he, as well as the Prince of Wales, was falling under Lady Julia Reynolds' spell, as Colonel Lake claimed? But of course not, he told himself sternly. He admired the Lady Julia, but he was not the type to fall in love. In spite of some very lovely mistresses over the years, and endless opportunities, he never had.

As he opened the morning-room door, Miss Ogilvie's gruff little voice exclaimed, "No, no, dear ma'am! Not a 'terrible candle.' I said the book was a 'veritable scandal'!"

Julia stepped inside the room to a burst of laughter from both ladies. They were seated across from each other, enjoying a cup of tea and a plate of muffins. And far from being intimidated by the elderly white-haired lady who was her hostess, or feeling shy and embarrassed, Edwina appeared to be having a very good time. Her discarded bonnet was on the floor at her feet, and she appeared very much at her ease.

As the earl shut the door, the countess and her uninvited guest turned toward the sound, and Edwina jumped to her feet.

"Aunt Julia!" she said, her voice somehow accusing. "What are you doing here?"

"More to the point, niece, what are *you* doing here?" her aunt asked. Then she turned to the earl's mother and curtsied. "Good morning, m'lady. I must thank you for entertaining this tiresome girl. You are too kind."

Lady Millicent wiped her eyes and smiled. "I have enjoyed it immensely, Lady Julia," she said, and then she chuckled again.

"Edwina, your manners," Julia said, indicating the earl with a speaking glance in his direction.

"M'lord," Edwina said, but her voice was cold and her curtsy a mere bob.

"I am sorry I was not here when you came, Miss Ogilvie," he said as he pulled up a chair for Lady Julia. "There was something you wanted to speak to me about?"

Edwina scowled at him, those heavy brows drawing together in a straight line. Before she could speak, he added, "Never mind. Lady Julia told me the purpose of your visit."

He sounded amused, and Edwina's scowl deepened. "I do assure you, Miss Ogilvie, that I am quite capable of seeing to this matter myself," he went on. "Your assistance will not be needed."

"But *will* you see to it?" Edwina demanded, thrusting out her lower lip and putting her hands on her hips. She sounded quite fierce as she went on, "Or will you just forget it, and settle for the bird in hand that you have?"

"Edwina!" Julia exclaimed. "I am ashamed of you! Whatever can the earl and the countess be thinking of you?"

Edwina tossed her head. "The time for politeness is past, dear auntie. Until the real culprit is caught, you are in danger. I shall not rest until your name is completely cleared."

"What culprit? He leered? What are you all talking about?" the countess asked, looking from one to the other.

"A private matter, Mother," the earl told her.

For a moment Lady Millicent looked as if she would like to ask a great many more questions, but then she rose. "In that case, I shall be off," she said. "I just remembered that I am late for an appointment. I hope I shall see you again soon, Edwina. I cannot tell you how much I have enjoyed your . . . er, your morning call."

As soon as she had left the room, Edwina turned to her aunt and grinned. "There, you see, ma'am?" she crowed. "She didn't think my coming here a bad thing at all! Besides, as I explained when she did question me in the beginning, I cannot be compromised, because I am not out!"

The earl's deep-set eyes crinkled shut in his amusement at this bit of feminine logic, but Lady Julia looked as if she would like to shake her niece, at the very least.

"You are, however, much too old for these pranks, Edwina," she said. "Come, we will go home now. We have taken enough of the earl's time, to say nothing of his mother's."

Edwina opened her mouth to protest, but the dangerous light in her aunt's hazel eyes warned her it would be most unwise. "Very well, auntie," she said obediently, and then spoiled this docile reply by muttering, "I only hope you do not live to regret it!"

As she picked up her bonnet and went to the mirror over the sideboard to put it on, the earl beckoned Lady Julia to his side. "May I suggest you write to Mrs. Andrews as soon as you reach home, and invite her to join you for a stroll in the park this afternoon, ma'am?" he asked quietly. "Send me word if she accepts, and I will contrive to meet you there, just by chance, you understand. And then, between us, we can take her measure."

"Certainly, m'lord," Julia agreed. "I shall also call on Lord Alvanley's aunt, Miss Whittingham, today. I do not really think it can be she, but she is elderly, and she has become a little strange in some of her actions and comments."

Trevor Whitney looked as if he would like to say more, but then Edwina was there, looking suspiciously from one to the other, as if she suspected them of planning some daring move from which she was to be excluded. Julia could see she was about to question them, and she hurried to thank the earl for all his understanding before she swept Miss Ogilvie before her from his house.

With Bess squeezed in beside them in the hackney, conversation was impossible. Julia dismissed the maid as soon as they reached home. Holding Edwina's arm in a firm grip, she marched her into the library and shut the door behind them. And then she delivered a pithy lecture about propriety, modesty, and manners that left Edwina gasping with indignation.

"But I was only trying to help, auntie!" the girl cried at last, when Julia paused for breath.

"Do me the kindness of not helping me so much, Edwina," her hitherto fond aunt said. "This is a very serious matter. It is not an exciting chapter in a novel. You are too young and inexperienced to do anything more than confuse things, and perhaps put yourself in danger as well. Whoever this blackmailer is, he will not take kindly to interference that puts not only his plans but also his person in jeopardy. That is why I decided to take the earl into my confidence as regards our suspicions. He is a man, and used to these intrigues, from what I can gather. And if I came to see the wisdom of not trying any detection by myself, surely any role you planned to play is even more unsuitable. Furthermore, if it became known that you have been meddling, it will bring censure down, not only on your own feckless head, but on mine, as your chaperon, as well."

Edwina hung that head, but she still looked rebellious, and once again Julia longed to shake her. "If I find you are not behaving yourself, Edwina, I shall send you home, no matter what my sisters say," she told her, her clear voice cool and determined. "This is positively the last time I intend to warn you. You may leave me now."

8

As soon as Lady Julia had received an enthusiastic acceptance to her invitation to stroll in the park that afternoon from Alma Andrews, she sent a note to the earl. Then she put on her bonnet again and took a cab to Grillon's Hotel, where she knew Miss Whittingham was staying for a few weeks.

As she was taken there, she wondered why the lady did not stay with her nephew, Lord Alvanley. Was this another instance of her peculiar ways? Of course, Julia had to admit that she herself would have been most reluctant to house such an eccentric. And Lord Alvanley, being such a leader of fashion, might well have refused to do so. Julia knew he was famous for his dinners, considered, as they were, the finest in London. Perhaps he did not care to have a dotty old relative peering at him from the foot of the table and making incomprehensible remarks when he entertained his cronies.

Fortunately, after she sent up her card, she found Miss Whittingham all eagerness to receive her. As she entered the lady's rooms, she discovered her seated by the window, a pile of mending in her lap.

As Julia greeted her, she wondered at this menial occupation, and at Miss Whittingham's attire as well. The old lady was dressed in a faded black dressing gown, her thin feet attired in a pair of bright red velvet slippers. They were embroidered all over with pink and orange cabbage roses and bright green leaves, and besides being impossibly garish, they did not fit, for they looked as if they belonged to someone much larger than the birdlike little lady bent so industriously over her sewing.

"How nice of you to call on me, Lady Julia," Miss Whittingham enthused, her faded eyes twinkling. She waved her needle at a chair set opposite, and said, "Do sit down so we may have a comfortable coze. You must forgive me for not rising. I am involved with a tricky seam. I employ no maid, you see, so I always do my own mending. It saves money. And you must forgive me as well for my *déshabillé*. I never dress unless I am going out. That way there is less wear and tear on my clothes."

"I hope I find you well, ma'am?" Julia asked as she took her seat, ignoring the lady's strange remarks.

Miss Whittingham peered at her as she snapped her thread. Taking up another length from the spool, she said, "Very well, thank you. Which is more than you are, my dear."

"I beg your pardon?" Julia asked, somewhat stunned.

"Oh, I did not mean you are not in blooming good health, m'lady," Miss Whittingham tittered, holding her needle at arm's length so she could see to thread it. "I only meant that your situation is not at all healthy."

"I am afraid I do not understand you," Julia said, trying for a calm and reasonable tone. Surely Miss Whittingham was even stranger than she had imagined.

"Well, look at you," her hostess told her, waving her needle now she had succeeded in threading it. "Young and beautiful—and alone. It is not healthy, my dear, not healthy at all. You'll dry up into a sour old prune if you're not careful, with that touch-me-not attitude of yours. You should have a husband again. I do not understand why you do not, after five years of widow-hood."

Julia stiffened. Although she had met Miss Whit-tingham many times, she was not an intimate of the elderly lady, and what she had just said was in very poor taste, coming as it did from a mere acquaintance.

"Now, don't ruffle up, Lady Julia, if you please," her hostess continued. "I knew your late husband well, you know. Yes, indeed. Nigel was some few years younger than I, but we came from the same part of Buckinghamshire. Everyone in the county thought him quite the fool to be marrying such a young gel, everyone but me, that is. I thought him very clever to have managed it, and I told him so, too. Were you happy?"

She peered at Julia, her needle poised above her work as she waited for an answer.

Julia took a deep breath and counted to ten. "But surely you know we were, ma'am. I believe the felicity of our union has been greatly remarked throughout the *ton*."

Miss Whittingham smiled. "You think you have evaded my question very neatly, but you have given me my answer, my dear. Oh, yes. Is your past marriage the reason you will not consider the state again?"

"I do not care to marry again," Julia said baldly. Besides a rising tide of indignation for the lecture she was receiving, she was in total confusion as to how to handle it.

"Once was enough, eh?" Miss Whittingham remarked, bent over her sewing once more. "Well, some unfortunate women are like that, I guess, but never would I have thought you were one of 'em."

"Like what?" Julia could not help asking.

"Sexually cold," the older lady said in a calm voice. Julia stifled a gasp. "No, you do not appear to be the type, not with that lush figger of yours," she went on. "How sad that looks can be deceiving! But perhaps all is not lost. Get yourself a lover your own age, or two, or three. You will be happier. Believe me, I know."

Julia had had enough. "I find it most unusual for you to be instructing me, ma'am," she said. "After all, you are a spinster yourself."

Miss Whittingham peered at her, those faded eyes twinkling again. "I do assure you, my dear, my single state does not mean I have not enjoyed a man's company many times. In every way," she added, as if to make the matter perfectly clear.

Realizing that the conversation was doing nothing to further her investigation of the snuffbox, and wishing badly to change the subject, Julia said abruptly, "Do you take snuff, ma'am?"

"Snuff?" Miss Whittingham asked. "How strange you should ask! I do not take it anymore. It was quite the rage in my youth, and I did try it, but I cannot say that I cared for it very much. Why do you ask?"

Julia was thinking quickly. "Someone remarked the queen's habit yesterday, and I have been wondering about it. They say she is never without her box. I had not realized that snuff was so addicting."

Miss Whittingham nodded. "That is true. The queen began using it when she was married in 1761. We always thought she did so to show off her fine arm and little hand. Because she made it the thing, many ladies began to use it as well. I myself had a pretty box I was fond of. Mother-of-pearl on silver, as I remember."

"Have you seen any of the modern boxes?" Julia asked next. As Miss Whittingham stared at her, she said, "The Earl of Bradford offered me snuff the other evening from a very handsome case."

"The Earl of Bradford, eh?" her hostess mused as she took another tiny stitch. "Now there is a man who might do very well for you, Lady Julia. It is true he has never married, but in his case it is not because he does not care for feminine company. I asked my nephew about that, for I wondered if the man was a pervert.

He is not. He has just never met a woman he wants to tie himself to for life. But the one who finally snares him will be fortunate, very fortunate indeed. Besides his title and wealth, he has kept his figger, which is more than the Prince has done. I swear Prinny's stomach grows daily, and that is so unpleasant in a lover, is it not?" She tittered a little as she stole a glance at her guest. "I do beg you to consider the lean-and-leggy earl, if not as a husband, then as a lover," she went on. "I am sure he would make a splendid one! Or there is Robert Hammond. I saw the way he looked at you the other day. He is definitely attracted." She paused to titter again. "Naughty man! But they can be the most exciting, you know."

Julia began to collect her things, preparatory to leaving. It appeared the conversation had come round again to her single state, and she had no desire to discuss it any further. As she rose, Miss Whittingham smiled as she broke her thread and put her needle in the fat red pincushion that sat on a table by her side.

"Going so soon, my dear?" she asked as she folded her sewing. "Well, run along then. But do think about what I have said. I do so hate waste!"

Julia made her good-byes and said she hoped to see Miss Whittingham soon again. This tiny social lie seemed to amuse the old lady immensely, for Julia could hear her chuckling as she closed the door behind her. Her cheeks felt hot, and she paused for a moment to put her hands to her face before going down the stairs. What a singular visit! she thought. The woman was mad, she must be. Imagine talking about sexual matters the same way you might discuss a book you had read, or a new recipe for pickled herring, and during a morning call, too. As she went out to the street, Julia was glad she had been the only visitor. She would not have put it past Miss Whittingham to have spoken as she had before any number of women.

She gave the cabby her address in Charles Street, and settled back on the squabs, deep in thought.

Putting aside Miss Whittingham's eccentricity, what
had she learned, if anything? The lady had not
appeared uncomfortable talking about snuff, nor had
she been unduly startled when Julia introduced the
subject. But she had mentioned the Prince, and as a
lover, too. Could the elderly lady know of his attentions to herself? Had she been warning her not to
become his mistress because she did indeed have the
case? And then there had been her references to thrift.
Was she in need of money? She might have picked up
the case planning to sell it, until she discovered its real
owner. It was hard for Julia to believe that any
relative of the wealthy Lord Alvanley's was in need!
But perhaps, as she grew older, Miss Whittingham had
become obsessed with the thought of possible poverty.
Julia's own grandmother had been like that, saving old
clothes and string, even though she had left a fortune
when she died.

As she stepped down and paid the cabby, Lady Julia
shook her head. She did not think she had learned
anything helpful this morning. It appeared she was
not cut out for intrigue, for all she had gained was a
most indelicate lecture about the evils of the single
state, and a great many instructions she could well do
without.

As Hentershee let her into the house, Julia reminded
herself that how she chose to live her life was no one's
business but her own, and most certainly none of Miss
Whittingham's. She would try to avoid the woman in
the future, and she heartily pitied Lord Alvanley his
eccentric relative.

Her enagement that afternoon was vastly different.

As the two ladies strolled together toward Hyde
Park, Mrs. Andrews kept up a light conversation about
London and some shopping she had done that
morning. Julia studied her as unobtrusively as she
could. Alma Andrews was a tall, slim woman, and
elegantly gowned and coiffed. Her blue eyes were
rather small and set too close together, and she had a

habit of opening them very wide, as if to make them appear larger than they were. They were her only fault. Her complexion was excellent, and her rosy mouth and cameo profile appealing.

"I cannot tell you how much I enjoyed myself, Lady Julia," Mrs. Andrews was saying now. "I must thank you for standing my friend. It makes such a difference when I am out in company, now that I have met a few people."

"It must have been difficult to come to town by yourself," Julia remarked.

Alma Andrews' expression did not change. "It was," she admitted. "But Harry, my husband, insisted. He said that his own inability to appear in public anymore was no reason for me to remain buried in the country. He is disfigured, you see, besides being crippled."

"How sad! I am so very sorry," Julia said. She thought Mrs. Andrews' smile was a little strained, and she did not wonder at it.

"I am accustomed to it now, my dear Lady Julia," she said bravely, and then, to Julia's relief, she changed the subject.

Lord Whitney must have been on the lookout for them, for they had barely entered the Stanhope Gate before he was beside them, making an elegant bow.

"Lady Julia, well met," he said with an easy smile.

His blue-gray eyes admired her companion, and Mrs. Andrews smiled, opening her little eyes very wide indeed. Julia introduced them, and he bowed again. "How fortunate I am to meet not one, but two lovely ladies this afternoon," he said. "May I join you? Such beauty should not be unescorted."

As he spoke, he held out both his arms. Julia was a little surprised that Alma Andrews took his right arm without a moment's hesitation. Neither had she glanced at Julia to see what her wishes in the matter were. Frowning a little, Julia tucked her hand in his other arm, and they strolled on together.

"How charming the park is today," Mrs. Andrews

remarked, tilting her sunshade over her shoulder in a way that exposed her classical profile for whatever perusal the earl cared to make.

"Are you from the country, ma'am, and fond of walking?" the earl asked.

Mrs. Andrews nodded. "Yes, I am from Kent. My husband was a great walker years ago, and I acquired the habit."

"You are a widow?" the earl asked. "My condolences, ma'am."

"Oh, I am not a widow, but I might as well be," Mrs. Andrews said, giving him a sideways glance and sighing. "My husband is one of Britain's naval heroes, but he was terribly burned and maimed in the Battle of the First of June, while serving under Howe."

"How very unfortunate for him—and for you, ma'am," the earl said.

Julia was listening hard, but she could detect nothing in that quiet voice. For herself, she was absolutely amazed at how quickly Alma Andrews had made her situation known to a man she had met only moments ago.

"I was just telling Lady Julia how Captain Andrews insisted I come to London by myself. Harry is so selfless! He always says it would be a shame for me to miss all the . . . the exciting delights that London has to offer during the Season."

Her voice had grown softer and huskier, and Julia realized that Mrs. Andrews had a definite talent for making the most innocuous statement fairly quiver with second meaning.

"And I am sure you will enjoy yourself a great deal, ma'am," the earl told her now, his mouth curving in a smile as he gazed down at her, admiration in his eyes. Alma Andrews smiled back.

As if he suddenly remembered the lady on his other arm, he turned to Julia and said, "My mother asked me to beg you to bring Miss Edwina to tea some afternoon soon, ma'am. She was much taken with the girl.

In fact, she says she cannot remember when she had such an amusing visitor. Of course, we depend on you to honor us."

Preparing another social lie, Julia said, "How very kind of the countess! I am sure Edwina will be as delighted to join you as I am."

"In what part of London do you reside, m'lord?" Mrs. Andrews inquired. On learning that his town house was in Portman Square, she said, "Such a distinguished part of town, is it not? I was admiring the architecture there only a few days ago, and wondering what the interiors of those imposing houses were like."

Julia could not be surprised when the earl extended a further invitation to tea, so Mrs. Andrews might see for herself. She was feeling a little uneasy until he turned to her again. One dark brown brow rose quickly, and she felt immensely better almost at once, especially when she saw the knowing little devil that lurked in his deep-set eyes.

"Yes, I am happily situated in the square," he went on, turning impartially to them both in turn. "However, Lady Julia's house in Charles Street is very fine, too. No doubt you have had a chance to admire it, ma'am?" he asked Mrs. Andrews. "Such extraordinary *objets d'art* she has, don't you agree?"

Alma Andrews was complimentary, saying she thought the large landscape in oils in the drawing room especially fine.

"You must ask the lady to show you her collection of snuffboxes sometime, ma'am," the earl said next. "It is very valuable." Julia gasped a little at his audacity, and his arm tightened, as if to reassure her.

"You collect snuffboxes, Lady Julia?" Mrs. Andrews asked, peeking around the earl's tall, lean form. "But what an unusual hobby for a lady!"

"Do you take snuff, ma'am?" the earl inquired. As she shook her head, he said, "I am not surprised. It is more a man's habit than a lady's. I myself have always felt women lost their femininity when they indulged."

"And you are saying we must ever be feminine to please you, are you not, m'lord? How typical that comment is of a man, is it not, Lady Julia?" Mrs. Andrews asked. Then, laughing a little, she went on, "Although I am sure most of us strive to be exactly what you men like, whenever we can."

"I am sure you do," the earl said smoothly before Julia was forced to think of a reply. "But snuff has always seemed masculine to me. And snuffboxes can come in so handy for a gentleman. Even when he knows a lady does not enjoy snuff, for example, by offering her a particular case, he can quickly and easily determine if she would be interested in enjoying . . . er, anything else. Are you familiar with that kind of snuffbox, ma'am?"

Julia's hand tightened on his arm, and she felt his muscles tense in response.

"I do believe I have seen one or two," Mrs. Andrews admitted, her voice demure.

Julia stared straight ahead, but she was sure, even without looking, that Alma Andrews' little blue eyes were open very wide indeed, for she had heard the contented smile in her voice.

The earl laughed. "I am sure you have, as lovely as you are," he said.

Julia glanced around and was delighted to see Lady Beaton, her son Percy by her side, waving to her from a carriage that was halted on the other side of the roadway.

"Why, there are the Beatons," she said brightly. "Do excuse me for a moment, Mrs. Andrews, m'lord. I would speak to them."

The earl released her arm and bowed, and Julia went across to the carriage, her back very straight. How could she ever have imagined she would care for Alma Andrews as a friend? she wondered. The woman was a terrible flirt! Why, just look how she had insinuated herself into the countess's tea party, and how boldly she had responded to the earl's remarks, practically making a dead set at him. It was obvious she not only subscribed to Miss Whittingham's persuasions, she was on the lookout for a lover to keep herself amused during her stay in town. As Lady Julia greeted the Beatons, she spared a sympathetic thought for the poor naval hero who was married to such a woman.

Lady Beaton asked her how she was feeling, and after a moment Julia remembered that she had fled the lady's ball the evening the Prince had arrived. "I have recovered completely, thank you, ma'am," she said. "I was so sorry to have to leave when I did, for it was a lovely party. You are both to be congratulated."

Lady Beaton smirked down at her. "Yes, it was well attended. Percy said it was a perfect crush, didn't you, son?" Without waiting for him to reply, she went on, her disagreeable voice complacent, "So charming of His Highness to honor us, was it not?"

Julia agreed, wondering if she had ever made so many untruthful statements in a single day before. Then, although feeling uneasy at leaving the earl and Mrs. Andrews alone, she decided to find out as much as she could from the Beatons.

"Forgive me for asking, m'lady, m'lord," she began, trying to look concerned, "but did you by any chance notice a snuffbox in my drawing room that afternoon you came to tea? I ask only because I am so vexed I have misplaced it. It had great sentimental value to me, for it belonged to my grandfather. I was sure I had it displayed on a side table there, but now it is nowhere to be found."

As Lady Beaton peered at her, Julia studied her carefully, but there was nothing written on her face but a little mild interest. Lord Beaton looked vacuous, but since this was his customary expression when he was not frowning, she gained nothing from it.

"Why, no, I can't say I did," Lady Beaton said. "Was it a valuable case, Lady Julia?"

"I do not know," Julia admitted, and then inspiration struck. "It had a painting of my grandmother in enamel on lid, and I am said to look exactly like her. You can understand my concern that it is missing."

"Servants!" Lady Beaton exclaimed in her piercing voice. "They can none of them be trusted! No doubt one of the maids pocketed it, my dear Lady Julia. I suggest you question them most stringently, and threaten them with the Runners. I am sure you will have your snuffbox returned in a trice."

Julia did not dare look at the Beaton coachman and grooms, although she wondered what they thought of this sweeping condemnation of their class.

"Perhaps I should do that," she said, and then she gave them both a little bow. "It has been so pleasant seeing you, but now I must return to my friends. They are waiting most patiently for me."

She smiled and left them, although she was not looking forward to rejoining the earl and Mrs. Andrews. As she came up to them, she wondered if Trevor Whitney had uncovered anything in her absence. So far, she herself had not discovered a thing from all her questioning. She could not help feeling discouraged.

"Now we can continue," the earl said, giving her a warm smile. "I trust you found the Beatons in good health, ma'am?"

Julia nodded, struck by how much handsomer he was when he smiled.

On his other side, Mrs. Andrews remarked, "How strange Lord Beaton is! I could not help observing him, and he never said a word. Nor did he in your drawing room the other day, Lady Julia. Is he, perhaps, a mute?"

The Earl of Bradford chuckled. "No, indeed. But he is very much under the cat's foot, ma'am. His mother insists on his constant attendance. I do not think poor Percy has ever had a day to himself in his entire life, and as for any friends of his own, or such beauties as I am escorting today, that would be impossible."

Now it was Julia's turn to peek around the earl's tall, lean figure when Mrs. Andrews had no comment to make about his revelation. As she did so, she wondered why the woman was looking so very thoughtful.

As they continued their walk, the earl guided the conversation into commonplace subjects, and snuff-boxes were not mentioned again. The trio stopped often to greet friends, Mrs. Andrews waiting expect-antly each time for Julia or the earl to introduce her to any members of the *ton* she had not as yet met.

When they reached the Stanhope Gate again, Julia waited for the earl to bid them both farewell. He sur-prised her, however, as he waved his hand to an elegant carriage waiting nearby.

"May I see you both home, ladies?" he asked. "Surely you have done enough walking today, and I would be delighted to drive you to your destinations."

Alma Andrews accepted at once, but when Julia would have refused, since Charles Street was such a short distance away, the earl tightened his arm, as if in warning.

Obediently she allowed him to hand her into the carriage. She was astonished at how smoothly he arranged to take Mrs. Andrews home first, even though Charles Street was on the way. The lady kept up a gay chatter as they drove to her rooms in Henrietta Place. Trevor Whitney took her up the steps, and bowed. As Julia watched, a few final words were exchanged, and Mrs. Andrews gave him a warm smile in farewell. Almost as an afterthought, she waved to Lady Julia.

As the earl came quickly down the steps, Julia wondered if Mrs. Andrews would lie down now, with a cool damp cloth over her little blue eyes. After the almost constant exercise they had been subjected to this past hour, she imagined they must be aching with strain, and then she scolded herself for such a spiteful thought.

9

The earl had a few words with his coachman before he rejoined her in the carriage and his groom put up the steps. Settling back on the leather seat, he turned to her and said, "I have ordered my coachman to take us on a short drive, Lady Julia. It occurred to me that we should compare notes while the events of this day are fresh in both our minds."

Julia could feel herself stiffening. There was no trace of a smile on his stern lean face now, and his voice was cold again. He might have asked if I had any other engagements, she thought with some resentment. What an autocratic, unpleasant man he is!

Her petulance increased as he asked, "What did you learn from Miss Whittingham this morning, ma'am? I could not tell from either your expression or your slightly tongue-tied demeanor if your quest had been successful or not."

"What do you mean, tongue-tied?" Julia demanded.

The earl looked at her impatiently. "You were practically as dumb as Percy Beaton all during our walk, ma'am. Why, you left everything to me."

"But you seemed to have the situation so well in hand, sir," Julia said sweetly, although her hazel eyes were full of a dangerous light.

The earl nodded a little, as if to thank her for a compliment she never intended. "That is one of the advantages of being thirty-nine, ma'am," he said. "You can talk about anything or everything without a blink of the eye. But come! First, what, if anything, did Miss Whittingham have to say?"

When Julia did not answer at once, he stared at her. He was surprised to see her biting her full lower lip, while her color rose slightly. Both of his dark eyebrows rose as well.

"She is very eccentric," Julia said at last, still not looking at him. She told herself she would never reveal the topic Miss Whittingham had chosen to discuss with her; there was no need for it, for it had no bearing on the case. "She spoke openly about snuff when I questioned her," she went on, "and she admitted she had used it in her youth. She also mentioned the Prince in a rather sly way, which made me wonder at the time. I also thought when she made a few remarks about thrift, and how she saved money, that she might have taken the box with an eye to selling it. But somehow I still cannot imagine her capable of blackmail. She is too . . . er, preoccupied with other matters."

The earl nodded. He was wise enough not to ask what those matters might be, for it was obvious that they had upset the Lady Julia. He thought her modesty refreshing in an age when sexual innuendos and *double entendres* were so commonplace.

"I also questioned the Beatons when I went over to their carriage this afternoon," the lady hurried on. Her voice was lighter now she had left the eccentric Miss Whittingham and all her peculiarities. "I told them I had misplaced a snuffbox that belonged to my grandfather, and asked them if they had noticed it the day they came to my drawing room." She turned to him then, and shook her head. "They had not. Lady Beaton accused my servants of theft, and neither she nor her son was in the least bit self-conscious."

"And Percy never spoke a word, of course," the earl

said. "But how quickly you sacrificed your grandfather to the cause, ma'am! Was he the . . . er, the type
to brandish such a box?"

Julia thought he sounded amused, and she said
stiffly, "He was a bishop, sir."

The earl chuckled in genuine amusement, and she
had to smile a little in response.

Then she sighed. "I fear I am not cut out for
intrigue, m'lord. I do not seem to get any further on,
no matter how I try. And perhaps Miss Whittingham
or one of the Beatons *is* guilty. I have no way of
knowing. Surely if you were the blackmailer, you
would be very careful what you said, and you would
be expecting just the kind of questions I have been
asking, and therefore be prepared."

Trevor Whitney's lips tightened for a moment, but
Lady Julia did not notice, for she was staring down at
her clasped hands in some dismay at her ineptitude.
"Shall we continue?" he asked. "As for the lovely Alma
Andrews, I could not determine any hidden guilt
there, could you?"

Julia was suddenly reminded of his words to the
lady, and she turned toward him, her hazel eyes accusing. "How could you say what you did, m'lord? I vow
my heart was in my throat when you mentioned my
fictitious collection of snuffboxes. Whatever am I to do
when she asks to see it, pray tell?"

The earl's cool blue-gray eyes stared into hers. "She
will not do so," he told her. "Alma Andrews is not interested in snuffboxes, except to be shown the same
kind you were," he said wryly. "Then, I am sure, her
interest would be intense."

As Julia made no comment, he went on, "I am surprised that you would take that kind of woman for
your friend, m'lady. She is most unlike you."

"I did not know she was like that until this afternoon," Julia defended herself. "She has never shown
me that side of her nature before, you see. You may be
sure our friendship will cool rapidly, however, now
that I do know."

Trevor Whitney nodded. "I doubt she will bother you anymore. She met so many people . . . er, gentlemen, I should say, this afternoon, did she not? I think she was only using you as the entrée to such introductions, and now, having gained the end she sought, will not seek your further intervention." He studied the lady by his side, and noting her lovely face and sensuous figure, he added, "She cannot care for the comparison, you see. You are a much more beautiful woman than she is."

Julia wondered why she felt such a lift of her heart at his calm words, and then she forgot them as he went on. "We are crossing suspects off our list at a rapid rate, are we not? If we discard Miss Whittingham, Mrs. Andrews, and both the Beatons, who is left?"

Julia frowned a little in thought, not even noticing that they were passing Marylebone Park now, and the scenery was becoming ever more rural.

"I have never considered Lord Alvanley a suspect," she said. "Do you agree with me, m'lord?"

The earl nodded. "No, blackmail is not his style. It is inconceivable that he could be involved in this. I shall ask him, however, man to man, if he noticed the snuffbox that afternoon."

"But that leaves only the Hammond sisters or their nephew," Julia said, trying to keep the discouragement she felt from showing in her voice.

"Ah, yes, Red Rob Hammond," the earl mused, caressing his strong chin with one well-shaped hand. "I believe I told you I do not know him, ma'am, nor his aunts? I am afraid the sleuthing must once again fall on your shoulders."

Julia shrugged, and he went on. "That is another acquaintance of yours that surprises me. I would not have thought a lady of your sensibility would favor a rake."

"I do not favor him, as you put it, m'lord," Julia told him, looking straight ahead once more. "I am slightly acquainted with his aunts because they were distantly related to my late husband. They brought

their nephew to my house uninvited; I assure you I did
not ask him." For a moment, she wondered if she
should tell the earl about Mr. Hammond's strange
remarks the evening of the Beatons' ball, but she
decided to refrain. His flirting with her could have
nothing to do with the snuffbox, she was sure.

"From what I have heard of the man, it is entirely
possible that it was he who took the snuffbox," Trevor
Whitney was saying now. "My contact at Carlton
House, Colonel Lake, has had him investigated. The
man is deep in debt. I gather he has always gambled
well beyond his means, and lives precariously, sometimes only a step or two ahead of being thrown into
debtors' prison. Surely blackmailing the Prince would
relieve a most pressing problem, would it not?"

He saw the hope that dawned in Lady Juliet's hazel
eyes, and he paused to admire it for a moment before
he continued. "Then too, I asked my mother to tell me
everything she knew about the man while we were
having luncheon. If only half of what she revealed is
true, his character is not at all—shall we say?—nice. I
suggest you make an effort to contact him soon, and
question him. We must make haste!"

Julia looked at him out of the corner of her eye, and
saw him frowning, his lean face taut with emotion.

"You have had a further letter, sir?" she asked in
some trepidation.

"No, we have not," he said, and then he reached out
and turned her toward him, his hands grasping her
upper arms firmly. For a moment, Julia stared at him,
her eyes widening as he searched her face. "It is very
unusual that we have not," he said at last.

Her chin came up, for she seemed to hear some little
condemnation in his voice. Her heart sank as she realized that the earl still believed her guilty. She was surprised when he sighed a little then and shook his head
before he put her away from him to bang on the roof.
When the trap slid open, he gave orders to return to
town, and Lady Julia's house on Charles Street.

They rode in silence for a few moments before Julia remembered the tea party. "Were you speaking the truth when you asked that Edwina be allowed to come to tea, m'lord?" she asked.

Before he could reply, she went on in a rush, "I was not sure, you see, that it was not a ploy you were using in your interrogation of Alma Andrews."

"No, indeed," he said. "My mother asked for her especially, ma'am, although I am sure I do not know why. From what she said, they spent the entire time they were together misunderstanding each other. But my mother said Miss Ogilvie made her laugh."

"She has not made me laugh lately," Julia said curtly. "She has made me very angry! This morning I threatened to banish her to Kent if she interferes in this matter one more time."

"The young are so often difficult, are they not?" the earl remarked. "I would not wager any large sum on the chance that she will obey you, however. From what I have seen of that young lady, she will continue to help you any way she deems necessary."

Julia rolled her eyes heavenward, and he smiled a little.

"Shall we say tea in three days' time, m'lady?" he asked next. "My mother has it in mind to ask several others as well, and she must pen the invitations."

Julia nodded her acceptance. "And one must go to Mrs. Andrews, of course," she reminded him.

The earl waved in impatient hand. "I doubt that Mrs. Andrews still expects an invitation." At Julia's curious look, he continued, "You see, while you were talking to the Beatons, I made my disinterest in any dalliance with the lady perfectly clear, and in such a way that not even she could misinterpret it."

He paused, and he looked so grimly amused that Julia eyed him askance.

"Weren't your ears red, m'lady?" he asked. "They should have been. I spent the entire time we were alone extolling your beauty, especially your *big* hazel eyes, and your modesty and ladylike refinement. I imagine that is why Mrs. Andrews was so interested in Percy Beaton. I swear I could almost hear her wondering whether she had a chance for a conquest there."

"What a rapacious woman!" Julia said, determined to ignore those compliments he had given her, which were not compliments at all. "I pity her poor husband!"

The earl shrugged. "He probably knows all about her and her activities. Perhaps that is even why he sent her to town. It cannot be pleasant for the man to have her flirting and carrying on in the country, so close to home."

Julia was not required to comment, for she noted with some relief that they had reached her home. The earl helped her from the carriage and bowed over her hand.

"Investigate the Hammonds as soon as possible, ma'am," he ordered. "If you would be so good," he added more mildly when he saw her raised brows. "I shall call on you presently, or you may send me word in Portman Square if you have any news."

Julia nodded distantly, and turned away, her head held high.

She had intended to go to her room to ponder the day's events until Hentershee told her Mrs. Lowden was waiting for her in the drawing room. Smiling, she gave him her bonnet and stole and patted her chestnut curls in the hall mirror before joining her friend. Now she could go over everything that had happened with Fanny, and ask her advice as to how she should proceed with the Hammonds. Nothing could be better!

She was about to enter the drawing room when her butler coughed and said, "Another bouquet has been delivered, ma'am. I took the liberty of placing it in the drawing room, since you were from home. And this letter accompanied it."

Avoiding his eye, Julia took the familiar cream-colored sheets, closed with that distinctive seal that proclaimed its royal sender as surely as if his name had adorned the outside in large black letters. "Thank you, Hentershee," she said, tucking it under her arm for perusal later.

She found Mrs. Lowden seated before the fire, leafing through a novel Edwina must have left there. Fanny put it down at once.

"My dear Julia," she said, coming to hug her taller friend. Then she drew back to search her face. "You are all right, my dear? I was beginning to worry about you, for Hentershee said you had been gone some time before I arrived."

"I have been playing sleuth, Fanny," Julia told her, leading her back to the sofa. As she sat down, she noticed she still carried the Prince's letter, and sighing, she threw it down on a table by her side.

"Another impassioned appeal, Julia?" Fanny asked, frowning a little.

"I imagine so, and singular only because it is the second one today," Julia told her, frowning in turn. "When will this end, Fanny? And *where* will it end?"

"What happened today, dear Julia?" Mrs. Lowden asked, taking her hand in hers and pressing it in her concern.

Julia spoke for some time uninterrupted, as she told Fanny everything she had done, up to and including her drive with the earl, and their conversation. Fanny smiled at her description of Miss Whittingham's shocking instructions, and even Julia had to chuckle a little. It did seem funny now, in retrospect. And when she mentioned the eager Mrs. Andrews, Fanny pursed her lips in disapproval and shook her head.

"The earl has just left me," Julia concluded. "He as much as ordered me to investigate the Hammonds as quickly as I can. I gather he expects another letter from the blackmailer momentarily. I myself feel that Robert Hammond is the most likely suspect; pray I do not make a botch of it when I question him, Fanny!"

Her friend reached out and hugged her again. "I am

sure you will be just splendid, Julia," she said. "Oh, by
the way, surely the earl considers me a suspect too?"

Lady Julia looked shocked. "Of course he does not!
He knows you are my best friend. I told him you only
came that day because I sent for you, and that your
visit was long after the others had left."

Mrs. Lowden nodded. "I have been thinking, Julia,
thinking hard," she said, her thin, homely face
solemn. "After all, I was here that afternoon. I have
tried and tried to recall if I saw the snuffbox at that
time. Of course, my attention was all for you in your
distress, but surely I must have noticed such an
unusual item, don't you think? But I did not. That
must be proof even the earl must accept that someone
at your party did take it after all, unless one of the
maids stole it, as Lady Beaton suggested."

Lady Julia shook her head. "I would be willing to
swear my servants are innocent. Most of them have
been with me since my marriage, and they are loyal to
me. The only newcomer is the younger footman, and
Hentershee keeps his eye on him, I know."

She turned to her friend and sighed. "Fanny, can
you think of anything else I should be doing? Or could
be doing? I must admit I feel helpless, the way things
are. And if Robert Hammond and his aunts prove to be
innocent, the earl will turn his attention to me again! I
am so frightened!"

Fanny soothed her and told her not to borrow
trouble, but even after she had taken her leave, Julia
remained in the drawing room deep in thought. At last
she rose. Spying the Prince's letter on the table where
she had dropped it, she decided she would return it to
him unopened. As she picked it up, her soft lips
tightened. Certainly that would make her intention
never to have anything to do with him clear!

Before she could start to worry about the protocol of
treating royalty this way, she went to her library and
sealed the unopened letter in another sheet of paper.
She gave it to Hentershee with instructions to have it

delivered to Carlton House at once, and she went upstairs relieved that she had taken this new step.

That evening after dinner, she was forced to go over her day's activities yet again. She had no engagement, and she could see Edwina was anxious to learn everything that had happened. Telling herself that she owed this much to her concerned niece, she gave her a carefully edited account. When Edwina would have engaged her in endless speculation, she changed the subject firmly, however. Perhaps if she treated the matter more lightly, she thought, Edwina would tire of it and turn her energies to something else. Julia shook her head at her optimism. Somehow, like the earl, she did not think her niece would do that.

Edwina did not smile when she learned they were to go to tea at the earl's house. When questioned, she admitted she considered the countess an old dear, but it was plain that she thought accepting hospitality in the enemy camp a foolhardy thing to do.

Julia made a morning call on the two Hammond sisters the next day in the house in Belgravia where they had lived for so many years. The elder, Miss Dorcas Hammond, welcomed her with a sunny smile, and insisted she take a cup of tea with them, and as Miss Daphne tripped away to order the refreshments, her sister assured Julia she would just adore Cook's new muffin recipe.

As they sat together and chatted of the Season, Julia inspected them both. They were ladies in their late fifties who bore a strong family resemblance. Their red hair, so like that which topped most Hammond heads, was graying now, and their pleasant faces were lined, but they had kept their figures. As usual, they were richly if not fashionably dressed in gowns that recalled their youth. Miss Hammond had once confided that the new flimsy Empire styles were not suitable for elderly ladies, although she had sighed a little in regret that she had never had the chance to show off her excellent figure in such a revealing, flattering way.

When Julia introduced the subject of snuff, both ladies looked at her in stunned surprise. Miss Daphne even put her cup down on the table so abruptly the spoon clattered in the saucer.

"I fear your remark has disturbed my sister, Lady Julia," Miss Hammond said, her eyes growing cold. Julia saw her glance at her younger sister and sniff, and she also noted that lady's flushed cheeks and lowered eyes.

"I do beg your pardon," Julia said in some confusion. She wondered what this was all about, and what she was to do now. If the sisters refused to discuss it, she could hardly persist.

"There was an incident involving snuff in my sister's youth that makes the subject very painful," Miss Hammond went on. "I am sure you understand."

Julia nodded, although she did not understand in the slightest. She looked at Miss Daphne again, her hazel eyes wide, and the lady blushed an even deeper shade of red, as she rose and excused herself in a few broken words before she almost ran from the room.

Julia turned to her elder sister in some confusion. "I am so very sorry, Miss Hammond," she said, wondering if she had discovered something at last. "I would not have upset Miss Daphne for the world! But surely her reaction at my just mentioning snuff was most unusual . . . ?"

Dorcas Hammond lowered her eyes and pursed her lips. "I see I must explain, Lady Julia," she said stiffly. "I am sure that you will keep in confidence what I am about to reveal."

She paused until Julia nodded, trying to look sympathetic and trustworthy.

"My sister has always liked pretty things, even as a small child," Miss Hammond said. "And when she was very young, she had a most unfortunate habit of taking anything she fancied and hiding it away. You do understand she was not consciously stealing, do you not?"

Julia nodded, although she wondered what else you

could call it, as the older lady went on. "Once, she could not resist picking up a snuffbox that belonged to a guest of our father's. It was a valuable sterling-silver box, covered with diamonds and rubies, which, of course, is why Daphne coveted it. There was a terrible fuss when it was found to be missing, and one of the maids was falsely accused. My mother found the box under Daphne's mattress. It was her favorite hiding place. Of course, my father was furious, and her punishment was severe. So severe, in fact, that she has never taken anything that did not belong to her again, and she cannot hear snuff mentioned without becoming distraught."

When she paused, her color high, Julia hastened to assure her she understood Miss Daphne's former unfortunate habit completely.

Dorcas Hammond smiled at her. "Thank you, you are very good. And you must not worry that Daphne is upset. She will return in a little while, and everything will be as it was before. Would you care for another cup of tea, my dear? I am sure yours is quite cold."

Julia accepted, and while Miss Hammond poured out, her younger sister slipped back into the room and took her seat again, as if nothing unusual had happened at all. Julia turned the conversation to their nephew. "Does Mr. Robert Hammond stay with you while he is in London, ma'am?" she asked.

"Oh, my, no," Miss Hammond told her, smiling now that the dangerous subject of snuff had been disposed of. "He has his own rooms. It is not that we have not invited him time out of mind, my dear Lady Julia, for heaven knows we have enough room! But Robert will heed none of our entreaties. He says he would not dream of putting us to the trouble. Such a dear, kind boy, is he not?"

She smiled fondly, and Lady Julia concentrated on stirring her tea, her hazel eyes lowered. She was sure Red Rob preferred his own rooms for vastly different reasons, but she did not comment.

"Of course, he does take us about, now and then,"
Miss Daphne joined in, now that she had recovered
from her earlier embarrassment. "And we have prevailed on him to dine with us many evenings as well.
We feel we stand *in loco parentis*, as it were, now that
our dear brother and his wife have passed on to their
glorious rewards."

Lady Julia wondered what Mr. Hammond thought
of being mothered by two old spinsters. He must be all
of thirty-five, she knew. And she wondered if his aunts
had any idea of his unsavory reputation. It did not
appear that they did, which she thought very strange.
As the two began a litany of his virtues, she listened
with half an ear. She was trying to think of some way
she might meet him, for she did not feel she could wait
for a chance encounter. The Hammonds had not mentioned the location of his rooms, not that Lady Julia
would have called on him there in any case. Perhaps
she should invite them all to dine some evening soon?
She hesitated to do this, for even though they were
distant relations of her late husband's, she had never
cultivated them. And, she admitted, she did not care
to encourage the rakish Red Rob. He might take such
an invitation as a sign of her interest in him, and make
her life miserable. And since the Prince and the Earl of
Bradford were doing that so well already, she really
did not need to add another difficult man to her
life.

She was about to make her excuses and leave them
when she heard a deep bass voice laughing in the hall.
Miss Hammond and Miss Daphne brightened, and
looked expectantly at the door.

A moment later it opened, and Mr. Hammond came
in, throwing a quip over his shoulder to the butler.
When he saw Lady Julia Reynolds sitting with his
aunts, he halted and put both hands to his heart.

"From the moment I woke this morning, I was sure
today was going to be a lucky one for me," he said in
his deep voice. "Now I perceive I was right. My dear
Lady Julia, how wonderful to see you again! Aunts,

you are looking very fetching today. I like that cap, Aunt Daphne. So frivolous!"

As he made his bows and dropped a kiss on each faded cheek, Julia studied him. He was only a little over medium height, and in his fashionable clothes that fit him so superbly, he did not look like a great rake. His brows and eyelashes were too pale, and his green eyes set too wide in his rather colorless face. The only unusual thing about him was his startling red hair. As a stray sunbeam touched it, it shone as if it were as hot as the glowing coals it resembled.

Julia settled back in her seat. If she remained a little longer, perhaps Mr. Hammond could be enticed to accompany her when she left. She would offer him a seat in her carriage, and take him wherever he wished to go after he had completed his duty call. And in doing so, she could question him as the earl had instructed her.

Her plans worked perfectly. When she excused herself and rose, Robert Hammond rose as well. In no time at all they were seated side by side and the coach was taking him to his appointment at his tailor's.

Perhaps it was because she was growing tired of the devious methods she had used before, or perhaps it was because she did not feel she had much time, but for whatever reason, Julia was much blunter in her questioning. She asked him outright if he had noticed a snuffbox in her drawing room the day he had brought his aunts to her house.

His pale brows rose, and those green eyes narrowed a little. "To be sure, I did," he said easily. "I thought it most unusual, too, for I know that you, like my aunts, do not have a man about the house. And in your case, m'lady, what a shame that is," he added, bending closer and giving her an intimate smile.

Julia could feel his warm breath on her cheek, and she forced herself to sit quietly and not shrink away. Her heart was beating rapidly now; surely she was very close to discovering Mr. Hammond's part in the snuffbox's disappearance.

"Describe it, if you would be so good, sir," she said, determined to make sure he had seen it indeed.

He looked astonished at her persistence, but he obeyed. "I saw it the minute we entered the room," he said. "It was lying on a side table. I must admit I wondered who it belonged to, for I have heard no rumors that you have become enamored of any gentleman lately." He laughed at her intent face, and went on, "But who would not have noticed such a lovely case with its gold filigree, those discreet diamonds and rubies on the clasp! And the lady depicted in enamels on the lid, so very like the lady in whose drawing room it rested."

He took her hands in both of his and pressed them. "Now, you tell me, if you please, m'lady, who is the lucky man?"

Lady Julia shook her head. "But I am sure you know already, sir," she said through stiff lips.

Robert Hammond laughed and dropped her hands. "I swear I do not. But perhaps it would be amusing to find out? Could it belong to a *married* gentleman and you worry about scandal? But you need not fear to give me your confidence, dear lady. I have been privileged to hear many a dainty confession, and I can be as still as the grave. Do tell me!"

Her head in a whirl, Julia continued to refuse. Robert Hammond whiled away the rest of the drive naming possible candidates. Julia thought they would never reach his destination.

At last the carriage came to a halt before Weston's establishment. Before he left her, he smiled at her again and raised her hand to kiss it. "You may be sure I shall continue to ponder this mystery, ma'am," he said, his deep voice silky. "You see, I've a mind to try for you myself, and I do not care for competition."

As Julia stifled a gasp at his brazen words, he added, "Do you attend Lady Barr's ball? Be sure to save me two waltzes."

Julia stared into his mocking, knowing eyes. She

could see he meant to use the snuffbox as a weapon, perhaps to force her into his arms lest he reveal its existence in her house and set the tattlemongers to gossiping.

He had barely closed the door of the shop before she ordered her coachman to take her to Portman Square —and at once!

10

As the butler opened the door of the earl's town house to her, Julia could hear someone playing the piano in the library. Even in her excited distress, she noted the excellence of the musician, and she wondered who it could be.

She asked for the earl, and the butler bowed. "M'lord is at home, m'lady. If you will be so good as to step into the drawing room while I ascertain if he can be disturbed?"

Julia nodded, although she was a little surprised at his response. Surely it would be more correct to say he would go and see if m'lord was receiving visitors?

After he left her in the large formal room, she paced up and down, unable to sit calmly as she waited. It seemed a very long time before the butler came back and asked her to follow him.

He led her to the library, where she had been before. The music had stopped now, and as she entered, she saw the earl standing before the piano, straightening some sheets of music.

"Was it you, then, playing just now?" she asked, her eyes admiring.

He nodded curtly, not a glimmer of a smile on his face.

"How well you play, m'lord!" she marveled. "I had not suspected you to have such talent."

"I have always been interested in music," he told her as he came toward her. "It is how I met the Prince so many years ago. I have accompanied him on the violoncello many times, and we often have trio music in this very room."

As he indicated a seat, he went on, "Now, shall we dispense with the pleasantries? It is obvious you came to see me about something important, and I am most anxious to hear what it is."

Julia sat down, her eyes searching his cold, lean face. His deep-set eyes burned into hers, and she felt a flutter of alarm. But then, remembering what she had discovered, she put up her chin.

"I saw the Hammond sisters this morning, m'lord," she said. "They both became agitated when I mentioned snuff, so agitated, in fact, that Miss Daphne fled the room."

The earl pulled up a chair so he could sit close across from her. "I am surprised," he murmured. "I had not thought a pair of elderly sisters capable of—"

"I do not think Miss Hammond had anything to do with it," Julia interrupted. "She pledged me to secrecy—oh, dear, and here I am breaking my word not an hour later! But what am I to do but tell you?" she asked in some distress.

"Do go on, Lady Julia," Trevor Whitney ordered. "What you reveal to me will be kept as quiet as possible. I can see you do not like to divulge a confidence, and I commend you for it, but in this instance, needs must when the devil drives, don't you agree?"

Julia nodded, biting her lip a little. "Yes, you are right," she said slowly, and then she took a deep breath and told him about Miss Daphne Hammond's light fingers as a child. "Miss Hammond assured me she had outgrown this compulsion to take pretty things, but I cannot help but wonder if a person ever does outgrow it," she concluded. "Might she not have slipped from grace, seeing the snuffbox in my drawing room? After all, it was a pretty case, and the lady on the cover had red hair." Her voice died away in some embarrassment.

The earl ignored her confusion. "It is a distinct possibility," he said. "And it would better explain her strong reaction when you brought up the subject this morning. I wonder how I am to investigate her bedroom, however. I must admit I am at a loss to think of any plausible way I would be able to check under her mattress."

Julia looked up at him, surprised to see the amusement gleaming in his eyes. The picture of the elegant earl skulking around the elderly lady's bedroom brought an answering curl to her lips, until he said, "I shall, however, have the matter investigated discreetly. Perhaps Colonel Lake can arrange to bribe a maid to check her room. In any case, Miss Daphne Hammond will be watched closely from now on."

He crossed his arms over his chest. "There remains only Robert Hammond, ma'am. Have you found a way to question him?"

Julia nodded. "Better than that, m'lord. Mr. Hammond came in while I was there. I contrived to offer him a lift in my carriage when the visit was over. He accepted. During our drive I asked him point-blank if he had seen a snuffbox at my house. He admitted without a moment's hesitation that he had, sir! Furthermore, he described it perfectly!"

Lord Whitney leaned forward, all insouciance gone. "Do you really think he would have told you he saw it, if he was the one who took it, m'lady?" he asked.

Julia shook her head. "I do not know. He was not at all reluctant to discuss it. He believes it is the property of my lover who left it there by accident. It occurred to me that he might already know the name of the owner, that that was just a ruse."

She paused, and Trevor Whitney saw the look of distress on her face, and the way she was holding her reticule so tightly, and he waited, knowing she was upset at what she had to say next.

"When he left me, he all but threatened to use the snuffbox as a weapon to expose this secret liaison," she went on after she had composed herself. "He said he had a mind to try for me himself, and he ordered me to save him two waltzes at the Barrs' ball."

As her voice died away, the earl rose to pace the room, his brows drawn together in a black frown. "Hardly a delicate, gentlemanly approach, was it?" he observed. "And yet, if he were already using the box to blackmail the Prince, why would he now think to use it to gain your compliance? It does not make sense."

He stared at her, and for a moment she stared helplessly back. His mouth twisted in a little grimace, and he turned away. Trevor Whitney had been thinking of the Lady Julia when she was announced by his butler. He had been playing the piano for some time, a few random melodies that did not require any concentration. As his long fingers wandered over the keys, his mind had been free to ponder the lady yet again. He often played music in times of stress. Somehow music soothed him, and when he rose from the bench an hour or so later, he would have the solution to whatever was bedeviling him. But that had not occurred this time. He had just become even more confused, and this had made him angry. After all, he was no green young man! He had had his share of love affairs, and he had been able to walk away from them, his heart intact, when the attraction of the moment faded. Somehow, what he felt for Lady Julia Reynolds was a completely different thing. It was not that he did not want her—he was honest enough to admit to himself that he did. But his physical longing to possess her was not his primary emotion where the lady was concerned. No, it was more than that. In every sinew and cell of his body he felt a deep need to exonerate her. He wanted to bring that wonderful smile of hers back to her face, that smile that turned her into a beauty.

He did not understand what was happening to him, for she was in his thoughts more often than she was not. Over and over, he wondered what her part in this really was. Sometimes he managed to convince himself that she was guilty, and that in time he would discover invincible proof of that guilt. But then his mind would play the devil's advocate, searching and discovering ways she must be innocent. He wondered why he wanted her so badly to be innocent.

Because he did not trust these new, strange feelings, his face grew even more cryptic, his expression colder and sterner as he regarded her.

"Perhaps he knows I have not become the Prince's mistress," Julia was saying now. Firmly he put his mental meanderings aside to concentrate on the problem at hand.

"If he did know that," she went on, "why wouldn't he think it possible to use the box not only to get money from the Prince, but to force me to accept him as well? How amusing he must find my dilemma!"

She paused, her eyes steady on his. The earl shrugged. "I still say your premise is very farfetched, ma'am," he said harshly. "It would be too dangerous playing such a precarious, double-headed game. He would concentrate on the money, first and foremost. I do assure you that lovemaking, no matter how much a man desired it, would have to wait its turn."

Julia read the disbelief in his eyes and in his cold voice, and suddenly she was as angry as she had ever been in her life. She rose quickly, and came toward him.

"Will you never try to see my side of it?" she demanded when she was close to him. "Must you always assume I am guilty? I am not, but I am tired of telling you that. From the very beginning of this horrible affair, you have badgered and bothered me, disbelieved me and accused me. I cannot stand much more of it!"

Her voice had grown higher and more breathless, and he could hear a tiny note of desperation in it. He grasped her arms to steady her, and made his own voice calm and reasonable. "As I have told you before, m'lady, what I believe has no bearing on the case. I will grant you that Robert Hammond is a possibility, as is his Aunt Daphne—the only two we have discovered."

"Other than myself, of course. Isn't that right, m'lord?" she demanded.

"Other than yourself," he echoed obediently. At the flash of anger in her eyes, he closed his own for a moment. He did not feel he could look into those sparkling, accusatory eyes for another second, lest he be forever lost.

Suddenly he felt the tension leave her body, almost, she slumped a little in his grasp. His hands tightened.

"What am I to do?" she asked. Her voice was quiet now, almost despairing, as if she had given up any hope of ever bringing him to her side. "You must tell me, m'lord, for I do not know how to handle this situation."

He squeezed her arms and led her back to her chair. Wonderingly she watched him as he went to pour her a small glass of brandy. When he brought it to her, she took it without protest. She had come very close to breaking in the past few minutes, and she knew she must not do that.

"Drink it, m'lady," the earl was saying as he bent over her chair. "You have had an upsetting morning. It is no wonder you are distraught." He waited until she had taken a small sip, and then he continued. "I must admit I think Robert Hammond a more promising suspect than his aunt. His character, background, his heavy debts and desperate need of money all point to him. Don't you agree?"

He waited until she nodded, and then he went on. "It is of primary importance that we—or, rather, you —keep him under surveillance. But it is not necessary for you to do anything at all. Go to the Barr party, and give Mr. Hammond his waltzes. Question him further, and try, if you can, to trick him into admitting his guilt."

He saw she was going to protest, and he added, "I shall be there as well. There is nothing to fear from the man, for I shall be watching him all the time. And if he tries to contact you before the ball, do nothing to alarm him or frighten him away. We must test Mr. Hammond, and unfortunately you are the only one who can do that."

Julia took another sip of brandy. She felt calmer now, although her skin was still crawling and her stomach churning. To think she had to play such a distasteful part! To think she was going to allow herself to be used as bait for a trap! But when she considered the alternative, she knew she had no choice. If Robert Hammond was indeed the guilty party, it was up to her to prove it. The earl could not, would not help her, not really.

She put the snifter down on the mahogany table beside her and rose. "Very well, sir," she said as she smoothed her gloves. "I shall do as you say. I quite see how important this is to me, but even though it is the only way I can prove my innocence, I must tell you that the course you have set me is most repugnant."

The earl nodded, those deep-set eyes devouring her face. He was staring at her with such intensity, Julia was sure he was trying to look inside her head and divine her innermost thoughts. She looked away.

She curtsied then, and he let her go without another word. At the door she turned back, her hand on the knob. Her chin came up, and she looked at him proudly. "I tell you again, on my honor, m'lord, I do not have that snuffbox. I am innocent, and I will do whatever I have to, to prove that to you. And when I have proved it, I hope I never have to see you again in my entire life."

She slipped from the library and closed the door behind her. As the butler went to open the front door for her, she heard the piano again. As she went down the steps, she could still hear the loud, dissonant chords, and she shivered at the barely controlled anger that resounded in that harsh, brutal music.

She did not see the earl again until the afternoon of the tea party. For the two days after her morning call on him, a certain uneasy peace prevailed. The Prince still wrote to her every day, and sent her gifts, which she returned without comment. Somehow, his persistence had no power to upset her further. Fanny called, and Julia found herself most reluctant to discuss the matter of Robert Hammond, even with her old friend. Instead she claimed that things seemed to be at a standstill. Fanny went away shaking her head at this new, reticent Lady Julia.

Edwina watched her aunt's new calmness with a frown between her heavy brows. Aunt Julia almost seemed resigned to whatever fate had in store for her. Edwina, thinking such a course of inaction paltry, spent a lot of time wondering what she might do to help her.

When the two were admitted to the Whitney drawing room, they discovered not only the earl and his mother but also several other prominent society members, although Julia noted that Alma Andrews had not come. She told herself she was glad of the company, for in such a large group she would not have to spend any time alone with the earl.

Much later, as they were leaving, she wondered why she was feeling so displeased and unsettled. She had chatted with Lord Alvanley and Lady Cowper, exchanged pleasantries with Lady Jersey and two gentlemen in her train, and she had spent some time with the countess and Edwina. The earl had not sought her out, but had kept his distance, speaking to her only when it was absolutely necessary, and then only with the politeness he would extend to any guest in his house. It was almost as if he were barely acquainted with her, she thought as she took her seat in the carriage beside her niece.

She was not aware that Edwina was studying her with some concern. Both she and the countess had noticed the unusual behavior of the earl and Lady Julia, and wondered what it meant. Edwina wished she might ask her new friend about it, but in a crowded drawing room amid general conversation, not even she had dared to be so rash. Besides, she told herself, she would have had to shout it into the elderly lady's ear, and everyone would hear her. As the carriage rumbled homeward, she set herself to thinking of a way she might question the countess in private. She knew she could not call on her alone again, for she was afraid this time Aunt Julia might send her home, as she had threatened to do.

By the time they had reached Charles Street, Edwina was smiling to herself. She could not call, but no one had forbidden her to write, now had they?

The morning of the ball there was another floral offering to join the Prince's spray of gladioli. Julia saw the nosegay of pink rosebuds at once, and she took up the note that accompanied it with some foreboding. She did not recognize the handwriting, but something told her she had better not open this note until she was alone.

In the library, with the door safely closed behind her, she slit the seal. As she had supposed, the nosegay was from Robert Hammond. She thought his written words almost proprietary, and she was angered by his bold assumptions. He told her he was looking forward most impatiently to their tryst this evening and that he expected to see her carrying his flowers.

Immediately Julia decided to wear the brown silk with the gold threads running through it. Pink posies would be impossible with such a gown, and would give her the perfect excuse for not obeying his orders. Besides, it was new and she had worn it only briefly the evening the Prince had come to the Beaton affair.

The day seemed to fly by for her. In no time at all, or so it seemed, she was having her hair done and dressing for the evening. She decided to arrive quite late, and she lingered over her dinner with Edwina. Later, she made an excuse to return to her room, saying she was sure her curls were becoming unpinned. Edwina shrugged and picked up the current novel she was reading. She had written to the countess, but as yet she had had no reply.

When Julia finally came downstairs again, the carriage was at the door, and she called her good-nights to her niece from the hall. She thought Edwina's reply sounded abstracted, and she smiled to herself. No doubt the girl had reached an exciting part of the story, she told herself.

Behind her, in the library, Edwina's blue eyes grew wide as she read on. Of course! she crowed to herself. Here was the perfect solution to Aunt Julia's problem! She would get busy on its completion this very evening.

The Barr mansion, besides being large and imposing, was set in a pretty garden that was unusual for its size, so close to town. As Julia entered the ballroom, she saw that the French doors to the terrace were standing open this warm June evening, and that lanterns had been placed around the garden, their pools of colored lights turning it into a place of enchantment. She promised herself that she would not, no matter how provocative the situation, put one golden sandal outside those doors.

Because she had delayed her arrival, a set was already in progress as she came in. She moved gracefully along the sides of the room until she saw some friends, and she was quick to join them. She was soon engaged in gay conversation, but as she wielded her fan and chatted, she looked about the large room. She saw the tall, lean Earl of Bradford almost at once. He was in a group of gentlemen some little distance away,

and even though she disliked him so much, she was
relieved he had come as promised. And then, leading a
very pretty blond through the set, she saw Red Rob
Hammond. His red hair shone under the glistening
lights of the chandeliers. Julia turned her back on him.

Unfortunately, the next dance was a waltz. Mr.
Hammond was at her side before anyone else could
claim her, and he bowed.

"I believe this is my dance, Lady Julia," he said,
holding out his hand.

As Julia took it, she saw his pale green eyes, intent as
they caressed her face, lingering on her mouth before
they went in leisurely inspection down to her throat
and lush figure. Julia had all she could do not to pull
away from him.

He held her close in his arms, much too close, she
thought, although she made no protest. The wiry hand
clasping hers was hot, and she could feel the heat of his
other hand on her waist right through the thin silk of
her gown.

As they began to dance, he said, "I see you do not
carry my posy, ma'am. Now, how am I to take that, I
wonder?"

Julia glanced at him briefly. "You may take it any
way you like, sir," she said evenly, although her heart
was leaping in her breast. Then, remembering the
earl's instructions, she made herself smile a little. "It
was so unfortunate that it clashed with my ball gown,
was it not?"

As his angry look eased a bit, she told herself how
much she hated herself.

"And are you going to tell me who my rival is,
ma'am?" he asked next. She could feel his thighs
pressing against hers, and she concentrated on not
shivering.

"No, I am not," Julia said. "The gentleman who left
the snuffbox in my drawing room is not a lover of
mine. I have no lovers."

"What a wicked waste," Mr. Hammond murmured,

his breath hot against her skin. "But I do not believe you, my lovely one," he went on. "It is impossible that such a luscious lady as you are is celibate. No, no, that cannot be."

"It is true, however," Julia said as he turned her in time to the music. "Mr. Hammond, if you please, I would ask you a question."

"Certainly, my dear. Ask me anything you like," he replied. "I am most agreeable, since all we can do at the moment *is* talk. Know, however, that I intend to have done with words between us in a very short time."

Julia leaned back against his arm, her hazel eyes regarding him steadily. "Did you take that snuffbox from my drawing room, sir?" she asked.

She felt him start, and she watched his green eyes narrow. "Are you accusing me of theft, ma'am?" he asked, his voice suddenly ugly.

Julia did not look away. He had closed his eyes a little, and it was hard for her to see his expression. Still she stared at him as she explained. "The box has disappeared, sir. It is nowhere to be found. I have searched, questioned both my servants and my guests that afternoon, and no one was even aware of the box but yourself. Surely you are the prime suspect, wouldn't you say?"

"The box was not that valuable, from what I could see of it," Mr. Hammond mused. He sounded as if he were struggling to keep control of himself. "Can it be that you are making this great stir about it because it is an embarrassment to you, Lady Julia? And to the very noble gentleman who left it there?"

As her eyes widened, he added, "Oh, I think I am safe in assuming he must be of high rank, ma'am."

Julia nodded. "You are correct, sir," she managed to get out. "He wants that case returned."

"But how desolate I am that I am unable to produce it for you instantly, dear lady!" Mr. Hammond said. She noticed that there were two distinct white lines bracketing his mouth, and his green eyes were blazing. "You see, in spite of your assumption that I am a common thief, I must tell you that I have never stooped to such depths. I will admit I am a rake and a gambler, even an adulterer and a duelist, if it please you, but I am not a thief. How dare you, ma'am?"

His hands tightened cruelly, and Julia had all she could do not to cry out. "You are hurting me, sir," she gasped.

For a moment his hands tightened still further, but then he saw her white face and the pain in her eyes, and he loosened his cruel grip.

Julia took a deep breath, and his angry eyes were drawn to her half-exposed breasts. "You are really very lovely," he said, his voice quieter now. "But even so, I cannot forget that insult. No, you may be sure you shall be punished for your accusation, ma'am. How I shall enjoy the task!"

Julia began to pray that the music would end soon, until she noticed that he was dancing her purposely toward the terrace doors. At once she stumbled, trying to resist. "Let me go!" she demanded, wondering where the earl was.

The music drew to a triumphant close, and all around them couples were drawing back and smiling as they bowed and curtsied to each other. Red Rob Hammond wasted no such time on the amenities. With one arm still tight around her, he drew her quickly from the floor and out onto the terrace. Julia felt powerless to resist without making a scene that could do nothing but humiliate her.

She was relieved to see other couples on the terrace, strolling up and down and enjoying the scented air. But Mr. Hammond did not linger there. He all but carried her down the shallow steps into the garden, and Julia realized that even though he was only of medium height, he was very strong.

"Stop at once, or I shall call out, sir!" she demanded, and she was shocked when his other hand came up to cover her mouth and he pushed her head hard against his chest. She began to twist in his arms, fighting to loosen his grip on her.

They had passed by some lanterns hung from a tree branch and were moving into the dark beyond when she heard that voice she had been praying for say, "But, my dear sir! That is no way to take a lady for a stroll. Is she so unwilling?"

Mr. Hammond spun around with his captive. When he saw the tall Earl of Bradford leaning against the trunk of a tree, his eyes narrowed and he let Julia go. As quickly as she could, she moved away from him, back into the circle of lights near the earl. She was breathing quickly in her distress, and for a moment both men were silent as they admired the rise and fall of her breasts under the taut silk gown.

"Not that any man could blame you for such impetuous behavior, nor do I," the earl said as he straightened up and came toward them. "However, I do find I object to having my dance preempted. You see, the Lady Julia is promised to me for the next set."

He took her hand, and then, as an afterthought, he bowed. "You must excuse us, sir," he said coldly. "But I beg you to remember that the lady is safe with me. Yes, very safe, for I intend to see that no harm shall come to her."

Slowly he began to stroll back to the house, Julia on his arm. They left a frustrated, angry Red Rob behind them. Julia concentrated on putting one foot in front of the other, for she had never felt more like fainting. The earl led her through the ballroom and into the hall, as if he could tell how close she was to giving way. It seemed only a moment before he was closing the door of a small antechamber behind them and leading her to a sofa. For a moment, Julia felt the room spinning, and she sagged against him. Immediately he put his arms around her to keep her safe. Julia realized how very unlike Mr. Hammond's cruel grip those comforting arms were, and she relaxed.

When he had seated her, he said, "Put your head

down on your knees, ma'am." It was an order, and all trace of the weary, elegant socialite was gone from his voice. "I do not care to have you fainting on my hands."

Feeling as if she might burst into tears of chagrin for her weakness, Julia did as she was bid. Soon the room stopped spinning and she felt better. She raised her head to see the earl leaning against the mantel, those blue-gray eyes observing her carefully. When he saw some color had returned to her white cheeks, he nodded and came to sit beside her.

"And now perhaps you will have the goodness to explain why you went outside with the man, ma'am?" he asked. "Surely you knew such a move in Red Rob Hammond's company was dangerous."

"He gave me no choice, m'lord!" Julia protested. "He was furious with me, and I could not make a scene."

Her eyes dared him to contradict her, and he shrugged. "And what, if anything, did you learn from the man?" he asked.

Not even trying to keep the disappointment from showing in her voice, Julia told Trevor Whitney what she had said and done, and how Mr. Hammond had responded.

"So, he was overcome with rage, was he?" the earl mused. "He is either innocent, which would explain his reaction, or, knowing you were bound to question him, an excellent actor. Of course, being able to act a part must be a valuable asset to a rake, don't you think?"

Julia stared down at her hands, wondering what would happen next. Surely the earl would not expect her to continue to question Mr. Hammond, not after what she had just told him. To her relief, he said in a calm voice, "I think it best if I take a hand now, m'lady. I shall set certain investigations in train, and question the man myself. I do not think it will hurt if I tell Mr. Hammond the box belongs to the Prince of

Wales. He either already knows it, or he does not have the snuffbox, and so cannot use it as a weapon."

He paused for a moment, and then he said, "By the way, I have spoken to Miss Daphne Hammond and her sister."

Startled, Julia looked at him, and he said quickly, "I did not mention the snuffbox. I had my mother introduce me so I could take the lady's measure. I agree she might have taken the box, with her history, but I cannot see such a nice old tabby involved in blackmail. And since we know blackmail is the motive, we must cross her from our list of suspects. Her older sister, being the stronger personality, would be more believable. Colonel Lake concurs with my conclusions."

Julia nodded, still feeling somewhat unsettled from her frightening experience in the garden. She had to wonder, in spite of what the earl had said, if either Miss Hammond or Miss Daphne had participated in the intrigue. They were fond of their nephew, after all. Why, they doted on him! For a moment she daydreamed a little. Suppose Miss Daphne *had* taken the box. She might well have confessed it later to her sister. And perhaps Miss Hammond had given the box to Red Rob, begging him to see it was returned to its rightful owner. Julia shook her head mentally. She was becoming as suspicious as the earl. The thief had to be Robert Hammond himself; all signs pointed to him.

She was surprised when the earl rose and held out his hand. "If you are quite recovered, ma'am?" he asked politely. She forced herself to rise and shake out her skirts.

"I am so sorry to have to burden you with my distasteful escort, Lady Julia," Trevor Whitney went on coldly as they walked to the door. "But I believe you must make the best of me for the remainder of the evening. I would not put it past that redheaded devil to try for revenge against you even now. Best that you stay by my side."

He turned to look down at her as if to gauge her reaction to his proposal, but she was looking resolutely ahead, and he could read nothing from her serene profile. When she did not answer him, his lips twisted in a grimace.

"By the way," he murmured as they walked back down the hall together, "I questioned Lord Alvanley as well. He says he cannot remember seeing a snuffbox in your drawing room, although he is in no way sure. And you will be interested to learn that another blackmail letter has arrived at Carlton House. It came through the post this time."

Julia's startled eyes flew to his face. She saw how stern it was, how cold, and how tightly his lips were compressed.

"It is printed in the same hand as before," the earl continued, as if he had not noticed her shocked surprise. "And it has the audacity to demand the sum of five thousand pounds for the return of the snuffbox. Now, what do you think of that, my Lady Julia?"

11

Julia was not required to think of a reply, for they had reached the ballroom again, and its crowd of guests. Almost immediately their company was claimed by two of the earl's friends, and the gay conversation that ensued had nothing to do with blackmail notes, missing snuffboxes, or angry, rapacious rakes.

As Julia smiled and chatted, she noticed Lady Jersey watching her with a little smile, and she wondered at it. But when she saw the lady's eyes go to the tall figure of the Earl of Bradford standing so close beside her, she realized that the lady must have seen them disappear. She was sure she also knew to the minute how long they had been gone.

Julia was exasperated, but she made herself smile sweetly at the Prince's former mistress, who unfortuntely was such a great gossip.

"Lady Julia, do say you will honor us," a Mr. Grant was saying now, and she forced her mind back to present company. She didn't have the vaguest idea what he was talking about, and she was glad when he went on, "You have such an outstanding voice! Do say you will join us for one of our musical evenings. We always meet at the earl's house, but it is not a performance, oh, no. We get together only to enjoy the

music ourselves. I shall promise to practice any songs
you care to sing on my violin until I have perfected
them, and I am sure Trevor would be delighted to
accompany you as well. Why, we might even prevail
on the Prince to join us that evening, what say you,
m'lord?"

Lord Whitney returned a noncommittal answer,
and Julia had to say it sounded delightful, even as she
made up her mind to come down with a putrid sore
throat if any such date was actually proposed.

Eventually the earl asked her to dance with him,
and she was forced to accept. As they moved through
the steps, she saw Mr. Hammond watching her from
his position against the wall. His face was set and cold,
and his eyes still burned with anger. Without thinking
of what she was doing, Julia moved closer to the earl.

Surprised, Trevor Whitney looked down at her, and
then over the top of her head. His face resumed its
usual cryptic expression. "You see I was right,
m'lady," he murmured. "Mr. Hammond still thirsts
for revenge. Be very careful for the next few days."

"I shall," Julia promised.

"I will make the matter clear to the man as soon as I
can," he went on. "I think mention of the crown will
discourage any further intervention on his part."

He sounded grim, and Julia was sure the way he
would handle the rake would be most effective, even
without bringing royalty into it. She was also sure she
had nothing more to fear from Red Rob Hammond,
and she marveled at how much trust she put in this
man she had come to hate.

The earl stayed beside her the entire evening, taking
her in to supper and treating her with calm formality.

Julia wondered why she felt so depressed. She began
to think the evening would never end.

As he escorted her to her carriage at last, she asked
him to call on her the next day. "I would hear more
about this latest letter, sir," she explained. "Will you
be so kind?"

Julia wondered if she were imagining his slight hesitation before he bowed. "Certainly, m'lady. I shall be with you at two."

She rode home alone, thinking hard. If Mr. Hammond did not have the snuffbox, the earl was left with only one suspect again—herself! It was all she could do not to put her head back and wail. Surely one of the people she had questioned had to have been lying, but she had no idea how she was to prove which one of them it was. They all swirled in her head in a mad dance. Dotty Miss Whittingham? Light-fingered Daphne Hammond or her sister? Either of the impossible Beatons? Hungry Alma Andrews? Perhaps, in spite of his anger, Red Rob Hammond? He had admitted seeing the box in her drawing room, and he was the only one who had. Was he innocent, or very, very clever?

It was a long time before she fell asleep at last, and even then she continued to dream of them in one macabre nightmare after another. When she woke the next morning, her eyes felt heavy, and she was still tired.

As her maid brought in her breakfast tray, Julia told her she would wear the dark green gown today. She had promised to go to the circulating library with Edwina, and then help her with some shopping. Neither activity seemed very amusing today.

Later, after she had left Edwina at the Rogerses' so she might visit with her friend Evelyn, Julia returned home. She was seated in the drawing room when Hentershee brought in the earl's card.

Until he had been served the sherry she ordered for him, they chatted lightly of the ball. But as soon as Hentershee had bowed himself away and closed the door behind him, Julia dropped her social pose.

"You said another letter in the same hand had been delivered, m'lord," she began. "Do you have it with you?"

The earl took out his notecase and handed her the folded sheet. Julia's eyebrows rose slightly. At least this time he was not keeping a firm grip on it. Perhaps he was beginning to trust her a little? she wondered.

She read the letter quickly, and as the earl watched her, she shuddered. The sunlight shining on her curls turned them to fire. He was thinking how silky and alive they looked, when she interrupted his reverie.

"But the letter does not say how the money is to be paid, sir. I do not understand."

"No, but if you read the last line again, you will see that we are to expect one more communication," he told her. "I am sure, as is Colonel Lake, that that final letter will contain our instructions."

"Won't that be the most dangerous time for the blackmailer, m'lord?" Julia asked, handing back the note.

As the earl put it away, he said, "It will indeed, ma'am. And you may be sure that wherever payment is to be made, we will be there and on our mettle to intercept whoever comes to claim it."

"You do intend to pay such a munificent sum, then?" she asked curiously.

The earl stared at her, his face expressionless. I wish I could see him smile again, Julia thought somewhat irrelevantly. He has such a nice smile.

"We have no choice, ma'am," Trevor Whitney said. "The snuffbox must be recovered. I very much fear that unless we can recover the money as well, there will be no keeping this from His Majesty."

He sipped his sherry before he went on. "You will like to know that I called on Mr. Hammond this morning. He was stunned—or at least he pretended to be— when I told him who owned the snuffbox. I also told him that he was under even more suspicion than the other guests, and he assured me that he had had no idea of the magnitude of the problem. I was not able to ascertain anything further, but he knows he will be under investigation, and watched carefully. I do not think you will be troubled by him again, ma'am."

Julia thanked him gravely. She was vastly relieved.

"But tell me, does the Prince pursue you still?" the earl asked next.

Julia nodded, biting her lower lip. "He is very

tenacious," she said. "Every day there is a letter or a gift, all of which I have returned."

"Do not be surprised if he calls here again, Lady Julia, and demands to see you," the earl warned her.

He saw how her face paled at the thought of such a visit. "I will not receive him!" she said quickly. "I will never be home to him!"

"I advise you to instruct your butler to that effect at once, then, ma'am," he said. "I have observed the Prince during many of his affairs, and I know his pattern. It rarely varies. If he does not gain a quick compliance, he becomes impatient and reinforces his letters with personal calls. I expect he will commence that part of his campaign to win you almost any day now."

"How horrible all this is!" Julia exclaimed. "I have half a mind to send Edwina home and retire to the country myself."

"You must not do that," the earl commanded as he put his empty glass down and rose.

Julia rose as well, looking puzzled. "Why ever not?" she asked. "Surely if I went where he could not find me, he would tire of his pursuit. Then, too, it might well be a way for me to establish my innocence. If a further letter comes, you will know I had no hand in this, after all."

She looked up eagerly, to see the earl shaking his head. "But the post travels the length and breadth of England, ma'am," he said.

As her face fell, he added coldly, "There is also the matter of a possible accomplice. I am afraid I must insist that you remain in town. Colonel Lake is in complete agreement. We cannot let you out of our sight, not yet."

Julia's head came up, and her face grew stiff and haughty. "I see. Of course, I should have known," she said proudly. "How disastrous if your chief suspect was not at hand to bully and accuse. I bid you good day, sir."

The earl nodded. Julia stood there she was, watching his tall, proud figure as he left her drawing room.

Then she sank down on the sofa, her eyes despairing.

She made it a point to tell Hentershee, a few minutes later, that if the Prince of Wales should come, he was to say she was not at home and that he had no idea when she would return. Her old retainer nodded, but he looked so distressed that she put her hand on his arm and pressed it.

"I know, Hentershee," she said. "This is all very unpleasant for you, as it is for me. But we must hope it will soon be over. Until then, I rely on you."

Hentershee bowed low as he assured her he would do his best.

Lady Julia spent the rest of the afternoon attending to her neglected account books and correspondence. When the room grew darker, and she heard rain striking the windowpanes, she called for a branch of candles. She was not at all surprised that the lovely day had turned dark and gloomy. It seemed such a perfect counterpart to her present mood.

Remembering the earl's comments about the Prince, she could not help starting up every time she heard the door knocker. Her account books contained several errors that day.

At last, when she heard Edwina's voice in the hall, she put her work aside and rose gratefully. She decided to have tea served here in the library. With the cozy fire on the hearth, it would be more pleasant than the large, formal drawing room.

As she opened the door to ask Edwina to join her, she was surprised to see Fanny Lowden beside her niece. She was handing a large umbrella to Hentershee.

"My dear Fanny!" she exclaimed. "What a lovely surprise. You are just in time to join us for tea."

Mrs. Lowden gave her a loving smile. "I came in to escape the rain, and I should be glad of a cup of tea, Julia," she said.

"If you would please excuse me, auntie, Mrs. Lowden," Edwina interrupted. "I had tea with Evelyn just a short time ago."

Julia was not at all reluctant, for she knew she could

not speak freely to her friend, not with her eager, inquisitive niece listening.

Edwina ran up the stairs, and the two friends took seats across from each other next to the fire.

"What a pleasant room this is," Fanny said, looking around the library at the soft green draperies trimmed with gold braid, the smart striped upholstery, and the play of the firelight on the highly polished furniture. "It is so comfortable, so cozy."

"I think of all the rooms in the house, it is my favorite," Julia said. "I did wonder if that pale green was not too feminine a shade, but it was such a relief after the deep purple Nigel insisted on."

Mrs. Lowden admired a bowl of freesia and iris. "From the Prince, my dear?" she asked, her thin brows drawn together in a frown.

Lady Julia nodded. She was staring into the flames, her head propped up on one hand, and she seemed distracted. Mrs. Lowden took her clue from her, and sat quietly as well until Hentershee brought in the tea tray.

Julia roused herself then, to prepare their repast.

"What has been happening to upset you, Julia?" Mrs. Lowden asked as she took the teacup from her hand.

Julia frowned, and then she told her about the ball, and Mr. Hammond's advances and threats. Mrs. Lowden's expression did not change.

"Well, you must expect such things, dear," she said at last. "You are too lovely to avoid them. But you say the earl discouraged him?"

Julia told her how Trevor Whitney had called on Mr. Hammond that morning before coming to see her. "And Fanny, there has been another blackmail note," she continued.

The Imperturbable One sat waiting quietly.

Julia related as much as she could remember of it. "I was surprised that there was no mention of how the money was to be paid, until the earl told me that would come in the next letter," she said, holding out a plate of tea cakes. Mrs. Lowden shook her head.

"He also said it would be the most dangerous time

for the blackmailer, for the Prince's men were sure to take precautions."

"Precautions?" Mrs. Lowden said. "What do you mean?"

"Why, of course they do not want to lose the money, my dear," Julia explained. "They intend to try to catch the blackmailer when he comes to get it, thus killing two birds with one stone." She sipped her tea, frowning a little.

Mrs. Lowden noted her unusual pallor, and the little downward droop of her mouth, and she said, "I am so sorry to find you blue-deviled, my dear. But soon, you know, this will all be over, and then you can be comfortable. The blackmailer will be making his demands soon again, and I, for one, hope the earl catches him red-handed! He is inhuman!"

Julia could only applaud this sentiment, but she could not envision ever being comfortable again. However, she made an effort to look more cheerful. "The earl also warned me that I must expect the Prince to become even more persistent. Oh, Fanny, he says he may well take to calling here and demanding to see me!"

"How tiresome the man is!" Mrs. Lowden said sharply. Her complete lack of any reverence when speaking of royalty made Julia smile in spite of herself.

"I have asked Hentershee to deny my presence, if he should do so," Julia went on. "But what do you advise, Fanny? Would it not be best for me to see him at least once, so I can tell him face-to-face that I am adamant in my refusal?"

Mrs. Lowden thought for a moment. Julia watched her eagerly, thinking how like a little bird she was with her dark, sleek head tilted to one side.

"Of course you must do what you think is best, dear Julia," she said at last. "If I were you, I would avoid the man. Seeing you can only fan the embers of his infatuation."

"Perhaps you are right, Fanny," Julia admitted.

"And is Edwina behaving herself?" Mrs. Lowden asked next.

Julia nodded. "Indeed she is. There have been no further contretemps since her morning call on the earl. I wish I could convince myself that her meddling is a thing of the past, but I am not so sanguine. I live in daily dread of hearing something perfectly horrid that involves her."

Mrs. Lowden shook her head as she put down her cup and picked up her gloves and bag. "You are much too kind, too easygoing, Julia," she lectured as she rose. "But I must be off. I really should not have stopped at all, for I have an early dinner engagement, but I could not bear not to know how you were, and how you were faring."

Julia walked with her to the library door. "My good friend," she said softly. "I thank you for all your concern. I do not think I could have borne all this without you to support me."

"Goose!" Mrs. Lowden said fondly, before she kissed her good-bye.

When Julia came downstairs two mornings later, she discovered that Edwina had been called for by the Lady Millicent Whitney. She had left a note for her aunt, telling her the countess had kindly asked her to go for a drive in the country, and a luncheon, and she did not know when she would be back.

In spite of the free day stretching ahead of her, and even knowing Edwina was so well chaperoned, Julia could not feel easy. At last she called for her carriage and made plans to make some morning calls herself. She knew she would feel better just to be free of the house and any sudden visit the Prince might decide to make.

She did not return to Charles Street until that afternoon, and she was surprised when Hentershee told her the Earl of Bradford had called and insisted on waiting for her in the drawing room.

Julia's heart was beating faster as she removed her bonnet and stole before she joined him. As Hentershee opened the door for her, she heard him at her piano.

She was relieved that the music he was playing with such proficiency and exquisite feeling was a soft little melody that had a certain sad sweetness.

He stopped as soon as she stepped inside, and he rose from the bench to study her face as she came toward him.

"I am sorry I was out when you called, m'lord," she said. "There was something important . . . ?"

He nodded, and she indicated a wing chair by the fire, before she took the seat across from him.

"There was something, indeed, ma'am," he told her, those piercing eyes never leaving her face. "Several of our suspects had decamped."

"Decamped?" she asked, and then her face darkened. "And so you rushed around to Charles Street to make sure I was not one of them, sir?" she asked in an outraged voice.

Before he could reply, the drawing-room door was thrown open and Edwina ran in. "Dear auntie, just look whom I have brought to tea!" she cried. As she caught sight of the earl, she skidded to a halt, her gay smile replaced by a ferocious frown.

Julia was about to call her to order when she noticed the beaming Countess Bradford, who was coming in on Hentershee's arm.

She rose quickly and went to greet her unexpected guest. "How pleasant to see you, ma'am," she said. "Hentershee, a tea tray, and perhaps some wine for the earl."

"What a surprise to see you here, Trevor," his mother said as she took a seat on the sofa and Edwina sat down beside her. "You were discussing the case of the mysteriously missing snuffbox with Lady Julia?"

At their surprised looks, the older lady chuckled. "Edwina has told me all about it. How exciting it is, although, of course, not for you, Lady Julia! But Trevor is very clever. He will discover the thief and bring him to justice."

The earl threw up his hands and then ran one of them over his dark brown hair. "Was there ever any way of keeping things from you, ma'am?" he asked in mock disapproval.

As the countess shook her head, he went on, "I should be glad to bring the thief to justice, but I may not be able to find him or her now. I was just telling Lady Julia that most of our suspects have left town."

Edwina leaned forward in her seat. "Who did?" she demanded, her eyes wide.

The earl eyed her with disquiet. "Miss Daphne Hammond has left suddenly for the country. Her sister does not even know with whom she has gone to stay, which I find very strange. Then, when I went to call on Mrs. Andrews, I discovered she had also returned home, leaving early this morning by post chaise. And Percy Beaton, for once, has been separated from his mother, for she left town last evening." His voice had been growing colder and Julia felt a shiver run up her spine. "In addition, Grillon's no longer has Miss Whittingham as a guest," he went on. "She has disappeared, and with her one of the older waiters." He looked confused. "I do not understand why that should be so, however."

Julia was not even tempted to enlighten him, as Edwina said eagerly, "Has Mr. Hammond gone too?"

"No, he has not," the earl told her. "He remains, as do Lord Alvanley and, of course, your aunt."

Edwina sank back on the sofa, the frown returning to her face. "But how very disappointing!" she said, as if to herself. "And I was sure it would work. . . ."

"What would work?" Julia and the earl asked together, their voices full of foreboding.

Edwina was not required to answer at once, for Hentershee and the footmen were even then bringing in the tea tray. While they arranged it, and poured the earl a glass of canary, the countess regaled them with an account of her day.

The door had barely closed behind the servants before Julia fixed her niece with a steady gaze and said, "You will explain your last remark, Edwina, and at once!"

Her niece's blue eyes were earnest. "It was just that I had this wonderful idea, auntie," she said. "I decided to send all your guests an anonymous letter. You see, I was sure when they read it, the guilty party would leave town at once, and then we would know his identity. But I never expected most of them to go haring off! It is so strange!"

Julia sat back, horrified, and the earl took up the questioning. "What did you say in this letter, Miss Ogilvie?" he asked.

Edwina scowled at him. "It was quite unexceptional," she assured him. "I copied it out of a book. You see, in the novel I am reading, one of the characters gets a letter that makes him very nervous."

"Bring me the book and show me the place, Edwina," Lady Julia demanded.

Everyone waited uneasily until the girl returned to the drawing room. Silently she handed the open book to her aunt, pointing to the place.

Julia began to read aloud, her voice expressionless. " 'Sinner!' " she intoned. " 'All is discovered. You must fly at once. A friend.' Edwina, how could you?" she asked, as the book slid from her nerveless fingers to the floor.

The countess began to laugh, at first softly, but then in an ever-increasing crescendo. It was only a moment before the earl joined in. Even Julia's mouth quirked a little, although she tried to look stern.

"But what are you laughing about?" Edwina asked, staring at each one of them in turn. "It is not *funny*!"

"Oh, but it is, my dear child," the countess told her as she wiped her eyes. "Oh, my, I haven't laughed like that for years."

"I don't understand," Edwina said, looking confused.

The countess patted her hand. "You will when you are a little older, my dear," she said. "You see, most people have something in their lives of which they are ashamed. Something they have done at one time which they can never forget, and fear to have discovered. When all Lady Julia's guests received their letter, most of them thought their secret sin had been unmasked at last."

"How depressing it is that adults are so deceitful," Edwina said, tossing her head in disdain. "Especially when they tend to go around pretending to be as good as gold. I think it serves them right if they were frightened!"

The earl chuckled again, and Julia admired his flashing smile and the way his deep-set eyes crinkled shut in amusement.

"But why didn't Mr. Hammond go too?" Edwina persisted. "I am sure he has many things in his life he is ashamed of, for he is such a great rake."

"Perhaps he couldn't decide which one had been discovered, and therefore was in such a quandary, he felt he must sit tight?" the earl suggested gravely.

This was too much even for Julia, and she burst into a peal of laughter. Trevor Whitney felt his heart lift at those clear, golden notes. He realized he had never heard her laugh before.

"Edwina, Edwina, whatever am I to do with you?" her aunt demanded when she could speak again. Then she pointed a finger as Edwina opened her mouth to defend herself. "And please do not tell me one more time that you were only trying to help! Now I know why Mary sent you to me. She was desperate for a few weeks of calm!"

"She is not at all a bad girl," the countess said, earning a warm smile of gratitude from Miss Ogilvie. "And what harm has it done?" she asked.

The earl put down his glass. "I cannot be sure," he said. "But if the blackmailer is someone who fled town, he knows he must return to collect the money. And if we receive another letter and he does come, we shall know he is guilty."

"Yes, that is true," Julia said. "And as Fanny pointed out to me some time ago, she did not notice any snuffbox here when she came later that day. It has to be one of them."

"There, you see, it was helpful after all, auntie!"

Edwina exclaimed. Julia gave her a darkling look of disapproval, and she subsided.

To Julia's surprise, it was an enjoyable tea party. She knew she had the countess to thank for that. The older lady chatted gaily, often brought Edwina into the conversation, and would permit no stiffness between her hostess and her son. Her occasional misunderstanding of a spoken word only added to the hilarity.

Julia wondered why she was so pleasant. Surely Edwina had told her of the earl's suspicions of her guilt. She did not realize that Millicent Whitney had become determined that she would see Lady Julia installed as the next Countess of Bradford, and was busy promoting the match. Lady Jersey had lost no time informing her of the earl's constant interest in the lady at the Barrs' ball.

At the end, the countess even had the last word.

As Edwina curtsied to him, the earl said, "May we assume you did not send a latter to your aunt, Miss Ogilvie? I forgot to ask."

"Of course I did not!" Edwina said hotly. "I know Aunt Julia is not guilty!"

"But you could not know if she has a secret in her past, now could you?" he continued, carefully not looking at the lady he was speaking of. "How unfortunate that now we will never know if she would have fled or not."

Edwina had to giggle in spite of her dislike for the man, and the countess was smiling as she bade her hostess good-bye.

"You must not mind him, m'lady," she said. "Trevor has such a peculiar sense of humor sometimes. I cannot imagine where he got it."

Even trying to look only passing interested, Lady Julia was hard pressed to preserve her dignity amid the laughter of the others.

12

The Prince called late the next morning. Hentershee bowed very low as he opened the door, although he was quick to announce in his most reverent tones that the Lady Julia had gone out of town for the day. To all his Prince's eager questions, he had only vague replies. He believed it had been decided suddenly, by a group of the lady's friends, and no, he did not know their destination or when she would return.

The Prince was forced to leave his card and the flowers he had brought. When Hentershee saw the priceless antique Chinese vase they were arranged in, he bore the offering with slow reverent steps to the drawing room.

Since Julia had been in the library all the time, she was forced to remain a prisoner in her own house for the remainder of the day, lest someone see her and tell the Prince. She found herself growing angry because of this, although in truth she had made few plans for the day.

Edwina naturally had to be apprised of the royal visit and what Hentershee had told the Prince, in case someone questioned her. She listened to all her aunt's instructions, and after promising not to say a word to anyone, went away shaking her head. Julia heard her saying as she closed the door behind her that she did

not think she would ever understand men, for surely
they were all of them very strange.

Lady Julia made herself keep busy that day. She decided she must redecorate her bedroom at once, for
suddenly the light blue brocade that adorned it now
seemed insipid. She decided a straw satin would look
much better, perhaps with pale orange and gold
accents. She next investigated the linen and still
rooms, told the housekeeper to set the maids to polish-
ing all the brass, and ordered one of the footmen to
draw up a list for her of the complete contents of the
wine cellar. Her own maid was instructed to remove a
flounce of lace from one of her ball gowns and see that
all her sandals were cleaned.

When she finally disappeared into the drawing
room to practice her music, the entire household drew
a sigh of relief.

Julia knew she did not have either the talent or the
technique of the Earl of Bradford, but she was
competent on the piano. After she had run through a
number of warming-up exercises, she found herself
trying to recreate the little melody she had heard him
playing the afternoon before. This annoyed her so
much when she became aware of what she was doing
that she immediately began to sing her scales.

It was some time later when she ended her solo
concert with a soft rendition of "Drink to Me Only
with Thine Eyes," which had been her father's and
mother's favorite. She had learned it when still a small
child, to please them.

Fortunately, the next day she was engaged with
friends on a riding expedition, and so she was not at
home when the Prince called again.

Hentershee told her in a sad old voice when she
came in that His Highness had been quite downcast to
find her still missing. Julia could tell the old butler
wanted her to receive the Prince and thus release him
from his awful task, but she had no intention of doing
that. Instead, she patted his hand and thanked him for

all his help, saying she did not know what she would do without him.

That evening she had been invited to a dinner party at Lady Ralston's in Eaton Square. She had hesitated to accept, for Lady Ralston was a great patroness of the arts. Her home was often filled with the leading artists, musicians, and writers of the day. Julia feared to meet the Prince there. But she had questioned the earl about that possibility while they had been dancing at the Barr ball, and he had assured her that His Royal Highness had another engagement for the evening.

Accordingly, she donned a slim gown of soft primrose and had her chestnut curls dressed high on her head.

Still a little nervous that the Prince might have changed his mind, she looked around with apprehension as she entered Lady Ralston's drawing room. There were several people there, some known to her, some unknown, but of royalty there was no sign. She was able to relax and begin to look forward to the evening.

And then, after she had greeted her hostess and moved further into the room, she found the Earl of Bradford confronting her.

"M'lord. I did not know you would be here," she said, glad to lower her eyes as she curtsied so he would not see her reluctance to speak to him.

"M'lady," Trevor Whitney said solemnly.

Julia would have moved on, but he took hold of her arm. "If I may have a moment of your time, ma'am?" he asked.

She nodded, and he drew her a little apart from the others. "I understand that the Prince has called in Charles Street again," he said in a quiet voice that only she could hear.

"Yes, he has, both yesterday and today," Julia told him. "My old butler is terribly upset at the lies he has to tell royalty." Her eyes darkened then, and she added tartly, "And yesterday I was forced to remain indoors all day because he told the Prince I had gone out of town."

She looked up at the earl then, her eyes despairing. "When will this end, m'lord?"

He took her hand in both of his and pressed it. Julia wondered why she felt so comforted. "I imagine in only another week or so, m'lady," he said. "The blackmailer is sure to complete his plans soon, and when we have accomplished his capture, you will be free to leave town—and the unwanted attentions of the Prince."

In the air hovered the unspoken thought that she would be able to avoid his attentions as well, unless, of course, she were indeed the guilty party. They stared at each other for a moment, and then Julia inclined her head a haughty inch. Trevor Whitney's stern face paled.

"Shall we cry truce, m'lady?" he asked in his coldest voice. "We are guests here together, and any animosity between us is sure to be remarked. It would be unkind to our hostess, to say nothing of the others."

"Certainly, m'lord," Julia said, her head high as she gave him a small social smile.

"Lady Julia, how wonderful to see you here," a breathless Mr. Grant exclaimed as he rushed up to join them. "Servant, Bradford," he added, almost as an afterthought.

Julia gave him her hand, and he peered up at her as he clasped it in his. "Do say you will sing for us after dinner, m'lady," he implored. "I know Lady Ralston plans to ask a few of us to entertain, and your performance would add so much to the evening."

Aware of the earl's tall figure so close beside her, Julia smiled. "I should be delighted, Mr. Grant, if Lady Ralston wishes it," she said calmly.

"I shall tell her at once! How delighted she will be!" Mr. Grant enthused before he rushed away. Julia had to smile. Mr. Grant, although an excellent violinist, was such a strange, darting little man, she thought. He was slight and pale, and although still only in his twenties, had begun to lose his hair. She thought he looked like a busy little insect.

"Yes, he is strange, but Amos is an excellent musician. I am very fond of him," Trevor Whitney remarked.

Julia spun around, her eyes asking how he had divined her thoughts.

"You have a very expressive face, m'lady," he explained. "You would never succeed in the diplomatic world."

"How fortunate that I have no aspirations in that direction then, sir," she told him. She was not at all displeased when another guest came up and claimed her attention.

At dinner, she found to her disgust that she had been seated beside the earl, and she steeled herself. On her other side, Lady Ralston had placed one of London's newest and most highly acclaimed poets. Since Julia had read his latest volume, she was able to turn to him and begin a discussion. The poet, a Mr. Reginald Cross, ignored his soup as he explained his poetry. Only when he asked which poem was her favorite was he able to eat his dinner.

Julia said that of them all, she preferred his *Ode to Diana,* although she was quick to praise his sonnet on the Thames as well. This approbation drew forth another burst of conversation from Mr. Cross, and it was not until some time later, during the fish course with its various removes, that she was forced to relinquish him to the lady on his other side, and turn to the earl.

"Do you also perform tonight, sir?" she asked, remembering to smile at him.

Trevor Whitney smiled back. A little light danced in his eyes, as if he were well aware of her reason for such excessive interest in verse. "Lady Ralston has asked me, yes," he said.

"Might I ask a favor then, m'lord?" Julia asked, shaking her head as the footman offered her more wine.

The earl looked amazed. "But certainly, m'lady," he said easily. "Anything in my power, of course."

"Then I would ask you to perform that melody I heard you playing in my drawing room the other day when I came in," Julia said. "I am not familiar with it, and I would hear it in its entirety."

"Ah, that one." The earl nodded. "That is a small composition of my own, ma'am, and a new one."

Julia stared at him, her Dover sole forgotten. "You compose, as well as play so well, then? What a great talent you have!"

Her voice was admiring, and Lord Whitney had the irrelevant thought that he and the Lady Julia were perfectly attuned, and would deal very well together. At least they would if the matter of the snuffbox had never arisen. Silently he cursed his absent Prince, before he thanked her for the compliment.

"Do you also arrange, m'lord?" she asked.

The earl admitted he did. "Sometimes I transpose from symphonic works and opera as well. It gives a trio or string quartet new scope and interest," he said.

"So that is why I have never seen you at society affairs," Julia mused. "Naturally, you would prefer evenings like this, among your fellow aficionados."

"I am beginning to think I have missed a great deal in not attending more social evenings, however," the earl said calmly as the footman removed his plate. He raised his wineglass in a silent toast, his blue-gray eyes intent on her face.

Julia was a little surprised until she reminded herself of their truce. The earl was behaving as he would to any lady seated beside him as a dinner partner. She must not make too much of his compliment.

Throughout the rest of the excellent dinner, they turned to each other often to continue their conversation. Julia found the earl a knowledgeable man, and not only about music. He was well grounded in art and literature as well, and as conversant with the latest trends as he was about earlier, better-known works. Indeed, he and Mr. Cross had a spirited discussion across her about ancient poetry as compared to the works of Byron that she found not only witty but also erudite.

She was almost disappointed when Lady Ralston rose and signaled her lady guests to retire. Both the earl and Mr. Cross rose too, and she curtsied to them in turn, thanking them in her clear voice for a most enjoyable dinner conversation.

When the ladies reentered the drawing room, they found that the seating had been arranged to face the front of the room and the grand piano. Music stands had been set up, and more candles lit.

"I am so delighted you will honor us this evening, Lady Julia," her hostess said, coming to her side. "I should have asked you to bring your music, however. I am sorry I neglected to do so."

"That will not be necessary, m'lady," Julia assured her. "I can perform without it. However, I suppose I must accompany myself, and I am only competent, no more. In this company, I do regret that."

Lady Ralston laughed. "But you must not despair, ma'am! The Earl of Bradford can play anything you like, from memory, too. He is such an outstanding musician."

She proved to be correct. After Mr. Grant, accompanied by the earl, had played several selections and had been warmly applauded, Lady Ralston asked Julia to sing.

As the guests murmured to each other and settled back to enjoy themselves, Julia went to the piano. "Lady Ralston says you can accompany me, sir. Do you dare, without any music, and no rehearsals?"

In the candlelight, Trevor Whitney's deep-set eyes sparkled. "Oh, I shall be on my mettle, ma'am," he said. "With what piece do you care to open?"

Julia at once selected a different aria that she would never have chosen if she had been playing for herself. The piano score was difficult and demanding. She looked carefully, but she could see nothing but amusement in his face as he nodded.

When key and tempo had been decided, he played a

chord. All conversation ceased as he began the introduction.

Julia stood beside the piano, her hands clasped before her. Her clear true voice soared in the intricate, melodic passages, and even when she slowed or quickened the tempo, Trevor Whitney followed her precisely. She had never had an accompanist like him, and during the storm of applause that followed the aria, and the cries of "Bravo!" she turned to him impulsively and exclaimed, "Thank you! What an excellent musician you are, sir! Why, you seemed to know instinctively when I was going to breathe, and when to soften or emphasize the accompaniment."

"It was a great honor, m'lady," he told her, his voice admiring. "You have the most beautiful voice I have ever heard. That soft high G—superb!"

Julia smiled, and this time it was not a social smile, and the earl caught his breath at her beauty.

She performed several more numbers, and then she held up her hand. "I must not monopolize the evening," she told the guests. "With your permission, therefore, I shall close with this little song that was my parents' favorite."

Turning to the earl, she said, "I am sure you know 'Drink to Me Only with Thine Eyes,' sir, do you not?"

He nodded, and played a soft introduction. Julia faced the guests again, but as she sang those simple words of love, she was very aware of the earl seated at the instrument behind her. She wondered why she had the greatest urge to turn toward him and sing those words for him alone.

She left the piano with only a short word of thanks to him, and hurried away to join the applauding guests, she was so unnerved by her thoughts. How could it be possible that she had longed to look into his eyes, those eyes that had so often been accusing and unbelieving? She told herself it was only his musical talent that had influenced her this way, as she accepted the compliments of Lady Ralston's guests.

She was glad to sink down on a sofa next to her

hostess, to listen as the Earl of Bradford performed some piano solos. He began with a difficult Bach fugue that had her clapping in stunned admiration at its conclusion. Then he played a Mozart sonata. She was wondering if he had forgotten her request, when he announced that like the Lady Julia Reynolds, he would close with a simple song, this one of his own composition.

The haunting, sad notes began, and a hush fell over the guests. The melody seemed to speak of love and longing, of disappointment and defeat.

Many a listener was reminded of the sweet intensity of first love, of wild hopes and shattered dreams. Julia found herself filled with an inexplicable yearning—for what, she did not even know. She stared at the earl's strong profile, the lean planes of his face under his cap of gleaming dark hair, as if she were mesmerized. In wonder, she lowered her eyes to his hands. His long fingers seemed almost to caress the keys, as if pleading with those thrilling notes to emerge and captivate them all.

There was complete silence for a moment as the last gentle notes died away, that silence that is a performer's greatest tribute. The earl remained staring down at the keys, frowning at them as if lost in reverie.

When the applause that broke out had finally died down, Mr. Cross called from the audience, "That was superb, m'lord! But it cries out for words. I should be honored to write them for you, if you will see I get a copy of the score."

The tall earl rose and bowed. "I thank you for your kind offer, sir. Unfortunately, the composition already has words."

When several guests clamored to hear them in an encore, he refused. "They are not quite ready to be performed as yet. Someday, however, I hope you shall all hear them."

"What do you call the composition, Trevor?" Lady Ralston asked.

He looked at her, and then his gaze went to Lady Julia's lovely face, where she sat beside her. "At the moment, it is untitled, ma'am," he said.

Although many people still begged for an encore of the song, he relinquished the stage to a woodwind quartet. Julia was always aware of him from then on, and where he was in the room, but he did not approach her again that evening. She told herself she was glad of it, for she was feeling unsettled and, somehow, shy, and she did not understand it.

Sometime later, as Julia was taking leave of her hostess and thanking her for a most enjoyable evening, Lady Ralston held her hand captive as she said, "I do not understand why I have never heard you sing before, my dear lady. You must come again, and to my salons on Sunday afternoons, as well. Your talent is outstanding! Extraordinary!"

"Thank you, I should enjoy that very much, m'lady," Julia said. "I have seldom sung in public of late. My husband did not care for music, you see, and he discouraged any performances of mine. I fear I lost the habit, and I never regained it after his death."

Lady Ralston looked not only indignant but also disgusted.

"My dear Lady Julia," she said in her deep, carrying voice, "you were most unwise to accept any such domination. My husband does not care for music or the arts either; he never has. But I refuse to let his dislike affect me or my plans. I simply tell him when I am going to have an evening like this, and he takes himself off to White's or Brook's. Husbands, my dear Lady Julia, should be kept firmly in their proper place, lest they become petty tyrants. And even the best of men will do so, given the least little bit of encouragement. I beg you to remember that when you remarry, as I am sure you will."

Julia was aware that everyone nearby had heard her hostess's lecture, and she curtsied without saying another word. As she turned to leave, she was not a bit surprised to see the Earl of Bradford standing only a little distance away, his deep-set eyes crinkled shut and his flashing smile much in evidence in his amusement at her predicament.

13

The Lady Julia Reynolds chose to remain at home the next day. Not even the thought of a possible visit from the Prince of Wales had the power to make her leave the house.

When Edwina wheedled and coaxed her to come for a ride in the park, she refused, saying she had a great many things that she must do today. Edwina finally gave up and shrugged, before she sent a note to Evelyn Rogers, begging her attendance instead.

In spite of her fine words to her niece, Julia accomplished very little. She went to the library to write to her sisters, but found herself staring down at a blank sheet of paper while the ink dried on her quill point. And when she tried to read a book, the words refused to make any sense.

At last, she permitted herself to think of the man who had disturbed her sleep the night before.

She marveled at Trevor Whitney still. Never would she have imagined that the cold, stern inquisitor she had known could ever have been so sensitive and talented. The earl had shown her only one side of his character, and she had been so naive as to believe that that was all there was to him. But if he could play like that, with such commanding strength and precision, compose such exquisite music, and interpret it so well, what an unusual man he was!

He was not only compelling in his powerful masculinity, he was perceptive and tender, emotional and artistic. She had never met anyone like him in her life, and she had to admit she was drawn to him more strongly than she had ever been drawn to any other human being.

She conceded that he intrigued her, nay, fascinated her, and this in spite of her dislike for him. And why do you dislike him, Julia? she asked herself sternly. Admit it is only because he suspects you of keeping the Prince's snuffbox and trying to blackmail him. But what can he think except that? You are the best suspect he has, Robert Hammond notwithstanding.

But someday he will discover that I am not guilty, someday soon, she thought, her heart quickening. What will I do when that day comes? And, more important, what will he do?

She rose from the desk then, to pace the room. She had never intended to marry again, in fact she knew she would be reluctant to do so even if the earl should ask her.

And what makes you think he will? her other self jeered at her. He is thirty-nine and he has never married. Why would he be tempted to now? The little admiration you have seen on such rare occasions in his eyes, his few compliments, are no sign that he is any more eager to give up his single state than you have been.

Julia sighed as she sat down and opened the book she had been reading. She made herself read it aloud so she would be forced to concentrate.

By late afternoon she had to admit to herself that she had been waiting for the earl to come to her all day. She told herself she was behaving like a witless, lovesick girl, and she was, after all, a widow in her thirties. She was absurd!

When Hentershee announced Mrs. Lowden, she wondered why she did not feel more welcoming. It was almost as if she were reluctant to receive her friend, and she did not understand herself. When Fanny came in, she gave her her warmest smile to make up for her treacherous thoughts, and insisted she join her in a glass of wine.

The two friends were soon seated across from each other, but when Fanny asked her if she had enjoyed herself at Lady Ralston's the previous evening, Julia found herself loath to mention the Earl of Bradford at all. Instead, she chatted about the other guests, and mentioned the music that had followed dinner almost as an afterthought.

"Did you sing, my dear?" Fanny asked. At Julia's nod, she said lightly, "How sorry I am now that I refused Lady Ralston's invitation! It is always such a treat for me to hear you perform!"

"I am sure you are my biggest supporter, Fanny," Julia told her. "Yes, I sang a number of selections, and everyone was very kind. Lady Ralston has asked me to attend her Sunday salons in the future. Perhaps you will come to one with me."

"I would be delighted, my dear," Mrs. Lowden replied. "Oh, by the way, Julia. Have you heard from the Prince lately?"

As she leaned forward a little in obvious concern, Julia admitted she had not. "It is most unusual, too, now that I come to think of it," she said. "But perhaps he is growing weary of my continued refusals. I can only hope so!"

To her chagrin, Fanny mentioned a most unwelcome subject. "And has the earl been badgering you again, my dear?" she asked. "Forgive me for prying, but you seem somewhat distraught and unsettled today. Since it is not the Prince who has upset your peace, I do pray the earl is not the cause of your unhappiness."

Julia's laugh was a little bitter. "Indeed, he is not, Fanny," she said. "He has not come near me all day."

Mrs. Lowden nodded before she rose and came and kissed her friend. "That is one thing to be grateful for,

then," she said. "But do look at the time! I must be off
lest I disgrace myself by still being here when Hentershee rings the dressing bell."

Julia made no attempt to delay her departure as she
walked with her to the front door.

But as she went up to dress for dinner, she could not
shake her feeling of depression. And even though the
Prince had not honored her today with another
personal visit, or sent so much as a posy or a small gift,
she did not feel any satisfaction. True, he had not
come, but neither had Trevor Whitney.

She had no engagement that evening, and after
dinner when Edwina picked up her latest novel to
read, she went to the piano to play. She did not feel
like singing. She wondered if she would ever feel like
singing again. Edwina lay stretched out on the sofa. It
was a very unladylike pose, and Julia had called her to
order for it before, to her niece's astonishment.

"But what can it matter, dear auntie?" the girl had
asked. "There is no one to see me but you, and it is so
comfortable. Besides, my mother does not mind, as
long as it is just the family, you know."

When Edwina rose at about ten o'clock and
stretched, Julia was surprised. Her niece was a comical
sight, with her homely little face contorted in a yawn,
although Julia felt no desire to smile at her.

"You have lost interest in your book, my dear?" she
asked.

The girl nodded, and yawned again. "This one is
not very good, I'm afraid. I shall return it tomorrow,"
she said. "Why any author should think his readers
interested in lengthy sermons on maidenly purity and
modesty, I do not know. Or in detailed descriptions of
Northumberland. It seems a bleak, uncomfortable
part of England. Will you forgive me if I go to bed
early? Evelyn and I rode for such a long time this
morning, I am tired."

As she came to kiss her aunt, Julia held up her
cheek. "Of course, my dear, go to bed," she said. "You
will feel much better after a good night's sleep."

After Edwina had left her alone, Julia made herself begin another selection. She told herself it was excellent practice for the times when she had to accompany herself.

It was almost ten-thirty when she heard someone banging on the front door, and her hands stilled on the keys immediately. Who could it be at this hour? Surely not even the Prince would come so late at night!

She waited, barely breathing, until Hentershee knocked and entered, bearing a card on his silver salver. His old face was lined with his concern as he gave it to her.

"Colonel McCarthy?" she asked as she read the card and frowned.

"He says he is one of the Prince's equerries, m'lady," Hentershee said, bending close to her to whisper, as if the colonel could hear him through closed doors. "He says it is urgent that he see you at once, most urgent!"

As Julia stared at her butler, he added, "I think you had better do so, m'lady. He does look that worried! And he said he intends to wait in the hall until you receive him, although he begs you to do so quickly, for time is of the essence."

Julia was frightened, but she rose from the piano bench. "Take him to the library, Hentershee, and tell him I will be with him in a moment," she said.

The butler bowed, and as he left the room Julia stood very still, wondering what this was all about.

Something seemed to tell her she must not delay. She smoothed her hair and her gown as she walked to the hall. Her visitor was not the Prince after all; she had nothing to fear.

A tall, burly military man rose as she entered the library, his sharp eyes intent. As Julia introduced herself and asked how she might help him, she told herself she had never cared for sharp black eyes and thick glossy black hair, nor for a high complexion, or lips as plump and red as any girl's.

"Thank you for seeing me, m'lady," the colonel said. His voice was curiously high in pitch for such a large man. "It is, as I am sure you must know, only an emergency that could bring me here at this time of night."

"What emergency would that be?" Julia asked as coolly as she could.

"It is the Prince, ma'am!" the colonel exclaimed, twisting his shako and gauntlets in his hands. In the scarlet and gold of the Prince's own regiment, he was an impressive sight.

His next words made her grasp the edge of her desk in shock, while her other hand went to her throat, as if to still the wild pulse that began to beat there. "He is dying, m'lady!" the colonel said.

"Dying? But . . . but he has not even been ill, has he?" Julia asked.

The colonel's full lips twisted. "Oh, yes, he has been ill, ma'am. His illness should not be unknown to you, since you have been the cause of it."

"I?" Julia asked, outraged at his boldness.

Her tone seemed to cause the big man to moderate his words as he explained. "He was melancholy all day and evening. Just a little while ago he tried to take his life by stabbing," he said. "He has been begging to see you, saying only you can save him, give him the will to live. I promised I would bring you to him. Say you will come with me, ma'am, if not for the love you bear our sovereign, then for the love of God himself!"

Julia leaned against her desk, trembling with fear and emotion. Was this possible? How could any man stab himself almost to death? Why, he had been here only yesterday, and surely Hentershee would have mentioned it if he had looked that melancholic and depressed. And then she remembered that Hentershee had mentioned it.

She turned away from the colonel and took a few steps. Was it possible that this was only a ruse? A trick to get her into his palace, where she would be unable to refuse him? Would the Prince of Wales, in all his majesty, stoop to such depths?

"M'lady, if you please! We must hurry!" the colonel urged.

Julia suddenly made up her mind. "You have your carriage here, sir?" she asked.

She thought he looked relieved as he said, "It is outside, ma'am. We can go at once."

Julia went around her desk and sat down as she took up a sheet of paper and a pen. "We can go as soon as I send this note to the Earl of Bradford," she said in an unplacable voice. "I shall go to Carlton House only if he accompanies me."

Colonel McCarthy's plump red mouth fell open in astonishment. "But . . . but that might be too late! I beg you to reconsider, ma'am!"

"You have my conditions, sir," Julia said as she folded the note and sealed it. "I shall send my footman running at once. You need not fear, he is very fleet and the earl does not live that far away."

She rose and went to the door. "Please let my butler bring you a glass of wine, Colonel. I shall rejoin you when the earl comes. Until that time, I must fetch my stole and get ready to go out."

Although she could hear him protesting behind her, and saying all she needed was her maid, she closed the door in his face before she called the youngest footman to her side to give him his instructions. As soon as he left the house at a dead run, she ordered refreshment for her visitor and went up the stairs. She did not like the Prince's messenger, and she had no desire to remain alone with him. The little knowing look in his black eyes had been almost insulting.

It was over fifteen minutes later before she heard Trevor Whitney arrive. She ran down the stairs, to find him standing in the hall staring up at her. He was bareheaded, but he had a dark cloak over his formal evening dress. Julia wondered bleakly what party of his she had interrupted, and then she scolded herself for such an inconsequential thought.

She told him as much as she knew in a quick

whisper. "I did not like to bother you, m'lord," she concluded, "but I could think of no one else."

Lord Whitney would have spoken then, but the library door opened and the colonel strode out, pulling on his gauntlets.

"Ah, it's you at last, m'lord! Come, we must be on our way," he said.

He hurried to the door, and the earl took Lady Julia's arm. "We shall follow you in my carriage, Colonel," he said.

The equerry spun around. "There's no need for that. I have the Prince's racing curricle here. Send your carriage home, sir, for we shall go in mine."

The earl's brows rose, but when they reached the street he went to have a few words with his coachman. He was beside Julia in another moment, as the colonel climbed to the driver's seat on the other side and took up the reins.

"It was madness to delay," Julia heard him mutter, and then, "Pray we are not too late!"

Her heart sank, but with the strong reassuring presence of the earl so close beside her, she felt comforted. The light racing curricle was hardly spacious, and she could feel both men's hard thighs pressing against her own as they raced through the night. She was even forced to lean forward a little to give their broad shoulders room.

The colonel did not stop at the front entrance of the Prince's palace, where it was well-lit and guards stood to attention, their weapons in their hands. Julia's eyes widened as he drove around to the back. There was only one flickering flambeau here, although a groom leapt to take the team in charge. It was obvious that they had been expected.

Julia could not help shivering, and she was glad it was the earl who lifted her down, and held her close for a moment, as if to give her courage.

At the colonel's muted knock, the door to the palace opened immediately. A man dressed in black stood there, holding a branch of candles high. "Lord Whitney, is that you, man?" he asked, as if astonished.

"As you see, Rodney, as you see," the earl said. Julia wondered at the grimness in his voice.

But then the colonel was striding forward and urging her up a winding stone stair. It was dark, and although warm enough, somehow airless as they climbed the stairs. Julia looked around. This did not appear to be a main part of the palace, for it was stark and unadorned, with not even a piece of drugget to carpet the stone stairs, and she had heard too many stories of the wealth and art with which the Prince had decorated his house.

At the top of the second flight, the colonel opened a heavy wooden door and held it for her to follow. Julia was breathing hard now, from the quickness of the climb, but she went along behind the two men obediently. The earl put his arm around her to support her, and she sent him a grateful glance. To her surprise, he did not notice, for he was staring straight ahead, a dark frown on his stern face.

As they moved along a deep, wide corridor, Julia wondered at the silence. It almost appeared to her fanciful imagination that the entire palace was holding its breath. She could not restrain a shudder, and the earl's arm tightened. She thought he must be affected by the atmosphere as well, for still he did not say a word.

Colonel McCarthy and the man the earl had called Rodney paused before a door at last, and opened it without knocking.

Julia blinked at the lights in the room. There were branches of candles on every table, and more in the sconces on the wall. It was also very warm, for a large roaring fire surely more suitable for December than June burned on the hearth. Julia loosened her stole as she inspected her surroundings. She appeared to be in a sitting room, for it was full of ornate gilt furniture and priceless bric-a-brac. The windows were closed and heavily draped in crimson velvet.

"M'lady?" Colonel McCarthy was saying, and she turned toward him to see him holding an inner door open. She hesitated for a moment, and Trevor Whitney bent down to whisper in her ear. "It is all right, m'lady," he said. "Go with him. I shall be right here. If you need me, you have only to call."

"Thank you," she said, and then she wet her dry lips.

She went past the colonel into another large room, and spun around as he closed the door behind her. It was much darker in here, although she could make out an enormous canopied bed set against one of the walls. She heard whispering on the other side of the room, and she turned toward the sound to see two men, also dressed all in black, observing her. In a moment they turned their backs on her and began to whisper again.

"Lady Julia? Can you have come to me at last?" a weak voice asked. The voice came from the direction of the bed, and steeling herself, she walked toward the sound.

In the antechamber, the Prince's equerries stood close together. Every so often, the colonel would glance at the Earl of Bradford, but that gentleman did not appear to be aware of their existence anymore.

When the door had closed behind Lady Julia, he had gone to one of the windows and thrown the draperies open. Now he stood there brooding down into the street. He was frowning still, his lean face taut and contained.

Lady Julia's note had been a complete surprise to him. That evening he had entertained some of his fellow musicians at dinner before they adjourned to the library, as was their custom, to play some new scores. The earl had been seated at the piano when his butler brought in the lady's note.

As the others argued about the interpretation of a certain phrase of music behind him, he had torn the note open and read it. And then he had risen so quickly

and excused himself in such a few terse words that Mr.
Grant had peered at him over his music stand as if he
could not believe his ears. There was no time for him
to question his friend, however, for the earl had
already left the room. The other men had looked at
each other and shrugged as they heard him calling for
his carriage as fast as it could be brought around, and
for a light cloak as well.

Trevor Whitney was remembering Lady Julia's note
now. She had begged him not to fail her, saying only
that she had been bidden to Carlton House on a
mission of the greatest urgency and she could not go
without him beside her. He remembered how his heart
had lifted at those written words.

Now he shifted from one foot to the other, remembering. He had spent a miserable day, and had almost
canceled the evening's arrangements because of it. He
knew he would never forget Lady Ralston's party, how
Lady Julia had complimented him on his talent and
musicianship, her face full of wholehearted admiration.

And he knew he would never forget how she had
looked as she sang. That full glorious throat that
trembled with the clear melodic tones that issued from
her lovely lips, her sparkling eyes that told him how
much she was enjoying herself! And when she had
sung that golden high note, he had almost misplayed
the chords that supported it. How rare a woman she
was, he mused. How lovely, and how talented. He
knew he would cherish the warm smile she had given
him for the rest of his life.

All day he had longed to go to her, although he
knew he must not, under any conditions. She was still
under suspicion. Just because she looked and sang like
an angel could not erase her possible guilt.

His musings were interrupted abruptly as he heard
the door to the Prince's bedchamber open behind him.
He whirled to see her standing there clutching the
doorjamb for support, her hazel eyes wide and staring

in her white face. He saw that even her lips were
white, and he hastened to support her.

As he put his arms around her, he heard the Prince
moaning, and he motioned to the colonel to shut the
door before he drew her away to the other side of the
room.

When her shivering increased and he heard her
sobbing a little, he swung her around to face him, and
enclosed her in his cloak so the other men could not see
her distress.

"Oh, m'lord," she sobbed. "The blood! There was so
much blood!"

Trevor Whitney's mouth tightened. "Do not speak
now, m'lady. You can tell me later," he said in a soft
undertone that was still full of authority. "For the
moment, keep silent until I can remove you from this
place."

He felt her nestle closer in his arms and reach up to
grasp his lapels before she nodded a little against his
chest. His throat was constricted as he whispered, "I
want you to pretend to faint, m'lady. Don't worry, I
have you safe."

Again he felt that little nod, and he turned her
toward the center of the room again. As soon as he
opened his cloak, she gave a little cry and sagged
against him. Prepared, he caught her up in his arms,
looking down only briefly at her still white face.

As he strode to the door, he said over his shoulder,
"Lady Julia has fainted. I shall take her home, for she
will need her own people around her to sustain her."

Neither man made any attempt to stop him, and at
the door he turned to them again, his deep-set eyes
raking them both impartially. "I shall return before
that, however, for I would speak to His Highness
myself. There is no need for you to tell him that his
ploy has failed."

He felt Julia start a little, and he left the room.

Julia was content to lie in his arms, held close
against his chest as he carried her down another set of

stairs than the ones they had come up only a short
while ago. She felt so weak she did not think she could
have walked in any case. She wondered what he had
meant by that last mysterious remark, but she knew
now was not the time to inquire. She could hear the
occasional rustle of a skirt or an apron, and people
whispering as they passed them, and she could tell by
the brightness against her closed eyelids that they were
in the main part of the palace.

She thought she must cry out in thanksgiving when
she heard some men click their heels together as they
came to attention, and the sounds of heavy doors being
opened at the earl's harsh command. In a moment he
had her down the steps and he was striding away. The
cool night air after the intense heat of the palace told
her it was safe to open her eyes.

"Where . . . where are we going, m'lord?" she
asked.

"Shhh," he said as he turned the corner. "It is only a
little way now. I had my carriage follow us here,
ma'am, for I suspected we might need it. Ah, there it
is, just as I ordered."

Julia saw a vehicle waiting a short distance away on
the dark side street, and the men in the earl's livery
who jumped down to assist them. The earl deposited
her on the seat of his carriage, and then he backed
down the steps.

"Will you be all right for a few minutes, ma'am?" he
asked politely.

Julia gazed into his lean face, and she could not
control a shudder. At once he put out his hand to
her, and she was ashamed of herself. "Yes, of course I
will, sir," she said in the strongest voice she could man-
age.

His flashing grin applauded her gallantry. "Good
girl!" he said. "I shall be as quick as I can, and you will
be quite safe with my men to guard you."

Julia watched him disappear around the corner
again, his cloak billowing behind him. Then she

leaned back against the comfortable squabs of his carriage and sighed in relief.

She had never been so frightened or so horrified as she had been this past hour. She doubted she would ever be able to forget it for the rest of her life. And when she thought of what had happened inside the Prince's bedchamber, she cringed. Trying to put it in the back of her mind, lest she faint in earnest, she wondered what the earl had gone back for, and what he was doing. At the thought of any possible danger he might be in, she felt a wave of nausea sweep over her, and she closed her eyes and swallowed.

It seemed a very long time before she heard him giving the coachman orders to return to Charles Street, but by then she had herself under better control. No good would come of her giving in to hysteria now, she told herself sternly. And how ridiculous that would be now that she was safe, and knew he was safe was well. She must try to be braver, more worthy of him, for he had, after all, risked a great deal for her this evening. And if the Prince died —although she refused to contemplate such an awful thing—he might well be banished or imprisoned for his part in helping her.

"You are all right, sir?" she asked, stretching out her hand to him as he climbed into the seat beside her.

As the carriage started to move, she was stunned to see the frown he wore between his brows. He nodded, and then he turned to her, a look of complete confusion on his lean face. Julia suddenly had a glimpse of what he must have looked like when he was a boy.

"Yes, all is well with me, m'lady," he told her. "But I do not understand it! When I went back to see the Prince, I was not allowed to enter his bedchamber. Colonel McCarthy told me the Prince had given orders to deny me. He told the equerry he could not bear the sight of such a traitor.

"He has never treated me in such a way, never! We

have known each other since we were eighteen. But I thought it wise not to press the issue when he was so distraught, and so I came away. But even though he discovered that I had come with you to help you, surely he knows that does not make me a traitor. This behavior of his is inexplicable to me."

He turned away then, to stare out the window, and on her side of the carriage, Julia gripped her trembling hands together tightly.

What had she done? Dear God, what had she done?

14

They rode on in silence. The earl was preoccupied, and Julia had no desire to interrupt his musings. She knew she must tell him what had happened in the Prince's bedroom, but she needed a few moments to put her thoughts in order first.

When the carriage drew to a halt before her house in Charles Street, the earl turned to her. "My pardon, ma'am," he said formally. "I'm afraid I have not been a very good companion, and after such a harrowing experience as you have suffered, too."

Julia shook her head, and then she had to clear her throat. "May I impose on you a little longer, m'lord?" she asked.

He nodded, and as the groom was letting down the steps and preparing to open the door, she said quickly, "Then I wish you would come in with me for a while. There is something I have to speak to you about. It is important, or I would not ask, at this time of night."

"Of course, m'lady," he told her as he stepped down and then held out his hand to assist her. "I had every intention of doing so, for there are things I must explain to you as well. Besides, I must make sure you are all right."

His hand under her arm was warm and steady as he

helped her up the steps and sounded the knocker. The door opened at once, almost as if Hentershee had been hovering there, concerned for her safety.

Julia made herself smile when she saw his worried old face. He took the earl's cloak and her stole, and she asked him to bring brandy to the library.

One of her footmen came after them to make up the fire, and Julia dismissed him for the evening after he had done so. When her butler brought in the tray and glasses, she dismissed him as well. "Go to bed, Hentershee. You are tired, and I can let the earl out and lock the door myself." She saw he was about to protest, and she added, "Come now! I insist on it."

As the old butler bowed and left the room, Julia moved closer to the blazing fire. It was not a cold night, but somehow the bright flames and warmth comforted her. How good it felt to be home, home safe!

She was recalled to the earl's presence only when she heard the chink of the brandy decanter on the crystal snifters, and she turned to find him holding one of them out to her.

"Thank you," she said, suddenly shy. "Won't you please be seated, m'lord?"

The earl waited until she sat down in her favorite chair, and then he took the one across from her. He swirled the mellow liqueur in his snifter between both hands to warm it, and then held it up to the light to admire the way the fire turned its amber to liquid gold. *It is just the color of her hair in the firelight*, he mused.

"I can't thank you enough for helping me tonight," Julia was saying. "I could never have gone without you. But I know I interrupted your evening, and yet you came so quickly! You are too good."

"I was only engaged with friends, playing some new scores," the earl told her. "They understood. But come! Drink your brandy, m'lady. You have had a shock and it will make you feel better."

As she obeyed, like a small child told to drink up her milk, he smiled at her. "And while you are thus engaged, shall I tell you what happened to you in the Prince's room?" he asked.

Julia looked startled. "But . . . but how can you know?" she asked.

Trevor Whitney smiled again. "Let us see if I am right," he said. "You received his emissary here late this evening. Colonel McCarthy told you the Prince had stabbed himself, in an attempt to take his life, and that he was calling for you, saying that only your immediate presence could save him. Is that correct so far, m'lady?"

Julia nodded, her brandy forgotten.

"When we arrived, we were taken up to him via the back entrance and the servants' stairs," the earl went on. "And, of course, you went in to him alone. No doubt you found him very pale and distraught, lying on his supposed deathbed?" The earl's lips twisted in a grimace. "There was a lot of blood on the sheets and coverlet, was there not, Lady Julia?"

She nodded again, unable to speak as she relived the horror of the scene.

"Perhaps he even went so far as to leave a basin of blood there?" the earl asked.

"Yes, there was a basin," Julia whispered. "But how do you know all this, sir? Why, you remained in the antechamber!"

"Much as I would like to keep you awed at my skill in detection, I must confess I know because he has done this before, m'lady," the earl explained. As Julia's eyes widened, he went on, "Yes, some sixteen or seventeen years ago, as I recall, he tried the same trick with Mrs. Fitzherbert. That time he sent his royal surgeon to her, with much the same tale that was told to you. Maria Fitzherbert felt she must go to him, but also like you, she insisted on having someone she knew come with her. The Duchess of Devonshire, snatched away from her supper, attended her. When the Prince told Mrs. Fitzherbert he would not live without her, she borrowed a ring from the duchess. She let the Prince put it on her finger as her pledge to him before the two ladies went back to Devonshire House, completely unnerved. Mrs. Fitzherbert came to her senses quickly, however. She and the duchess wrote a statement to the effect that promises obtained in such a manner were entirely void. She was so concerned about what he might try next that she left the country the following day."

He saw that Julia was leaning forward enthralled by the tale, her brandy forgotten. He pointed to it, and obediently she took another sip.

"The Prince has always believed in the beneficial effects of drawing blood, m'lady," he went on. "He learned to use the lancet himself years ago, to open a vein, for his surgeons would not always accommodate him, and he swore it made him feel better. I suspect that is what he did tonight. Do not worry about him. He will not die. He never had any intention of dying, so you will never have that on your conscience."

"But that is terrible, horrible!" Julia exclaimed, her voice rising. "How could anyone behave in such a callous, premeditated way, merely to gain a reluctant mistress?"

"The Prince has seldom been denied anything he wishes, ma'am," Trevor Whitney told her. "And so, when he is thwarted, he does not behave in a normal manner. But come, tell me. Is that essentially what happened?"

Julia nodded. "Almost exactly," she said. "But supposing I had been taken in by it, supposing I had agreed . . . ?" She shuddered.

"Why didn't you?" the earl asked curiously. "It was plain to see when you came out of his room that you were as much affected by it as poor Mrs. Fitzherbert must have been."

Julia looked down into her snifter and frowned. "There was something about the whole thing that did not ring true to me," she said. "That dash through the dark streets, the surreptitious way we entered—the back stairs, that silent lonely hall. It was most unusual, surely, not to see footmen there, some of his attendants, even maids, was it not? And I was struck by the way the men I did see wore black, almost as if they were already in mourning. And finally, the two men in his bedchamber who whispered together on the far side of the room. At the time, I thought them his doctors, but now I wonder who they were."

Trevor Whitney knew they had probably been gentlemen of the chambers, and their whispering concerned only the amount of money they were wagering on her capitulation, but he did not say so.

"Besides, there was the way the Prince's room was lit," Julia went on. "After that brilliant antechamber, so few candles, and those so strategically placed. It was almost like a scene from a play."

The earl nodded. "Yes, Prinny is fond of theatricals. He would have made sure his stage setting was perfect."

He was silent for a moment, and then he said, "But I am a little surprised, even so, ma'am, that he could not convince you, in spite of your intuitive feelings that something was wrong. What did he say?"

Julia leaned back in her chair and closed her eyes for a moment. The earl never took his intent gaze from her face. "He told me he was dying, that only the promise of my love could save him," she said, her voice so soft the earl had to lean forward to hear it. "I was frightened then, especially when he said his death would be on my head and I might well be punished for it. Then he changed completely. He said that if I would agree to be his mistress, he would shower me with wealth and his eternal devotion. It was when he began to speak of the joy we would know in each other's arms that I am afraid I lost my head."

She paused, and the earl saw her cheeks flush in sudden embarrassment. He waited, to give her time to recover herself, before he prompted gently, "You lost your head?"

Lady Julia looked up at him, and he was stunned to see her eyes pleading for his understanding. "I told the Prince I could never love him, m'lord. I told him my heart was already given to another."

Suddenly she raised her handkerchief to her lips, and the earl felt a premonition that, instead of making him recoil, filled him with elation.

"And the man you named, m'lady?" he asked in that same quiet voice.

"Forgive me, sir," she said quickly. "I named you! You were the only one I could think of that he would believe! It is common knowledge among the *ton* now that we have often been together, although not for the reason they suppose. Besides, Lady Jersey saw us leave the ballroom that evening at the Barrs'. She gave me such a knowing smile when we returned to company! I fear we have become an *on-dit*, sir."

The earl rose, and she watched him, her heart beating fast as he moved toward the fireplace. "So that is why he called me traitor," he mused, leaning against the mantel and trying to keep his voice even over the singing in his heart.

"I am sorry for that. I . . . I never thought of the possible consequences for you. I was only trying to escape, save myself. It was selfish of me, and no doubt you hate me now. Indeed, I am truly sorry," she said.

She bent her head, covering her eyes with her handkerchief and stifling a sob. To her surprise, he came and lifted her from her chair and drew her into his arms. He held her close, until he felt her relax against him.

There was nothing Trevor Whitney wanted more than to tell her how glad he was she had spoken as she had, how much he wanted it to be true, for he loved her more than he had ever thought it possible to love any woman. But as they stood there in the quiet, well-ordered library, he realized he must not do that. Not yet, while she was still a suspected blackmailer. If his brain had not been so overheated and his heart so overjoyed, he knew he might well have had the thought that her confession was possibly a ploy of her own. If it had come from anyone but Lady Julia Reynolds, he would have suspected immediately that she was offering herself to him to still his suspicions, perhaps even as a bribe.

At last he held her away from him and looked down into her face. It was almost as white as it had been when she came from the Prince's room, and he led her back to her seat.

"Finish your brandy, ma'am," he told her. When she made no move to do so, he took the snifter and put both her hands around the stem. "Sip!" he ordered.

As she did so, he retreated to his own seat again. He knew it was dangerous to be so close to her. "What you did does not matter, m'lady. I doubt my reputation will be ruined by your revelation," he made himself say.

"But the Prince!" she exclaimed. "He called you traitor, and you may be in serious trouble! I am so ashamed!" She hung her head.

"Look at me, if you please, m'lady," he commanded. He waited until she raised those hazel eyes before he went on. "I am not in serious trouble. It is true I shall be *persona non grata* for some weeks at the palace, but I believe I can survive not being summoned every few days to those overheated rooms. The Prince is too fond of me to banish me forever. Why, who else can accompany him on the violoncello with such skill?"

He saw the dawning of hope in her eyes, and he smiled at her. "Be assured, ma'am, he will forgive me just as soon as his hot eyes light on some other beautiful lady. Knowing the Prince as well as I do, I expect I shall be back in his good graces within the month. And I do not say that to insult you, ma'am. The Prince has always loved wildly and completely . . . and briefly."

The clock standing against the wall struck midnight then, and he put down his empty snifter and rose. "It is late," he said, wishing he could stay with her for hours more. "You should be in bed after this traumatic evening, and I will not keep you from it any longer, m'lady."

Julia rose obediently. As they walked to the door, she said, "You must allow me to thank you again, sir, for the help you gave me so willingly, and the inadvertent help I exacted. Without you beside me, surely I would have failed."

Her voice caught a little on the last words, and the pain in it that was echoed in her eyes made Trevor Whitney throw caution and cool common sense away as if he had never practiced them at all in any of his thirty-nine years. He caught her in his arms and stared down into her lovely face as if he would never have done with looking at her. Julia stared back at him, her lips opening a little in her surprise. It was very quiet in the large room, so quiet she could hear his sigh and the beating of their two hearts, just before he bent his head and kissed her.

For a moment, Julia thought to escape him. But only for a moment. No matter how wrong this was, she knew she would do nothing to evade his embrace. His lips were warm and insistent on hers; gentle, yet still relentless with a man's deep passion. With a little sigh of her own, Julia gave herself up to the sensations his kiss evoked. She quivered with weakness, but she knew she was safe in the circle of his arms. Trevor Whitney would not let her fall. He would never let anything happen to her. As his kiss grew even more insistent and urgent, she responded with all her heart.

When he raised his head at last, he drew back a little so he could look down into her face again. His blue-gray eyes searched deeply, and then one strong finger came up to caress her lips, as if to commit them to memory through his touch. He put his hand softly on her cheek for a moment, before he smoothed back her chestnut curls and felt them twist around his hand, as if to capture it. It was then he knew how willing a captive he was. He did not speak as they stood there, still locked together by the strength of his arms.

He let her go at last, and she reached out with both hands to grasp a chair back for support. Her heart was beating rapidly. Surely he would not just leave her like this! she told herself. Surely he would speak to her, tell her what was in his heart, and ask her what was in hers.

But the earl did not speak. Instead, he bowed and left the library. Julia remained standing exactly where she was. She did not even move when she heard him close the outer door behind him as he left the house.

The early did not sleep at all that night. Even reliving the sweetness of her kiss could not erase from his mind the enormity of what he had done. He had left her abruptly and without a single word, because he had not dared to remain. He had known then that if he had not done so, he would have poured out his love for her. How he had ached to tell her of it! But in the one tiny corner of his mind where sanity still reigned, he had known that any confession of his was impossible under the circumstances. He had behaved like a fool, an undisciplined fool, for what if she were the blackmailer, indeed? What if he had fallen in love with such a woman? After all these years, how would he be able to bear it if he found out that he had given his heart at last, to such as she? But on the other hand, how could he stand to live on alone, without her, no matter what she had done?

And then he told himself it could not be she, it could not! She was too fine, too good, those beautiful hazel eyes too clear and honest to hide any such duplicity.

He was so confused, and so ashamed of himself for his loss of control, that he rose from his rumpled bed to pace the room and chastise himself. Finally he managed to doze off in an armchair near the window,

just as the dark night skies began to lighten into gray
dawn. His valet was stunned when he came in to open
the draperies sometime later, but he made no
comment as the earl stretched and yawned.

"I'll bring your tea immediately, sir," Hennings said
just before he left the room.

The earl did not appear to hear him, for he had
risen and was leaning on the sill as he stared out the
window in the direction of Charles Street.

As soon as he had been shaved and dressed, he went
downstairs. His butler intercepted him in the hall.

"The countess begs you to excuse her this morning,
m'lord. She has gone walking with Miss Ogilvie. And
this has just come from Carlton House, sir," he said as
he presented a note.

The earl took it from him, slitting it open as he
walked toward the breakfast room. He was frowning
as he read it, and then he crumpled it in his hands.
Colonel Lake had written to tell him that the expected
blackmail note had arrived, complete with details for
leaving the money this very day, and recovering the
snuffbox. He begged the earl to receive him in an hour
so they could discuss the note and make their plans.

Trevor Whitney wondered, as he ate his breakfast,
if he should send a note to Lady Julia. Surely she
would wonder if he did not write or come to her, he
told himself. Then his lips tightened. He knew he
could not do that. He did not trust himself when he
was near her. No, he must stay away until this fiasco
was over, for better or for worse.

As he buttered a piece of toast, he tried to cheer
himself up by telling himself that possibly as soon as
tomorrow she would be free of suspicion. And then
how quickly he would go to her and take her in his
arms again. He had felt her respond to him last night,
and he knew she would not have done so if she did not
care for him. He began to dream of her, and their life
together, when this dark cloud that hung over her had
been dispersed.

Behind him, at the sideboard, his butler coughed, and he was recalled to his breakfast. His toast was stiff now, and his beef, eggs, and coffee cool. He called for fresh servings before he went to the library to await the Prince's equerry.

The colonel was prompt to their appointment. As the butler closed the library door, he came and shook the earl's hand. "Thank you for receiving me here, m'lord," he said. There was a little twinkle in his eye as he added, "I thought it more appropriate, for I doubted you would have cared to come to the palace today."

Trevor Whitney tried to smile. "So you have heard, have you, sir?" he asked.

The colonel snorted. "Of course I have! It is being talked about in every nook and cranny of the palace. Believe me when I say I did not know the Prince was planning a deathbed scene, or I would have tried to stop him. I must say I was surprised that you consented to serve as the lady's cavalier, however. At least I was until I realized you were merely keeping an eye on her. Was the Lady Julia quite undone by the experience?"

He did not sound too concerned over whether she had been or not. The earl returned a quiet answer.

"It was shrewd of her to name you as her lover, m'lord," Colonel Lake went on. "But then, as we both know by now, she is a very clever woman."

When the earl did not comment, he went on, "But let us hope that this time she has outsmarted herself." He held out the latest communication from the blackmailer. "Read this, and tell me what you think, sir," he said.

Trevor Whitney read the note quickly, and then again with more care. He was frowning as he said, "This is ingenious, sir. For if we leave the money in Hyde Park in that specific location, and at the specified time, we will have little chance to observe who comes to get it. The park is crowded at that hour, that is true, but if that makes it easier for our men to mingle in the throng, it also makes it easier for the blackmailer to escape without being detected."

"You are right," the colonel agreed. "I went by the place on my way here. That particular bench near the Serpentine is completely exposed, although it cannot be seen from the roadway. The only hiding place is a stand of trees and a few bushes. Surely anyone picking up the money would check them first. And any observer on the other side of the lake would be too far away to identify the person, especially if she wears any kind of a disguise. And you will mark Lady Julia's warning. She will expose the Prince to the journals tomorrow if we try to watch. I must admit I am stumped for a solution, m'lord."

He paused for a moment, and then he added, "I did think of setting a man to watch her home, and those of the others involved as well, but I came to see that would be too dangerous. No, we shall intercept her on the spot. Catch her red-handed, as it were."

The earl closed his eyes. Colonel Lake thought he was trying to picture the scene in his mind's eye. In reality, the earl had done so to hide the pain he felt that the equerry should name her the blackmailer still.

"No, we cannot risk any watchers on the ground there, lest they give the game away," the earl said when he had regained control of his expression. "We can, however, have the gates watched. If the money is put in a distinctive enough package . . ." He paused and ran a hand over his dark brown hair. "But what am I thinking of?" he muttered to himself. "The black-mailer will put the package into another bag or parcel at once. No, that will not work."

He sat quietly without speaking for several moments. The colonel watched him anxiously. Suddenly the earl sat up straighter, and a grim smile of satisfaction twisted his lips.

"I have it, sir!" he said, his voice exultant. "I said we could not risk anyone on the ground near that particular spot, did I not? But what if the watcher was someplace the blackmailer would never suspect, and he had a perfect view of the bench as well?"

Colonel Lake threw out his hands in defeat, "And where might that be, m'lord?" he asked.

"Up a tree, sir," Trevor Whitney told him. "Up a tree."

As the colonel leaned forward, his interest caught, the earl went on, "And I do think it had better be me who is perched in that tree. I know most of the suspects by sight now, and so I will be able to recognize whoever it is quickly, from my vantage point. Besides, that way we will not have to risk men following the thief, and perhaps alarming him into flight. Because the park is so crowded at that hour, they would have to follow closely, and they might well be noticed. The thief is sure to be nervous and extremely suspicious. This way we can let him think the plan has succeeded and he is free to return home in safety. But we will be there to intercept him, to regain possession of the five thousand pounds, and to relieve him of the Prince's . . . er, indiscretion."

"How very creative, m'lord!" the colonel complimented him. "I think it has an excellent chance of success, indeed, I do."

The earl leaned back and put his hands behind his head as he continued to plan. "It is fortunate that it is June, and the new leaves are so thick. I shall dress in green and brown and make sure my shirt and cravat are covered up. If I keep my face turned away until the blackmailer actually reaches for the package of money, I do not think I will be seen. The thief will be looking around, after all, not up."

The colonel had been thinking as well. "But you will have to be in place a long time beforehand, m'lord," he pointed out. "If the park is being watched—and we cannot know that it is not, even now, by either the blackmailer or a possible accomplice—you run the risk of being seen when you take up your position." He eyed the earl's lean, masculine figure with concern. "Can you remain up a tree for that length of time, sir?"

The earl smiled. "Like every boy, I was adept at tree climbing in my youth, sir. I am sure I can perch on a branch for as long as you like. But perhaps we can arrange a diversion about the time I am climbing into the tree? Perhaps a runaway team? A small grass fire? I am sure you will know what would be best. Any watcher's attention, no matter how intense, would be caught by such an incident. And all I will need is a few seconds."

"At what time do you think you should take your place, m'lord?" the colonel asked next.

The earl consulted the note again. "It says the money must be placed under the bench at precisely five o'clock. I do not think the blackmailer will come at once, but surely he or she will seek to retrieve it before the park begins to empty. However, just to be on the safe side, I will climb into place at four."

The two men continued to plan, making sure they forgot nothing. Every contingency was explored, and possible solutions decided. It was almost noon before the colonel looked at the clock and rose in haste.

"But I must be off at once!" he said. "I have a great many things to do in the next four hours. How will you occupy your time until then, sir?" he asked curiously.

Trevor Whitney smiled as he walked with him to the door and opened it. "I shall be lying on my bed trying to sleep, sir," he said. "I spent a restless night."

The colonel looked around, and when he saw the hall was empty, he said in an urgent voice, "I beg you will go armed, m'lord! This could be dangerous for you even if it works as planned. And, as you know, there's many a slip . . ."

"Never fear, I shall be well prepared, sir," the earl told him. "Until four, then. I shall expect a very superior diversion near the Serpentine at that time."

"You shall have a royal one," the colonel said,

pumping his hand in farewell. "If only the Prince knew what a good friend of his you are, and how much you have done to find this blackmailer! I know he would not have spoken as he did last evening, if he were aware of it."

The earl walked with his guest to the front door. After a few last words, the colonel hurried away, and Trevor Whitney went back to his library.

Behind the slightly open door of the small salon the countess used as her own when she was in town, Edwina Ogilvie drew back, her eyes as round as her mouth. Lady Whitney had been called away a few minutes before to deal with some problem in the kitchen. Edwina had told her she would let herself out, and the older lady had left her in the salon.

Now she was glad she had tarried as she had, leafing through an interesting novel the countess was reading. If she had not stayed, she would have missed this most thrilling development.

Every nerve aquiver, Edwina tiptoed past the closed library door and quietly let herself out of the house. She felt a certain self-satisfaction. All she had to do was to be in Hyde Park near the lake at four, and on the lookout for the earl. She still had a chance to help her Aunt Julia.

She was honest enough to admit to herself as she hurried home that there was rather more to it than that. She knew she wouldn't have missed all this excitement for the world, Aunt Julia or no Aunt Julia.

15

The earl found it impossible to sleep, but remembering the cramped position he was about to be subjected to for such a considerable amount of time, he was glad to stretch out on his comfortable bed and rest.

At three he rose and summoned his valet. Hennings was hard put to control his expression when the earl told him the clothes he intended to wear that afternoon.

"If I may suggest, sir?" he said, looking pained. "I rather think that particular shade of green would look much better with the biscuit breeches. The darker brown ones and the gloves to match will not complement the jacket at all."

Trevor Whitney's lean face was intent as he searched one of his drawers. "I am not attempting sartorial splendor this afternoon, Hennings, and I am in a hurry," he said.

The valet saw him take two businesslike pistols from the drawer, along with some ammunition, and understanding dawned in his eyes.

"Certainly, m'lord," he said, hastening to lay out the required clothing. Hennings was still getting occasional information from the footman on Charles Street; he knew that particular problem had yet to be solved.

At three-thirty the earl entered one of his closed carriages. He ordered his coachman to circle the park, the team at a steady trot. When he did not see any of the suspects in the case, he rapped on the roof as they were approaching the wooded section where he had decided it would be best to proceed on foot.

Lord Whitney glanced around quickly before he stepped from the carriage. There were a few people strolling a little distance away, and some carriages approaching, but no one was close enough to remark a hatless, caneless Earl of Bradford disappearing into the bushes like any common sneak thief.

He felt more secure as soon as he was out of sight of the road. Behind him he could hear his carriage drawing away, as had been arranged earlier. As quietly and as quickly as he could, he edged forward. His deep-set eyes were keen and intent, and he was listening hard. He reached the edge of a little wood and stopped behind a large tree.

Before him was a stretch of green grass that sloped slightly to the ornamental water that was the Serpentine. In plain view was the bench the blackmailer had designated. There was no one in the immediate vicinity, and he breathed a sigh of relief. It had occurred to him the spot would make a perfect place for a tryst, and he had no desire to endanger the mission lurking behind a tree when he should have been climbing up it, just because some young buck was meeting his lady there and was lost in a passionate embrace.

The earl looked up. The thick oak tree he was sheltering behind was much too tall, and the lowest branches too far above the ground for him to even attempt climbing it. A little worried now, he inspected the other trees nearby. There was one that looked promising, and he moved toward it after checking again to make sure he was still unobserved.

He was delighted to see there was a branch of the tree he could reach easily, and above it, one that would make a perfect perch. He could only hope that when he was in position, he would have a clear view of the bench, if not the approaches to it.

He slipped behind the tree and consulted his pocket watch. It was almost four. Buttoning his jacket to the throat, he covered his white linen. The artful arrangement of his cravat suffered, as did his starched shirt points, but he knew he could not risk any flash of white once he was in position.

Suddenly he heard a great commotion from the direction of the roadway, people calling out, and the thunder of hooves. He did not hesitate. Jumping to grasp the branch directly overhead, he swung himself up, to climb to the branch above. He was glad it was sturdy, for he knew he was no lightweight, in spite of his lean physique. As he settled down on it close to the trunk, a runaway horse galloped across the grass some little distance away. On its back, a screaming girl clung to the horse's mane. She had lost her hat, and her long blond hair whipped out behind her. Several men on horseback were in hot pursuit. Idly the earl wondered who she was and how the colonel had found her so quickly.

He looked around. He could not see anyone within sight who appeared to be at all interested in either the stand of trees where he was hidden or in the black-mailer's bench. Two children who had been sailing boats had risen to point to the runaway horse, and their nanny was hurrying to them to ensure their safety. Several strolling couples watched as well. The ruse had worked perfectly.

The earl settled himself more comfortably on the hard limb. He was well aware that he would be stiff and cramped before his surveillance was over, but he was resigned to it, and to observing the utmost patience as well. It was entirely possible that the blackmailer would not pick up the parcel until dusk, but Trevor Whitney hoped that whoever did so would be so greedy he could not wait that long.

He checked to make sure he had a clear view of the
bench. Because of the position of the other trees
nearby, he would not be able to see anyone approach
it. It was less than an ideal location, but he knew it
was the best to be found in the short time he had dared
to risk exposure.

Knowing the money was not to be placed under the
bench until five o'clock, he leaned his head against the
rough bark of the trunk and closed his eyes to rest
them. Lady Julia's lovely face with those great hazel
eyes danced behind his eyelids. He tried to think of
something else, but he found it impossible. He could
picture her as clearly as if she were seated beside him;
those soft lips that had been so yielding and yet so shy
under his, the color coming and going in her cheeks,
the full round column of her throat. And, of course,
those springy, shining tresses that had curled around
his fingers last evening.

He was so lost in reverie that for a moment he did
not notice the sounds of someone approaching. His
eyes flew open only when a twig snapped. Whoever it
was, was behind him, and very cautious. He would
hear some faint movement, and then, silence. Trevor
Whitney held his breath. It had to be the blackmailer!
He prayed that he or she would not decide to recon-
noiter right under his dangling feet, or worse still, hide
there until the money was delivered.

There was a crackling in the bushes some few feet to
his right, and he turned his head very slowly and
cautiously. He saw a pair of white-gloved hands part
the bush before a head emerged and turned to look this
way and that.

The earl inhaled sharply, his anger rising as Miss
Edwina Ogilvie stepped out into the open and stared
intently around.

He put aside his initial thought that she was the
blackmailer. As clever as she was, she was too young
and naive to have engineered such an intricate plot,
and he knew instinctively that even if Lady Julia was

the blackmailer, she would never involve her young niece in anything criminal.

No, somehow Miss Ogilvie had learned of the latest demand and of the location where the money was to be left. Thinking hard, he remembered his butler telling him that morning that the countess was with Miss Ogilvie. He remembered the colonel's last remarks in the hall as well. Had she been somewhere near, and heard them? She must have, and she must have followed him. Drat the girl! he muttered to himself.

She was edging closer to his tree now, and looking so suspicious as she did so that even a person of the meanest intelligence would have known that there was something unusual afoot. He could wait no longer, for surely it was a miracle she had not been noticed before this.

"Miss Ogilvie!" he called in a harsh whisper.

She gave a little squeal of fright and spun around toward the sound of his voice, her hands clasped to her heart.

"It is Trevor Whitney. Come here at once!" he ordered.

She looked around puzzled. "Where are you?" she asked, fortunately keeping her voice low.

"Up here," the earl whispered. "In this tree."

Her blue eyes were wide with shock as she came toward the tree. When she was beneath it, she put her hands on her hips, and, staring up at him, said, "How dare you frighten me so! And what in the world are you doing up there?"

"I am waiting for the blackmailer, of course," he said. "But there is no time to lose. Since you have stumbled onto our plot in your own inimitable way, Miss Ogilvie, you must join me. I cannot risk you wandering around the vicinity, lest you alarm the person I am so eager to catch. Give me your hand!"

As he had been speaking, he had moved down to crouch on the lower branch again, and now he reached out to her. He was glad when she extended her hand without making a fuss, and at how agile she was as she scrambled up beside him.

He noted she was wearing a dark green gown. It was not at all the color of the new leaves, but at least it was not scarlet, and that was a help.

The earl pointed higher, and she climbed to the next branch, showing most of her petticoats and silk stockings as she did so. She did not seem afraid of the climb, nor embarrassed at her immodesty, and silently he blessed the brothers she must have.

He followed her, but when the branch he had been sitting on creaked a little, he ordered her to climb to one higher up on the other side of the trunk. He thought she was going to argue, so he told her in a few terse words exactly why it was important. When she was seated on the branch, he took up his former position.

"Tuck your skirts around your legs, Miss Ogilvie," he whispered. "No trace of white must show. And now, although there are a great many things I would like to say to you, miss, we will preserve a perfect silence. There must be nothing to alarm the black-mailer, do you understand?"

Miss Ogilvie agreed in such a thrilled little whisper, he longed to spank her.

"And even if a bee stings you, or an ant crawls up your leg, you must not make a sound, nor any movement. Do you understand?" he asked between gritted teeth. "And take those white gloves off!"

"Certainly, m'lord," she whispered back.

For several minutes she remained perfectly still, but eventually he heard her shifting on her perch. "Be quiet!" he said, and if a whisper could be said to thunder, the earl's most certainly did.

A deadly silence prevailed from that moment on. They both watched as Colonel Lake sat down on the bench shortly before five. He put a neatly wrapped parcel beside him and opened a newspaper he carried.

At precisely five, he slipped the parcel under his feet and out of sight. Then he looked at his pocket watch, and, as if startled by the time, folded his paper and hurried away.

The earl knew the real wait was about to begin. He was growing a little stiff, but he dared not move. There was not a sound from Edwina Ogilvie. He hoped she would not become impatient and ruin the plan that up to now had worked so perfectly.

Five-fifteen came and went, and five-thirty as well. It was a lovely June afternoon, the sky as blue as if it had never known a cloud. Faintly, behind him, he could hear the chatter of the *beau monde* as they strolled along, greeting their friends and exchanging gossip, and the thoroughbred teams and smart carriages as they rumbled over the cobbles. No one came near their tree, nor the bench.

He was beginning to wonder if something had gone wrong when he heard the bushes crackling below him again. He held his breath and froze, and he prayed Miss Ogilvie would have the sense to do the same.

This person was even more cautious than she had been about coming out into the open.

It seemed an age before the figure of a woman carrying a large satchel emerged from the bushes and walked quickly to the bench and sat down. Trevor Whitney peered at her, but he could not determine who she was. She was dressed in a severe gray gown with a light cloak over it, and her hair was covered by a large turbanlike hat. Large plumes obscured her face as she turned a little to inspect her surroundings. When she was satisfied that she was unobserved, she reached under the bench. In a moment she had the package in her lap, had opened her satchel, and placed it inside. She rose then, and the earl willed her to turn in his direction, if only for the briefest of moments.

As if obeying his command, she turned to inspect the woods behind her. He heard Miss Ogilvie's little gasp of shock, and was hard put to control one of his own.

In a moment, the woman was hurrying away around the Serpentine, and soon she disappeared from sight.

Even before she was barely out of earshot, Miss Ogilvie whispered, "Mrs. Lowden! I cannot believe she is the guilty one! But, m'lord, surely we should go after her at once!"

The earl began to climb down. "There is no need for us to do that, Miss Ogilvie. I know exactly where she is going."

Edwina thought his cold voice so utterly devoid of emotion it made her shiver as she prepared to follow him to the ground.

"Take care as you come down," he warned her. "Your muscles are no doubt as stiff and sore as mine are from our long wait."

He reached the last branch and lowered himself until he was swinging from it before he dropped lightly to the ground. He reached up to catch her as she did the same.

Edwina straightened out her crushed skirts. He noted bleakly that her eyes were shining with excitement. "I never in all the world suspected her," she confided as they walked away. "Why, Auntie Julia will be so shocked! Mrs. Lowden is her best friend, you know. It just goes to show you, doesn't it?"

"Goes to show you what, Miss Ogilvie?" the earl made himself ask. His jaw was beginning to ache, he was gritting his teeth so.

"Why, that you can't trust anyone," Edwina said, skipping a little to keep up with his long stride. "It is too bad!"

"You most certainly can't trust anyone," the earl agreed as they reached the carriage road. He saw Colonel Lake's barouche a short distance away, and he took Miss Ogilvie's arm and headed in that direction.

When they reached the barouche, Trevor Whitney introduced his young companion to the colonel. The equerry frowned.

"Do you mean to tell me she is that vile, m'lord?" he asked.

Edwina stared at him in confusion.

"Not at all, sir," the earl said as he helped Edwina to a seat in the carriage. "Miss Ogilvie was merely an observer. The person who picked up the blackmail payment was Mrs. Fanny Lowden."

Before the colonel could comment, he said, "Do me the kindness of driving me to Lady Julia Reynolds' in Charles Street, sir. I must see Miss Ogilvie gets home safely, and I have another errand there. A most important errand. I will need two of your men."

The colonel noted the hard, set planes of his face, the white lines around his thinned lips, and his icy blue-gray eyes, and he nodded.

"Very well, sir," he said. "And I shall go to Mrs. Lowden's rooms in Wimpole Street. Just in case, you know," he added as he signaled to some men on horseback a little distance away. They took up their positions behind the carriage as it began to move.

"I doubt that will be necessary, sir," the earl told him, still speaking in that cold, strangled voice.

Edwina looked from one man to the other, completely at sea. There was something about the earl's posture and stern profile as she peeked at him that made her decide it would be best not to initiate a discussion of the exciting experience they had just shared. Besides, she remembered only too well how angry he had been when she had appeared on the scene. No doubt he was taking her back to her aunt's so he could administer a mighty scold. She was not looking foward to it at all. She knew, however, the adventure had been more than worth it, no matter how he ranted at her, or how fast her aunt sent her home to Kent.

When they arrived in Charles Street, the earl helped her from the carriage. She waited while he leaned back inside for a few further words with this Colonel Lake before he marched her up the steps. They were followed by two of the colonel's men.

The earl did not speak as they all entered the hall, and he still gripped her arm. Edwina was beginning to feel very alarmed.

"You will go upstairs to your room, Miss Ogilvie, and you will remain there until your aunt sends for you," he said.

Edwina opened her mouth to protest his autocratic behavior, but as her eyes encountered the barely controlled anger in his, she closed it at once. She tried to climb the stairs slowly and with dignity, but she had gone no more than halfway up the flight before she began to scurry as fast as she could. Below her, the earl turned to the old butler.

"Lady Julia is at home, Hentershee?" he asked.

The butler bowed. "Indeed, m'lord. But she is receiving Mrs. Lowden at the moment. If you would just wait here—"

The earl interrupted, shaking his head. "I shall announce myself. I am here on crown business." He turned to his companions and said, "Wait here. I will call you if I need you. Make sure no one leaves the house."

He strode purposefully to the drawing-room door. The three men behind him saw him hesitate for a moment, his hand half-extended. Then he straightened his shoulders and opened the door.

The earl walked in, shutting that door behind him. The two women in the drawing room were standing before the fire. They both looked startled at his abrupt appearance.

His icy eyes grew even bleaker when he saw the satchel Lady Julia was holding. As he watched, she put it down on a chair beside her.

"There was something you wanted, m'lord?" she asked. With deep despair he noted the constriction in her voice. Even if he had not caught her red-handed with the money, that voice would have told him of her guilt.

Julia had spent a miserable day. After she had gone

to bed last evening, she had surprised herself by falling asleep at once, although she had been awake again at dawn. Her first thoughts had been of the Earl of Bradford, and as she lay in her comfortable bed, still drowsy and warm, she had recalled the evening before. It had begun badly, and it had ended that way. There had been only a few exultant moments of happiness in it for her. Now, as the long shadows of late afternoon began to fall, she knew they had not really been happy moments at all. She might have thought the earl had kissed her as if he cared for her deeply, but then he had gone away without a single word. She did not understand; she did not think she would ever understand.

All today she had felt as if she were waiting in breathless anticipation. She had been so sure he would come to her, or, if unable to do that, write. Surely he owed her some explanation for his behavior? But as the hours passed and there was no word from him, her spirits had sunk. Did he consider her beneath contempt because she had named him as her lover? But he himself had said the Prince would not banish him, that he had nothing to fear. That could not be the reason he held aloof. Had his kiss only been exacted payment for her untruthfulness? His absence and his silence seemed designed to show her how little he honored her, how casual that kiss had really been.

Now she stared at him, wondering why he looked the way he did. His face appeared to have been carved from marble, and his piercing eyes, now more gray than blue, seemed full of accusations.

It seemed a very long time before he strolled forward, removing his gloves to toss them on a table. "So, the colonel was right all along," he said coldly. "Of course, neither he nor I had any idea the two of you were in this together. I congratulate you on your acting ability, m'lady. You were superb, but even so, I wonder at our stupidity."

"What are you talking about?" Julia asked, frowning in puzzlement. She moved a little closer to her friend. She noticed Fanny seemed frozen where she stood, and her breathing was quick and shallow.

The earl reached down and opened the satchel. Julia put out a hand in protest as he rummaged through it. When he withdrew a sack of money, and the guineas clinked as he brandished it in her face, she gasped. "You know what I am talking about all right, m'lady," he said harshly. "This is the money we left for the blackmailer this afternoon. I watched Mrs. Lowden pick it up from under the bench where we had left it not half an hour ago. Of course she brought it to you at once. Were you about to divide it, ladies?" he asked, his voice sarcastic. "How very unfortunate that you will not have the chance to enjoy your ill-gotten gains!"

Lady Julia now was as frozen as her friend. Her hazel eyes were huge in her pale face. As Trevor Whitney watched, one trembling hand went to her throat. Then she turned, almost reluctantly, to Mrs. Lowden.

"Fanny?" she whispered. "It was you all along? You, my best friend? But when you came in, you told me the satchel contained only some books you had just purchased—that you had stopped here to rest because they were so heavy. How could you do this to me, you who have said you love me? How *could* you?"

The earl felt despair such as he had never known. The confusion and disbelief in her stricken voice proved she was innocent after all, and he had just accused her of guilt and complicity.

Suddenly Mrs. Lowden moved. Reaching into her reticule, she took out a small pistol. "Put the money back, m'lord," she ordered, pointing the gun at him. When he obeyed, she snatched the satchel and clutched it to her thin bosom. Then she began to back away.

"Stay exactly where you are, m'lord," she ordered, her thin, homely face serious with intent. When Lady Julia took a step toward her, her imploring hand outstretched, the pistol swung to cover her too. "Stop there, Julia," she said. Lady Julia obeyed.

"You ask how I could do it, m'lady?" Mrs. Lowden asked. "How could I not? I saw the snuffbox that first afternoon. It was on the table where I left my hat. After I heard your story about the Prince's visit and his proposition, it took me only a moment to slip it into my reticule before I put on my hat as I was leaving."

"But why, Fanny, *why?*" Lady Julia asked, her voice anguished. "Why did you do it? And then to advise me, console me, pretend that all you wanted to do was help me! You, of all people, have seen the trouble it has brought me, the agonies I have suffered. How could you let something like that happen to me, your friend?"

"Because I needed the money!" Mrs. Lowden hissed, her face contorted. "You are a beautiful woman, Julia, sought after and admired. You can have your choice of any man you want, up to and including the Prince! But no one will ever offer for *me* again, take care of *me!* Besides, you are wealthy, without a worry in the world. Did you really think I liked living in rooms in Wimpole Street, my dear? I did not! I was forced to sell my town house and take those rooms after my husband died and I found he had left me almost penniless with his incessant gambling and his debts." Her voice was sarcastic as she went on, "And did you really think I preferred to walk everywhere, even in the rain, instead of keeping my own carriage? Turn down invitations, claiming the parties bored me? You are so imperceptive, so naive! I could not attend parties often because I did not have enough new clothes to wear, for I could not afford them. And did you really believe I *liked* the company of the Jennings sisters?"

She put back her head and laughed. At the bitter, mocking sound, Lady Julia dropped her imploring hand. She did not even notice the earl moving closer to her, as if to support her.

"Stand still, m'lord, or I'll put a bullet through

you!" Mrs. Lowden said quickly, the pistol once again
trained on his heart. The earl had to obey. He knew
that if he tried to reach for his own pistols in the
pockets of his jacket, she would shoot him before he
could draw and cock them. There was nothing he
could do, and he cursed himself for his carelessness. He
had been so distraught to discover Julia's supposed
guilt, he had forgotten to be cautious.

"I cultivated the Jenningses because they are such
great gossips," Mrs. Lowden went on, as if anxious to
tell them the whole story. "That is how I have supported myself, my dear, *dear* Julia! I found out things
about the *ton* from them, and then I made those who
had been indiscreet pay for my silence. The Prince's
snuffbox was a gift from heaven—a windfall I never
thought to gain. And this money is enough to set me up
in style once again. Of course, it is unfortunate that I
must remove from England to do so, but I do not
repine. I can always make new friends."

She seemed to notice Lady Julia's heartbroken,
anguished expression then, for she went on in a quieter
voice, "I knew you would not be in any real danger
from my blackmailing. Oh, yes, it meant an uncomfortable time for you, but that would last only a little
while. There was no way the earl could tie you to my
scheme, and after I had the money safe, I intended to
return the box. The whole thing would have dwindled
into an unsolved mystery. Surely your inadvertent
help was not too much to ask. I have always helped
you, now haven't I, goose?"

The earl saw Lady Julia shudder, and he wished he
might put his arm around her.

"What you have done is terrible, Fanny, terrible!"
she said in a broken voice. "I do not feel I have ever
known you at all."

"No, you have never understood me, my dear,
lovely Julia," Mrs. Lowden agreed with a thin smile.
"You see, I am not only the Imperturbable One, I am
the Unfathomable One as well."

Chuckling a little, she began to edge backward to the door. The pistol she held never wavered.

At the door, she put the satchel under her arm so she could open the door a crack. "Hentershee, get me a hackney cab at once," she called.

She did not wait to hear his assent, for she closed the door again quickly.

The earl hoped his men could take her by surprise when she left. He himself planned to step in front of Lady Julia so she would be out of the line of fire when that dangerous moment came.

It seemed an age before there was a knock on the door, but no one broke the heavy silence. "Yes?" Mrs. Lowden called.

"The hackney is here, ma'am," Hentershee said.

Slowly, Fanny Lowden reached for the doorknob, the satchel still held tightly under her arm. "You will remain here until I have made my escape," she ordered the earl and Julia. "If you do not, I shall shoot Hentershee."

Julia inhaled sharply, both hands to her heart. Still covering them with the pistol, Fanny Lowden backed through the door.

The moment she was out of sight, Trevor Whitney moved to put Lady Julia behind him. He held his breath. Suddenly Mrs. Lowden screamed. The pistol shot that came in concert with that scream sounded very loud in the quiet drawing room.

He pushed Lady Julia gently into a chair before he ran to the hall, his own pistols now in his hands. He found Mrs. Lowden held tight in the grasp of one of his men, while the other wrestled both the pistol and the satchel from her grasp. She was screaming and cursing, her thin face contorted with rage. The earl ordered the men to take her to the Tower, saying he himself would tell the colonel what had occurred. He searched her reticule, and when he found the Prince's snuffbox in the bottom, he put it into his pocket, along with his unused pistols, without making any comment or giving it more than a cursory glance.

When they had tied her hands before her, Fanny Lowden fell silent, almost as if she had resigned herself to her fate. The earl waited until the men led her from the house before he asked a footman to bring his mistress some brandy.

"Bring some brandy for Mr. Hentershee as well," he ordered when he noticed the old butler sitting on a hall chair, his wrinkled face working with shock as he stared up at the blackened hole in the ceiling where the pistol shot had gone.

Trevor Whitney looked up the stairs. Somehow he was not at all surprised to see Miss Ogilvie there, clinging to a newel post, her eyes as wide as saucers. "Summon Lady Julia's maid at once," he called, and she nodded before she ran out of sight.

When he went back to the drawing room, he found Lady Julia sitting exactly where he had left her. She was staring straight ahead, her eyes unseeing. Tears streamed down her face.

Silently the earl took out his handkerchief and gently wiped her face before he knelt before her and took her icy hands in his. She did not look at him as he rubbed them, trying to restore their warmth. He wished with all his heart that he might take her in his arms and comfort her, but he could see how very close she was to hysteria. The arms of a man who had believed in her guilt would be no comfort to her now. He would have to wait until she had recovered a little.

As her maid hurried in and curtsied, he rose. "Your mistress had had a bad shock. See to her," he ordered.

The wide-eyed maid nodded, bobbing another curtsy as he went and picked up his gloves.

"I shall return tomorrow, m'lady," he told the silent figure who was still staring at the wall. "Go to bed and stay there until morning. This has been a terrible experience for you, but it is over now. Know that I shall see that nothing ever hurts you again. My promise on it."

16

Trevor Whitney called in Charles Street as early as he dared the following morning, but even so he discovered the doctor had been before him.

The butler shook his head sadly as he told the earl the bad news. "Lady Julia hasn't said a word, m'lord, not one word since yesterday afternoon. Her maid tells me she just lies there in bed staring at the ceiling." Hentershee's voice quavered with his concern, and the earl's lips tightened.

He had spent the previous evening alone in his library, thinking of Julia and making plans as he played the piano. He knew it would be difficult for her to forgive him his accusations and suspicions, but he also knew he loved her so much, he would never rest until he had that forgiveness.

He had come to see that a life spent without her would only mean endless days and nights of unhappiness for him. Surely he would be able to convince her of his love, his caring, and his concern. But he had to see her to do so, and he wanted it to be soon.

Accordingly, he asked Hentershee for Miss Ogilvie. He paced the library as he waited for her, his eyes going often to the ceiling. Julia was up there somewhere, still distraught. He had to go to her, infuse her body and spirit with some of his own strength, make her well.

Miss Ogilvie was frowning as she slipped into the library, and she only whispered his name in greeting.

"She has not spoken yet?" the earl asked, frowning in turn.

Edwina sighed as she took a seat. "No, she is just the same as when you left, m'lord," she said. "The doctor can find nothing wrong with her, not really. But he says she has an emotional disorder."

Trevor Whitney sat down across from the girl, never taking his eyes from hers. "She has had a tremendous shock," he said.

"But I don't understand it at all," Edwina protested. "True, it was hard for her to learn her best friend was the blackmailer, but surely she could overcome that, don't you think so, m'lord?"

The earl stared into her earnest blue eyes, knowing full well that his own behavior yesterday was part of the problem.

"Has she said anything at all?" he asked.

Edwina shook her head. "Not a single word. She will drink a little, but she refuses to eat. And she won't talk, not to anyone. Why, she won't even talk to me!"

He saw her shiver before she added, "I am so frightened, sir!"

Trevor Whitney was frightened too, but he saw no good would come of telling a sixteen-year-old that. "Yes, I can see where you might be," he said, trying to sound calm and assured. "I think I had better see Lady Julia myself. I might be able to help."

"In bed? In her nightgown?" Edwina asked, sounding shocked.

The earl was not even tempted to laugh at this horrified display of misplaced maidenly modesty, even coming as it did from the unpredictable Miss Ogilvie.

"Exactly," he said wryly. "You will stay in the room, of course, and her maid as well. That should observe the proprieties. Now, run up and make sure she is ready to receive me."

After Miss Ogilvie left him, Trevor Whitney began

to pace the library again. It seemed an age before Hentershee came to escort him upstairs.

The butler knocked on one of the front bedroom doors, and Edwina opened it at once, motioning the earl inside. Standing at the foot of the bed, very much on guard, was the maid he had seen yesterday afternoon. Edwina drew her over to the window, so they were a little apart from the drama about to unfold.

The earl had no eyes for anyone but Lady Julia. She lay propped up on a number of lace-trimmed pillows, and she was staring straight ahead. She was dressed in a white nightgown that buttoned to the neck, and her chestnut hair streamed over her shoulders, so rich and full of life it made a mockery of her pale, still face.

"Good morning, m'lady," Trevor Whitney began in his normal, deep voice, although his heart was beating in an alarming way.

He watched carefully, but he could see no sign that she had heard him. Her eyes remained fixed on the same spot on the wall. She did not even blink.

"I cannot tell you how distressed I am to find you like this, m'lady," the earl went on, coming to stand close to the bed.

He waited, but when there was no response, he went on, "It is such a beautiful day too. The kind of June day when everyone should be outside. There is only a little breeze, and the sun is delightful."

He paused again, his eyes going from her still face to where one of her hands rested on the blue velvet coverlet. It looked so defenseless, palm up with the fingers curled a little, that he sat down on the bed and picked it up to hold it gently.

"Julia, listen to me!" he ordered, completely forgetting the interested audience by the window. "You must not do this to yourself! You must fight with all your will. Come, my dearest, speak to me! Look at me!"

Edwina and the maid held their collective breaths,

but when Lady Julia did not respond, her niece sighed
and the maid stifled a sob.

The earl did not speak again. Instead, he reached
out to take Julia into his arms, to cradle her against his
chest and rock her a little. One strong hand caressed
her chestnut curls. Then he lifted her chin so she was
forced to look at him. "Julia," he said quietly. "Julia,
my love."

Still heedless of the two others in the room, he bent
his head and kissed her lips. He could think of nothing
else to do, since his words had had no effect on her at
all.

For a long moment he thought he had failed. She
made no response. It was like kissing a loved one who
had just died, even though he could hear the steady
beat of her heart, feel her breath and the scented
warmth of her skin.

And then, just when he felt the utmost despair, he
felt something else. A tear touched his lips, and then
another. Trevor Whitney had never tasted anything
so wonderful. He was sure even nectar from the
gods could not compare to the warm salt of her
tears.

He raised his head to see her hazel eyes overflowing,
her face contorted as she cried.

The earl drew her back close to his heart, his strong
arms holding her safe there as his hands caressed her
back. "Yes, love, cry," he whispered in her ear. "Cry
until all the pain and disappointment are gone. And
then come back to me. I cannot live unless you come
back to me."

He felt her shuddering and sobbing, and he raised
one hand to the maid, snapping his fingers for a handkerchief. When Julia's sobs died away into a series of
little hiccups, he laid her back across his arm and
wiped her face.

"Blow!" he ordered, holding the handkerchief to her
nose.

She did not even think of disobeying. She stared up

at him, her eyes huge in her pale face. When he saw
the recognition in them, he felt the heavy ache in his
heart lighten.

"What . . . what are you doing here?" she asked,
looking around in wonder, as if she could not imagine
why he was in her bedroom. "You must go away at
once!"

"I shall go away just as soon as you tell me you will
eat a good meal and then get up and dress," he said in
his old autocratic way.

She seemed about to protest, but something deep in
those shining blue-gray eyes made her bite her tongue
and nod.

"Tell me you will," he insisted.

"Very well, I will do as you say," she said a little
breathlessly. "And now, sir, leave me at once!"

"I will be waiting for you downstairs, Julia," he
warned her as he picked up her hand and kissed it. She
snatched it away, some color coming to her cheeks,
and he smiled. "And if I hear from Edwina that you
are not doing as you promised, I will be back up those
stairs again before the cat has time to lick her ear. Do
you understand? You will dress, m'lady, if I have to
dress you myself!"

It was well over an hour later before the drawing-
room door opened softly and Lady Julia Reynolds
slipped inside. Trevor Whitney was seated at the
piano, playing some aimless melodies, but he stopped
and rose as she came toward him.

She was wearing a simple morning gown of soft
green, and she had a matching ribbon threaded
through her curls. He studied her face carefully. It was
still and composed, but there was life in it, and in the
wide hazel eyes that looked so steadily into his.

"Should you care for some coffee, m'lord? A glass of
wine?" she asked like a perfect hostess.

The earl came and stood close before her. All he
could do was shake his head as he stared down at her.
Julia lowered her eyes in some confusion.

"Before I say anything else, I must beg your forgiveness, m'lady," he said. His voice seemed to plead for her understanding. "I am ashamed that I thought you guilty. But when I saw you with the satchel actually in your hands, I was so distraught, I . . . I lost all sense of reason. Tell me you will forgive me that mad moment of doubt, Julia, I beg you."

She looked at him and the earl held his breath until she nodded. "Won't you be seated, m'lord?" she asked, moving away to take a straight chair near the window.

Trevor Whitney frowned. Her voice was emotionless. She was a lady receiving a gentleman caller, no more, no less. He was confused.

"Julia, look at me!" he ordered, coming to kneel before her and take her unresisting hands in his. "I want more than your forgiveness, my dear. I want your love. You see, I have known for a long time how much I love you, but I could not tell you of it, not when you were under a cloud. As much as it hurt me, I had to wait until your name was cleared. You do see my dilemma, don't you?"

Julia steeled herself against those fervent, pleading eyes, that lean face that was set with such emotion.

"That night we went to Carlton House and you told the Prince you loved me, you will never know how much I wanted it to be true," he went on. "And then, back here, I lost control of myself just before I left. I could not bear to go without holding you in my arms, kissing you. I knew it was wrong, but I could not help myself, and I was so overcome, I had to leave you without a word, lest I tell you what was in my heart then and there. The next day, when I learned of the blackmailer's scheme to collect the money, I knew I could not come to you, nor even write, until he was in custody. I spent a very long day, my darling. I hope it was a long day for you too."

Julia removed her hands from his, and he rose, a puzzled frown between his brows.

"Please be seated, m'lord," she said, indicating a

chair nearby. "If you continue to speak so wildly, I shall have to ask you to leave. I do not want your love, and you shall never have mine."

The earl sat down, keeping his eyes locked with hers. "You say that because you have been hurt, not only by your friend's duplicity but also by my behavior. But in time, I am sure—"

She shook her head. "No, I will never change. This has been a terrible experience for me, but it has only served to confirm my resolve. I never intended to marry again, and I never shall. And most certainly not to a man who has put me through what you have, m'lord."

"So you have not forgiven me after all," he remarked sadly as he rose. His face was pale now, and he turned to pace the room. Suddenly he turned and pointed at her. "But you cannot deny that you returned my kiss that evening, Julia," he said. "Returned it with passionate fervor."

He stared at her, and watched the color stain her cheeks.

"I was upset, distraught," she said. "I did not know what I was doing—"

"I am, of course, desolate to have to contradict you, m'lady, but you knew exactly what you were doing," he told her. "How could I ever forget that response, and your complete surrender?"

As she flushed, he went on, "And why don't you want to marry again, Julia? A woman as lovely as you are, whose first marriage was known to be so happy—"

"That is none of your concern," she interrupted. "Suffice it to say, I am adamant. I do not care to marry, not you or anyone."

The earl started toward her, and when she saw his determined eyes and the purposeful set of his lean face, she realized she would have to be more brutal if she were to convince him.

"However, you remind me of my manners," she said

lightly. "I have been quite remiss not to thank you for bringing me back to life this morning. Sad, is it not, that as Prince Charming, your kiss could only awaken Sleeping Beauty, not make her love you?" She made herself smile as if in regret, and then she shrugged.

Trevor Whitney stopped and stared at her without speaking. Clearly they both heard the mantel clock as it ticked off the minutes. The homely little sound seemed to mock the charged atmosphere between them, almost as if it wanted to remind them that for the rest of the time it would tick off the minutes of two lives that by her decision must now be lived apart.

"There is something else I must ask you, m'lady," Trevor Whitney said into that painful silence.

Julia told herself she was relieved to hear those cold tones he had so often employed in the past when speaking to her, in spite of the pain she felt at their return.

"It concerns Fanny Lowden," he went on. "The Prince has decided to be magnanimous, since we have recovered both the money and the snuffbox. Mrs. Lowden will be freed as long as she promises to leave England and never return. There is a condition to her freedom, however."

"Yes?" she asked. "A condition, you say?"

"It is that you must agree to it as well. If you want her to be prosecuted for the pain she has caused you, it shall be done."

Now it was Julia's turn to rise. She rubbed her hands together as she thought, and then she sighed. "No, let her go," she said softly. "I have no wish to be vindictive, perhaps because I feel it was all my fault, in a way. I was not perceptive enough to see into her heart and understand her. And I never even once suspected her. Let her go."

The earl nodded before he bowed. "As you wish, madam," he said. "I beg you will excuse me now, since our business has been concluded."

He walked away, and she stood very still, staring

after him. Just before he opened the door, he turned back. "Once you said that when this was all over, you hoped you would never have to see me again in your entire life. I shall do my best to honor that request, ma'am, since it appears it is the only thing I *can* do for you. Good-bye."

As the door closed behind his tall, proud figure, Julia sank down into a chair and put her face in her hands. It was over. And since she had gained the very end she sought, why did she feel so perturbed, so lost? Surely it was incomprehensible!

While she had been eating and dressing this morning, she had thought only of Trevor Whitney, as she had most of the time since Fanny Lowden had been unmasked. It still hurt when Julia remembered that he had thought her the blackmailer, but that was not the reason she had come to the plan of action she had employed just now. She knew she could have forgiven him for his mistake easily, for she was aware that she had always been the prime suspect in the case. No, that was not the reason at all. It was that he had suddenly reminded her of her late husband, Marquess Hastings, and how he had always mistrusted her as well. Those years of her marriage had been one ugly, agonizing, unchanging scene. To the public they had appeared the happiest couple in England, he so attentive, so full of loving concern for her well-being, so constant in his attendance. But in reality, Nigel had been consumed with jealousy, sure she was cuckolding him behind his back with one lover after another. Julia grimaced. Even if she had been so inclined, how could she ever have accomplished it when he never let her out of his sight? She had spent those years with him dreading any man's light compliment or easy smile, praying she would not be asked to dance or converse.

She knew she could not ever, ever go through such a marriage again. And even though she felt such warmth of feeling for the earl, and he for her, she knew that would change after their marriage. He would turn into an autocratic, demanding, untrusting husband too. His suspicions of her when he had come in and found her with Fanny had been a revealing clue to the type of man he really was. And one of them in a lifetime was enough.

She knew she would often regret this decision, for his kiss had awakened stirrings she had never even been aware she possessed. But she had been celibate for a long time; she would grow accustomed to remaining celibate, especially if the earl kept his word and she never saw him again.

A week later, Lady Millicent Whitney and Miss Edwina Ogilvie were taking a morning drive in the park. Miss Ogilvie was trying to speak with great clarity, although sometimes she forgot in her intensity.

"I never thought Aunt Julia could be so unreasonable, ma'am," she was saying now. "She not only refuses to speak of the earl, she will not allow me to do so either. Grown-ups are so strange!"

The countess patted her hand. "Indeed they are," she agreed. "Why, Trevor has turned into a perfect bear! He rarely goes out or receives his friends; he even canceled a musical evening! He stays in his library alone most of the time, playing the piano. The most melancholy tunes, too, dear Edwina. I swear they are enough to give anyone the mopes. It is obvious he loves her very much. Now, how are we to solve this, I wonder?"

Privately Edwina thought this new tangle of star-crossed lovers she was involved in not only silly but very tame, after the excitement of catching a blackmailer. But since it was all she had to deal with at the moment, she was determined to give it her best effort. Now she frowned, deep in thought.

"How would it be if I did something bad, ma'am?" she asked eagerly a few minutes later.

"Sad? What do you mean, sad? How would that help?" Lady Millicent asked.

"B. B. Bad!" Edwina enunciated in her gruff contralto. "Perhaps if I got involved in a crime, the earl would investigate it, and then he would have to see Aunt Julia again."

She saw the countess shaking her head and looking solemn, and she added in a wheedling voice, "Just a little crime, dear ma'am?"

The countess denied her the treat. "Absolutely not, Edwina. Besides, I think it is time I played a more major role." Sensing the girl's disappointment, she added, "You would not deny me that, would you? After all, you have had all the fun up to now, and it is not in the least fair."

Much struck by this logic, Edwina said she supposed it was only right. "What do you intend to do, ma'am?" she asked.

"I am not entirely sure, as yet," Lady Millicent said. "Tell me, does Lady Julia remain at home this afternoon?"

Edwina nodded. "She doesn't go anywhere anymore, either. I would be bored to tears, myself, just drooping around the house, holding a book I never bothered to read."

"Then I think I shall call on your aunt today, my dear Edwina," the countess said with decision. "A private call; you must be nowhere in the vicinity, do you understand?"

When Edwina agreed with a sunny smile, the countess rapped on the carriage roof. When the trap opened, she ordered her coachman to drive to Charles Street, and then to Portman Square.

Several hours later, Countess Bradford descended from the selfsame carriage and sounded the knocker at Lady Julia Reynold's home. Edwina had promised to go and visit her friend Evelyn Rogers that afternoon, her only stipulation being that the countess must remember everything that happened and give her a full, unedited account.

Handing her card to Hentershee, the countess said

in an imperious manner that would have amazed her
son, "I know Lady Julia is home. Miss Ogilvie assured
me she would be. You may tell your mistress I come on
a matter that will take only a moment of her time, and
I do not intend to be fobbed off."

She bent down and fixed the old butler with a steely
blue eye. "You understand me, my good man? Excellent! Off with you, then!"

Hentershee bowed, at a complete loss for words. He
went with measured tread to the drawing room.
Actually, he was not at all reluctant to do so, for he
had seen the lost look in Lady Julia's eyes all this past
week, and he regretted whatever was causing her
sorrow. If this Countess Bradford could bring her out
of the megrims, he would be the first to applaud.

He was back a short time later to announce that
Lady Julia would receive her guest. The countess
swept past him at the drawing-room door and closed it
firmly in his face.

Lady Julia rose from the chair where she had been
sitting reading. "My dear countess, what a surprise!
Won't you be seated and let me order you some refreshment?" she asked as she came forward. She was
wearing a smart afternoon gown of green moire
trimmed with darker green velvet ribbons, and her
hair was arranged in a stunning style. Still, she did not
look well. Her face was too pale, too set; her smile,
when she remembered to employ it, too fleeting.

"No, no, I do not stay," the countess said briskly. "I
have come only on a brief errand, and then I will be on
my way."

Julia looked a little confused as the older lady began
to rummage in her old-fashioned, roomy reticule.

"Now, where did I put it?" she muttered to herself,
before she smiled and nodded as she withdrew a
tightly rolled scroll that was tied with a piece of
ribbon. "Here it is!" she said, waving it triumphantly.

The countess held the scroll out to Julia. "I cannot
understand why Trevor did not return it to you," she

said. "I found it this morning in the library. And knowing that the two of you had decided you would not suit, I thought to spare you both any further encounter. Take it, dear Lady Julia! It is yours."

"Mine?" Lady Julia asked, eyeing it in confusion.

"Why, yes, it must be," the countess told her, pressing the scroll into her unwilling hands. "It has your name on it."

Julia turned it around until she saw her first name written in the earl's distinctive handwriting.

She looked up to see the countess closing her bag with a great air of duty done and mission accomplished. "There!" she said, brushing her hands together.

"Did the earl send you here with this, ma'am?" Julia asked, her hazel eyes flashing.

The countess started. "Trevor? Good heavens, no! I merely thought to tidy up the loose ends, you know. I cannot abide loose ends. And this way, both you and my son will now be free to pursue the unhappy courses you have set for yourselves without further ado."

She came forward and patted Julia lightly on the cheek. "I shall never understand it, of course, but then, everyone knows that mothers are notorious for seeing their children through rose-tinted glasses. To me, Trevor is everything any woman could dream of in a husband—handsome, talented, and sensitive, with a wealth of love and kindness to give. But, as I say, your refusal to consider him is a private matter, and none of my concern. Good-bye, my dear."

Bemused, Lady Julia watched her walk to the door, to wave before she disappeared. She stood where she was until she heard the front door close behind her unusual caller, and only then did she untie the ribbon and open the scroll. It consisted of two sheets of music. Julia went to the piano, smoothing the sheets as she did so, before she placed them on the rack above the keys. She picked out the melody with one finger, and discovered it was the earl's composition that he had played at

Lady Ralston's. Her eyes went to the title. In his strong, clear hand was written "Julia's Song." Wondering, she read the words he had written under the music, and her cheeks grew warm. What a touching tribute they were, she thought in spite of herself, so full of his longing and admiration.

She sat down and began to play the music, singing his words softly. But when she reached the last two lines, her throat seemed to close, and she was forced to stop.

" 'Yet though my Julia scorns my love, yet will I stay forever; For in her hand she holds my heart, with bonds she cannot sever,' " she whispered.

Julia's hands stilled on the keys, but still she seemed to hear the music echoing in her head, as well as his deep voice saying the words she had just read.

She was miserable. She had been miserable ever since she told the earl she would not marry him. Even knowing she had made the right decision, the only possible decision, did not stop the pain. It seemed to grow stronger every day, no matter how many times she told herself how much better she was feeling with the passing of time.

She stared straight ahead of her, a little frown between her brows, and then she rose from the bench. She did not dare to look at those sheets of music again. Instead, she made herself go back to her chair and pick up the book she had been trying to read.

It was well over an hour later when Hentershee knocked and came in with another calling card. Julia took it with listless fingers, but when she saw the earl's name, she sat up straighter, her breathing becoming shallow.

"M'lord begs a moment of your time on a matter of some urgency, m'lady," Hentershee told her, looking as impassive as he could. "He says he will not detain you for long."

"Very well. Show m'lord in," Julia said, putting down her book and rising. While she waited, she smoothed her gown with fingers that shook a little.

Trevor Whitney came in and bowed to her. His piercing eyes were eager, and she read such longing in them that she almost cried out. But when he spoke, his voice was cold and formal, and a mask came over his face. "I have just seen my mother, m'lady," he began. "I must ask you to forgive her for her impertinence in calling on you."

"I was glad to see her," Julia protested. "It was no impertinence."

"No?" he asked, strolling closer. "But it was an impertinence for her to leave the music here that she did. I have come to retrieve it. I am sure you cannot be interested in it."

"I am very interested," Julia found herself saying. "What woman would not be honored by such a tribute?"

The earl stared at her for a moment, and then he went to the piano. "You are kind to say so of my poor effort, ma'am, but I believe I will relieve you of it even so. You see, I intend to burn it."

Julia ran across the room to him and took hold of his arm with both hands. "Oh, do not burn it, I beg you!" she cried. "I could not bear it!"

He looked down at her. In wonder, she watched his cold, haughty face change, become warm and eager. Without saying a word, he took her into his arms and pulled her close. Julia hardly dared to breathe as she stared up into his unusual eyes, those eyes that searched her face as if he had been hungering for the sight of her all these long days and lonely nights. She raised that face to his. As his fervent lips covered hers, she closed her eyes and gave herself up to the wonderful sensations she had known but briefly before.

It was wrong, it was dangerous. She knew that eventually it was going to make her unhappy, but she could deny her love for him no longer. Her arms went up around his neck, and her hands lost themselves in his thick dark hair.

When he lifted his head at last, she clung to him, her eyes still closed as if to savor the lingering memory of his kiss.

"Julia, my love," he said simply. "Do not fight me anymore. You must know, as I do, that we were meant to be together. If you persist in refusing to admit that, you condemn us both to lives of unhappiness. Tell me you love me! I can feel it in your kiss, the touch of your hands, but I would hear you say it. And know the words I wrote for you are true. You have all my heart in your keeping. Marry me, my sweet Julia!"

"Oh, Trevor, I do love you," she whispered. His sensitive fingers cupped her face, and although they were gentle, she felt their warm strength. "If only I were not so afraid!" she whispered.

The earl did not take his arm away as he drew her down on the piano bench. "What are you afraid of, Julia?" he asked, puzzled.

Julia looked down at the hands she had clasped in her lap. "Of you . . . marriage . . . jealousy . . . domination . . . mistrust—all of those things!" she told him.

"I think you had better explain, my dear," he said. "I do not understand."

She nodded. "Yes, yes, I will. You know I have been married before and how everyone thought it was such a happy union. It was not. My husband was years older than I, and he was a man consumed with jealousy. He did not remain by my side because he could not bear to leave it, but because he was sure I was being unfaithful to him. I was not, Trevor! I was never unfaithful!" she cried. His arm tightened in understanding, but he did not speak. She turned away for a moment, her lips trembling, and then she faced him again. There was nothing but loving kindness and concern for her in his expression, and she took a deep breath. "You see, our marriage was never consummated," she said. The hand at her waist tightened. She could feel the muscles of his arm tense on her back as well. "Nigel was impotent," she went on. "He did not want a wife, a real marriage. He wanted a beautiful companion that other men would envy, a doll that he could put on display and then hide away. He . . . he never left my side. I rarely had a moment to myself, and I . . . I hated it! As I hated his mistrust of me. I am so afraid you will be the same, especially since I have seen how suspicious you can be."

The earl spoke at last. "But I was suspicious only because of the Prince's missing snuffbox, my dear," he said. "Our marriage will not be like that, I promise you. As much as I love you, you may have as many moments alone as you like. Why, I myself have never married because I could not see myself being happy in anyone's constant company. At least that is what I thought until I met you. But you can believe me when I tell you I have my own life to live—my books and my music. They keep me so busy I need hours to myself every day. And at heart I am a solitary man. Why, I'm practically a hermit!"

Julia's unhappy expression had brightened as he spoke, and now she smiled a little as she said, "One wonders if you will even have time for the ceremony, to say nothing of a short wedding journey, sir." Her voice was demure, but he could hear the teasing note in it.

Trevor Whitney looked down at her, that wonderful smile that made him so handsome and alive coming over his face. His eyes crinkled shut in amusement. "Oh, I imagine I will be able to find a few moments for you every now and then," he told her as one finger traced the contours of her face. As she turned her head to lay her cheek in his palm, he added, his voice a little ragged, "I promise I will never mistrust you, either. Indeed, I plan to keep you so happily occupied, you will not have time to be unfaithful to me, ever. You see, I do not suffer from your late husband's unfortunate malady, m'lady. I think you may count on an extended wedding journey of several weeks . . . no, months!"

Julia's laugh was just as he remembered it, gay and happy. He reached into his pocket then to withdraw the Prince's snuffbox. Silently he held it out to her. As her eyes widened, he flicked it open. Julia looked down at it, and her color deepened.

"The Prince of Wales has forgiven us both, m'lady," he told her. "He did not know how much he pained me when he gave this to me, for at the time, I thought I had lost you. But now I am glad he did so. Although I am not a jealous man, I would dislike knowing this was in anyone else's hands. The Prince told me that since I had captured the . . . er, the original, he thought it only right that I also have this poor copy." He smiled down at her, and then he said softly, "I am sure it is a very poor copy. Would you care to indulge with me, ma'am?"

"Why, I should be delighted to indulge," Julia told him.

As he felt her touch his hand, he looked down, amazed. For what seemed an endless moment, her fingers hovered over the open box, and then they closed the lid with a soft, decisive click.

As her arms went around his neck again and she lifted her lips to his, she whispered, "But not, m'lord, in snuff."

About the Author

Although Barbara Hazard is a New England Yankee by birth, upbringing, and education, she is of English descent on both sides of her family and has many relatives in that country. The Regency period has always been a favorite, and when she began to write seven years ago, she gravitated to it naturally, feeling perfectly at home there. Barbara Hazard now lives in New York. She has been a musician and an artist, and although writing is her first love, she also enjoys classical music, reading, quilting, cross-country skiing, and paddle tennis.